Beatrice Meier was born in Germany and studied literary translation at Düsseldorf University. She then went on to complete a scriptwriting programme at Munich Film School in 2002, and attended the Cologne International Film School in 2006. She won the Best Screenplay Award at the German Film Festival in Ludwigshafen in 2013 for the feature film *Offside Trap*, which was screened at festivals, the European Parliament and at trade union events. *The Vintage Springtime Club* is her first novel. A German television adaptation was broadcast in spring 2015. Beatrice Meier lives and works in Strasbourg.

the VINTAGE SPRINGTIME CLUB

Beatrice Meier

Translated from the German
by Simon Pare

ABACUS

First published in Germany in 2015 as *Alleine war gestern*
by Verlag Kiepenheuer & Witsch
First published in Great Britain in 2016 by Little, Brown
This paperback edition published in 2017 by Abacus

1 3 5 7 9 10 8 6 4 2

A CIP catalogue record for this book
is available from the British Library.

ISBN 978-0-349-14176-3

Printed and bound in Great Britain by
Clays Ltd, St Ives plc

Papers used by Little, Brown are from well-managed forests
and other responsible sources.

MIX
Paper from
responsible sources
FSC® C104740

Little, Brown
An imprint of
Little, Brown Book Group
Carmelite House
50 Victoria Embankment
London EC4Y 0DZ

An Hachette UK Company
www.hachette.co.uk

www.littlebrown.co.uk

There are many ways to live an adventurous life. You don't have to travel the world or take up extreme sports.

If you want, you can find the unexpected at your front door.

And, if you *really* want, even . . . just behind it.

1

'Six months?!' asked Ricarda.

'At the very least,' said the chubby, blue-overalled work-man with a nod. His eyes wandered over the living room's white-painted beams. Two of them were sagging slightly. 'It looks as though three floors are affected now. The whole house needs renovating.'

'The whole house?'

'Dry rot's the worst thing that can happen to a building. Do you own your flat?'

Ricarda nodded in despair.

'It's going to cost you a pretty penny.' He checked that the strands of hair combed across his crown concealed his bald patch properly.

Ricarda looked up from his balding head to the mouldy spot next to the wooden beam that ran across her bright living room. The management company had given her a preliminary cost estimate, but this was the first time anyone had told her that she would have to move out of her flat for six months.

'Okay, but where am I supposed to live during that time?'

'I've no idea. I'm just the mould specialist,' said the man with the comb-over. He picked up his toolbox and walked to the door. 'I'd gladly put you up at my place, *Fräulein*, but I don't think my wife would be very amused.' He shook her hand, and with a cheeky grin he was gone.

Ricarda wasn't sure what upset her most: the dry rot, his total indifference or ... that *Fräulein* stuff. *Fräulein*? Seriously?

She checked her watch. It was a quarter past nine, and she was running late. She grabbed her handbag and glanced one last time in the mirror. She didn't look sixty-one. Her face was still virtually wrinkle-free, she dyed her hair chestnut-brown, and she kept fit by doing Pilates and swimming. The years had taken their toll on her body, of course, but Ricarda was fighting hard – and by and large she was winning. She decided, amidst all this madness, that she would at least take that *Fräulein* as a compliment.

She stepped out into the busy street. The morning sun was dazzling. To her left the cathedral towered into the sky. Six months? At the very least? Where on earth was she meant to go for all that time? Maybe she could move into Stella's place for a while; her daughter had taken an interpreting job with a company in Granada for three months. Or had she sub-let her flat?

Ricarda searched for Stella's number on her mobile and dialled it. Straight to voicemail. Glancing at her watch, she saw that her first appointment would be arriving in twenty minutes. She hurried down the street. Her psychotherapy practice was on the far side of the cathedral. She climbed the steps to the square in front of the great monument, the wind billowing her skirt.

She could ask Berthe, who shared the practice with her. But did she really want to spend her evenings with her chatty colleague as well as her days? Given the choice, she'd prefer to rent a small flat for a time and . . .

'Ricarda?' A man's voice interrupted her thoughts. She spun around. The tall man, dressed in jeans and a white T-shirt, was peering down at her in surprise. It took her a moment to recognise him.

'Philip?'

It really was Philip. Philip Kreuzer.

'What are *you* doing here?' she asked.

'I'm back in Cologne.' His clear grey eyes twinkled. He was every bit as surprised as she was.

'So you're not in Mali any more?'

He shook his head. They held each other's gaze for just a little too long, then he laughed.

'Now isn't this something!' said Ricarda, returning his laughter.

They had studied together. Philip had been best friends with her then boyfriend Herbert, whom she had later married. After graduation Philip had gone to work for Médecins Sans Frontières in Mali. He only occasionally returned to Cologne. Herbert had visited him a couple of times in Africa, but they had lost touch over the years.

As Philip explained that he'd left Mali for good, she studied his face in amazement. He looked like a completely different person – and at the same time he seemed unchanged. They had once known each other inside out. His fine features had grown more prominent with age. He wore his hair a little longer now, and his three-day stubble lent him a cool and casual air. His hair was streaked with grey, but that suited him.

'How about you?' he asked. 'How are you doing?'

'Oh, I . . . Oh, don't ask!' She blurted out her story about the dry rot. Now it was his turn to study *her* face. The wind whipped her hair around as she tried to hold her skirt down. 'Six months! Just imagine! Where am I supposed to go for that length of time? And to top it all off the guy calls me *Fräulein*!'

Philip grinned. Once again his eyes lingered on her for a second too long. She looked at her watch. 'Philip, I've got to go, let's—'

'Move in with me.'

'Excuse me?'

'You can move in with me if you like.'

'Hang on – move in with you?' She couldn't just shack up with a man with whom she'd once been at university but hadn't seen in ages.

'It's a flatshare.'

'What? A flatshare?'

Flatshare. The word unexpectedly catapulted her back to a time that hadn't entered her mind for God knew how long. 'Flatshare': a word synonymous with long, smoke-clouded, debate-filled nights, blocked plugholes, overflowing ashtrays, rickety chairs, piles of dirty plates in the sink, cleaning rotas that went unheeded, red wine served in mustard jars, tears and fits of laughter, pre-exam stress, broken hearts . . .

'Yes,' Philip said with a nod. 'There's still one room available.'

'You're offering me a room in your flatshare?'

'Yeah.'

'Well . . . that's so great! You're my saviour!'

'It looks that way.' Philip grinned.

Ricarda couldn't believe it. What a coincidence!

2

Ralf was being difficult again. Philip dragged him up the stairs, and Ralf panted as he scraped his belly over the dark wooden steps of the Art Nouveau stairwell. After five steps Philip took pity on him. He picked him up and carried him to the top.

Ricarda ... What kind of trick of fate was this? Thoughts of her had been swirling through his mind ever since he'd got back to Cologne. He'd been meaning to call her, but had kept putting it off, day after day. He was still haunted by the memories. Even thirty-five years in Mali hadn't expunged them.

When she had suddenly appeared in front of him earlier that morning, outside the cathedral, he'd actually stopped breathing for a moment. The wind was ruffling her hair. She had little creases around her eyes, but her gaze, her lively gaze, was the same as ever.

She'd talked about her colleague Berthe, who might be able to put her up; her daughter Stella, who'd moved out seven years ago but had probably sub-let her flat; about the dry rot and the workman ... She'd looked calm, but inside she was in turmoil, he knew that. Even back then, Ricarda had always needed everything to go to plan. And, whenever something didn't go to plan, she would make sure that things were swiftly back on track.

'"Move in with me" ... Good grief, Ralf, did I really say "move in with me"?'

Ralf looked up wearily. The staircase light went out. Philip pressed the button again and climbed the last flight.

His mother's flat was on the third floor. Elfriede Kreuzer had died three weeks earlier, at the age of ninety. Philip had been in the middle of surgery when the call came through. It'd been his last operation in the bush. He'd decided three months ago to return to Germany and look after his mother, had been planning it and working his notice – and then she'd died. Just like that. Three days before he got home. What was it his old friend Harry had said as he offered Philip his condolences? 'People never die according to plan.'

Once back in Cologne, Philip had needed to choose a coffin, look up his mother's friends and invite them to the funeral, which had taken place last week. He'd also had to sort out the paperwork and get all the other administrative aspects out of the way.

And there was Ralf, his mother's beloved dachshund, whom he'd just taken for a short walk around the block and was now carrying up the stairs, jammed under one arm.

Philip liked the dog. And at the same time he didn't, for some reason. The fat brown long-haired dachshund with the devoted gaze had spent more time with his mother than he had. The dog had been there as her health gradually deteriorated; he had been there when she fell asleep for ever. Ralf – the embodiment of his guilty conscience on four legs. Four stumpy little legs.

As Philip reached the top of the creaky stairs his heart beat faster – and not only because of the three flights. Ricarda's account of the problems she was having with her flat had flicked a magic switch in his brain, and his voice had announced, as if of its own accord, that she should move in with him. He regretted the words almost as soon as he'd uttered them, thinking, *What are you talking about?* When she'd flinched a little, his voice had briskly added that it was a flatshare. Ricarda had hesitated but eventually said that she was in. And there was that flicker in her hazel eyes. Just like the old days! The old days, when they would concoct plans for some protest or other, or a campaign to change the world.

That was exactly what Philip was doing now: he was changing the world. He could hardly believe it himself.

The only hitch with this particular campaign was that

the flatshare was a mere fifty-five minutes old and so far it existed purely in his mind. That was because he'd actually been on his way to an estate agent to visit an apartment by the Rhine and to put his mother's spacious pre-war flat up for sale.

Philip reached the front door. He smiled again at his spontaneous white lie. It was a bit naughty, but that didn't matter: the main thing was to have achieved the right result. He set Ralf down. By way of thanks the dog peed on the doormat, which announced 'Be My Guest'.

Be my guest. How appropriate.

Ralf glanced up at him, and then away again – the kind of look dogs gave you when *they'd* been a bit naughty.

Philip unlocked the door and went into the flat. Ralf and the stained mat would have to wait. First he needed to find some flatmates.

3

Timmy was making a good job of this. He crammed the weed into the thin cigarette paper, carefully licked the adhesive strip and stuck it down to form a cone. Harry watched his grandson affectionately and packed his coffee-stained Peace and Love mug, two plates and his mother's quaint old teapot into the cardboard box. *I'm going to miss Timmy*, he thought, *but nothing else*. He ran his hand back through his thinning hair to the grey plait and scanned the sparsely furnished granny flat his daughter had fixed up for him in her basement. A black leather two-piece suite, a bookcase, a small table and two chairs. Behind the TV set French windows led out on to a terrace. Other than that, the room was bare.

Ever since his old friend Philip had rung him up two months ago to ask him whether he was 'on' for sharing a flat, Harry had been 'on' for sharing a flat.

Initially he'd said, 'Oh, come on, Phil, aren't we too old for that?' but then his gaze had settled on the garden, where Misha, his daughter's new boyfriend, was pottering about among the tomato plants. 'Okay. When?' he'd said. He hadn't even asked who else was in on it: the main thing was to get out of here.

Harry took the joint from Timmy, rolled it critically between his chapped, rough fingers, and nodded. 'Nice work, *compañero*,' he said in a Western drawl, tousling Timmy's dark, fluffy hair. Timmy smiled, revealing the gaps where his incisors had once been.

Someone flung open the door to the garden, causing the two cowboys to look up. A man was heading for their saloon. Harry screwed up his eyes against the blinding spring sunlight. Misha was a small silhouette in the doorway. His daughter had met the sociologist six months ago, and three months ago the guy had moved into Britta's terraced house. Talk about nailing their colours to the mast. But Misha's arrival had turned out to be the final nail in the coffin for Harry, as it had put an end to the peace and love in his granny flat. If there was one thing Harry couldn't stand it was being patronised. And if there was something he could stand even less than that, it was being patronised in a limp, do-gooder's voice.

'Timmy's six years old,' the do-gooder's voice said.

'Got to get their hand in early.' Harry nodded, and grabbed the keys to his taxi. He'd rather drive people

11

around than talk child development with a wimpy sociol-ogist. In the doorway he bumped into Britta, who spotted Timmy at the table clutching Grandpa's joint.

'That's not on, Dad!'

'Calm down,' Harry grumbled, as he walked across the small eco-friendly garden to his taxi. 'Tomorrow you'll be rid of me.'

4

'Don't you think, what with his prostate, it would be better to put Harry in the first room on the left next to the loo?' asked Philip on his hands-free, tearing the sticky tape off the packing case. His voice came echoing back from the bare walls. With the exception of a few pieces of furniture such as his mother's wingback chair and his father's desk, he had had the entire flat cleared and renovated; the room still smelled of fresh paint. He was wearing a faded MSF shirt which hung loosely over his jeans.

He'd been on the phone to Ricarda for the last ten minutes, discussing the final details before they at last swung into action the next day.

'On the left? Oh, he'll be pleased about that!' There was a rustling noise from the other end of the line: Ricarda was obviously cradling her mobile between her ear and her shoulder. Philip heard the screech of a roll of sticky tape being unwound. 'As long as it's on the left!' said Ricarda, giving a throaty imitation of Harry's voice. Philip had to grin. Ricarda and Harry had squabbled even in their university days.

'I'll be intrigued to see how things work out between you and Harry.' Philip took a carved female figure out of his packing case and placed it on the old oak desk. A village elder had given it to him as a farewell gift.

'Me too!' said Ricarda, taking a deep breath.

A terrible clattering sound assailed Philip's eardrum. He ripped out his earphones and heard a swear word spill out from them. He put the thing back in his ear. There was more rustling and crackling.

'Everything okay?' he ventured.

'Hey,' her voice said hesitantly down the line, 'you know your mum's old dinner service? You haven't by any chance kep—'

'Ric. It's all gone. You asked me to sell off the entire contents of the house.'

'Oh . . .'

'We're bound to have enough crockery between the five of us.'

'Hmm . . .'

Philip could hear shards of china scraping on bare tiles. He smiled. Ricarda and her obsession with organisation – dashed on the hard floor of reality. That must hurt. He could see her standing there, sullenly sweeping broken crockery together with her foot.

Philip slumped into the bright, flowery wingback chair, ran his hands along its threadbare satin arms, and gazed across the hallway into the empty room.

'I'm looking forward to this,' he said softly.

'So am I.'

From her words he imagined that she was smiling.

5

Ricarda pushed another half of a cup on to the heap of broken crockery. She had actually gone off the dinner service a long time ago – but still. Forgetting to assemble the bottom of the box properly! How stupid was that? Out in the hallway stood a ready and reassuring stack of packed and tidily labelled boxes. The next day was moving day, and the complete renovation of her building was due to start the week after.

'I'm looking forward to this.' The way he had said those words . . . Ricarda fetched the broom from the larder – *oh, God, I've got to clear that out too* – and swept the pieces together.

It was incredible how much you could accumulate in a flat over the years. Four weeks ago she had decided that she was going to move into the flatshare, not on a temporary basis, but once and for all. Her current 1,300-square-foot apartment had felt far too big anyway since Herbert had succumbed unexpectedly and all too rapidly to cancer five years previously.

Ricarda had been toying for a while with the idea of letting out her flat and looking for somewhere smaller, but she had never really got around to it for one reason or another.

Philip's flatshare had arrived as if on cue. A twist of fate. More than once, all those years ago, Philip, Herbert and she had built castles in the air: one day, when their children had flown the nest, they'd move in together, smoke cigarettes, drink whisky and pick up where they'd left off as students. She had to smile. They'd been a funny old bunch.

Philip's flat itself was a dream. It was centrally located in a quiet street lined with knobbly, hoary old plane trees in the Agnes quarter of town. It had five large bedrooms, a spacious living room, high ceilings with mouldings, wooden floors, and a beautiful stone balcony leading off the kitchen-cum-dining room.

She liked her flatmates too. There was tomboyish Uschi Müller, who had cared for Philip's mother a little; Eckart Fröhlich, a retired bank clerk and the Kreuzers' account manager, whom Philip had run into again at the funeral; and, of course, Philip's old schoolfriend Harry, who had dutifully enrolled at university along with Philip, but had then preferred to practise his social skills at the pub instead of pursuing a sociology degree! He hadn't changed one jot –

he was still the same old troublemaker. Tough, but with a heart of gold.

Yet it was Philip who had been the crucial factor in her decision.

Shortly after they'd first bumped into one another, they had agreed to meet up for dinner at a local brewery restaurant. They were rather shy to begin with, both of them, as though they barely knew each other. Then the beer had begun to loosen their tongues. Old stories came up, anecdotes from their university days including the immortal story of Professor Drissen, who had genuinely dozed off during one of his own lectures, like Professor Hastings in *Sesame Street*. They talked and talked and laughed a lot, mainly about the fact that the dry rot had enabled them to put into action the plan they had hatched all those years ago. If it hadn't been for all the bother with the dry rot, Ricarda wouldn't have been rushing to her practice like a lunatic, and she wouldn't have bumped into Philip. They chinked glasses and congratulated themselves once more on their extraordinary stroke of luck. By candlelight Philip's features looked almost as boyish as ever; he had that old twinkle in his eye.

It was strange to see Philip with wrinkles. That might have been what initially created a peculiar, minute distance between them – nothing personal, just a gap that had widened over the years. Those lines were like little markers of how much time had passed, a reminder that despite their familiarity (and that came flooding back!) it had been decades since they'd last met; they had almost no idea what the other had been through in all those years and months and days.

Their paths had crossed briefly once ten years earlier at Christmas in a bar in the south of the city. Harry had arranged a get-together in his former seminar room – in other words, his old pub. There must have been twenty university friends there. Herbert and she had chatted with Philip for a while. He'd told them about his health post out in the bush. It'd been absolutely fascinating, but he had had to head home soon after, as he'd promised to have dinner with his mother. When he'd left, Ricarda had realised that she would have liked to talk to him for longer. Oddly, she missed him; she had forgotten how nice he was and how fond she was of him. She had stepped outside and cadged a cigarette from a former fellow student.

Herbert had suddenly developed liver cancer a few years later. He'd suffered terribly, and the doctors could do nothing for him apart from relieve his pain. Ricarda had spent every day at his bedside, and the end, at least, had come mercifully quickly. In a matter of months her whole life was turned upside down. She'd tried to keep her chin up, and as always she had managed – to a degree.

She'd invited Philip to the funeral too. He'd had a wonderful wreath delivered, with the message 'To my old friend' printed on a lime-green ribbon, and Ricarda had secretly hoped that he would come, for these words had stirred up old memories in her, a kind of nostalgia. But he hadn't. Two weeks later she'd found a letter, pasted with colourful African stamps, in her letterbox. He hadn't been able to get away from Mali; he couldn't abandon his bush health post at the drop of a hat. He wished her strength.

Ricarda bent down and swept the broken china into the dustpan.

'I'm looking forward to this.' She whispered his words to herself again and smiled. She'd had a slight nagging doubt at first. Now and then she wondered whether the offer of a flatshare had merely slipped out in his enthusiasm at their chance encounter – and, once uttered, had been hard for him to take back. He'd been evasive during that first dinner when she had asked him about his other flatmates, and he'd put off introducing them to her. Maybe it was because he'd first needed to ask the others whether she was welcome.

They had all finally met up ten days later at the Ludwig museum café. It was certainly odd: a man freshly returned from Africa offers four virtual castaways a room each in the apartment he has inherited from his mother, which he says is 'in any case too big' for him on his own. Typical Philip. It soon became clear that they were quite a random bunch, but they got on extremely well. This ragtag dimension brought a little levity to the project, a youthful abandon. This was an unexpected fresh start for them all; none of them had any preconceptions or fixed expectations. That trendy café had felt almost like an African village, with their chief assigning their huts.

Shortly after that first meeting they had spent two weekends by the North Sea to get to know each other better and gauge whether they would really be able to live together. After the second weekend Ricarda had decided that she was fully committed to the flatshare.

She tipped the first dustpanful into the bin and glanced over at the heap of broken pieces that remained. What on earth was she going to do for crockery now?

She studied her lists on the kitchen table, running her finger over the various headings and names, then she picked up her mobile and dialled Eckart Fröhlich.

6

The tall narrow headstone jerked back and forth in the damp soil. The muffled sound of a mobile ringtone – Bach's Fugue in G minor – filled the air. Eckart pulled his phone from the pocket of his brown corduroy trousers just as the gardener finished levering the piece of granite out of the ground. *Lotte Fröhlich, née Penzer. 1949–1995.* The bronze lettering had taken on a faint greenish hue over the years.

The gardener pushed the stone on a wheelbarrow through the well-tended garden to the street.

'I've just donated my crockery to the council,' Eckart answered into the mobile as he trudged after the gardener. 'You said you didn't want two lots of everything . . .'

'I know, I know. I was simply wondering whether you might still have it,' said Ricarda on the other end of the line.

'Unfortunately not,' replied Eckart, unlocking the car boot for the gardener. 'But while you're there, about the . . .

what's it called again? ... the raclette machine. Should I ...? No? Three? Oh, I see. No, that's too many. OK, yes, see you tomorrow, Ricarda.' He switched off Ricarda's voice.

The gardener groaned as he heaved the stone out of the wheelbarrow and, bent double, swung it towards the boot. Eckart leaned close to him. 'Hey, you wouldn't have any use for a ... raclette machine, would you? You know, one of those things with the little pans and wooden scrapers ...'

'Ahhh ... not – right – now,' the gardener spluttered. Eckart gasped as his dark blue Passat dipped a couple of inches with Lotte in the back.

Eckart stood in his garden for a while, gazing at his house with its nice brick facing. Lotte and he had built it them-selves twenty-five years earlier. They had saved up for it, a little at a time. He had decided, with a heavy heart, to sell it after his son Christoph had broken the news to him three months ago that he was intending to follow his girlfriend to New Zealand to grow kiwis. Christoph needed money for his new project, and in any case the house had no purpose now; the people for whom Eckart had built it with such love and devotion were no longer there. Back then, Lotte had longed to have her own little house; that was her idea of happiness and the good life. As things turned out, they'd lived in it for less than five years. He glanced at his watch. It was time. Christoph's flight left in three hours.

Three hours.

7

'Fair enough! As long as it's on the left!' Harry gave a throaty laugh. He couldn't care less which room they gave him. He was talking to Philip over his hands-free kit while driving his taxi. The lights were just turning amber, so Harry put his foot down and accelerated across the junction the second before they changed to red. He could feel the young woman staring at him from the back seat. On the dashboard a plastic Hawaiian girl swayed her grass skirt and a model dachshund wiggled its head.

'Everything's sorted with Eckart for tomorrow morning, by the way,' Harry continued. 'His movers still have some room in the lorry. What a nice guy. Nah, I haven't got that much. A bed, a bookcase, my records. Yep, see you tomorrow, Phil.'

'Are you moving house?' asked the passenger in the back amiably.

'Flatshare,' Harry said with a nod.

'Oh, how lovely.' The woman gazed out of the window with a benevolent look on her face.

'What?' asked Harry.

'Old-age flatshares are such a lovely idea,' the woman remarked. 'A nice boost at the onset of the third age. Being there for one another when someone needs help. Doing things together, cooking together, going to the theatre and the cinema, playing sports . . . ' She leaned forward kindly. 'What were *your* reasons?'

Harry narrowed his eyes like Clint Eastwood as he sized her up in the rear-view mirror. 'Old-age poverty,' he said through gritted teeth. His mobile rang again, and Morricone's 'The Good, The Bad and The Ugly' filled the taxi with its whistling. He pressed the button for hands-free mode.

'Yes?' Out of the corner of his eye he clocked the reaction of the friendly woman on the back seat: he loved to provoke people.

'Crockery? Nooo . . . See you tomorrow, Ric.'

8

'I didn't fit,' said Uschi as she forced the hunk of beef through the mincer.

'What do you mean, you didn't fit?' asked her colleague Hedwig, who was standing next to her behind the meat counter.

'My hips were too wide,' Uschi replied, and she turned to the customer, holding the minced meat out in front of her green 'Delicatessen rhymes with Flessen' apron. 'Anything else, madam?'

'Into what?' the customer asked.

'Mrs Müller dreamed last night that she wouldn't fit into her coffin,' Hedwig explained.

The customer stared at her trusted sausage supplier in bafflement.

'My hips were too wide. They didn't fit,' confirmed Uschi

with a smile and showed off her round hips, squeezing them to emphasise the point. Her hips were no dream, unfortunately.

'I thought you wanted to be cremated?' asked Hedwig.

'I can't help it if I don't remember in my dreams that I want to be cremated,' said Uschi. And anyway that wasn't the point. The point was that she couldn't lie down in the coffin during the fitting because of her wide hips.

'That's terrible, Mrs Müller,' said the customer. 'What ghastly dreams you have!'

You can say that again, thought Uschi. *But what can you do about your dreams? Well, the night-time ones anyway.*

'Do you think semi-retirement's to blame?' Hedwig asked.

It wasn't such a stupid suggestion. Uschi had been sleeping badly ever since the branch manager had abruptly announced that he was reducing her hours to part-time. His voice gnawed away at her, especially at night: *Isn't that right, Mrs Müller? You'll have a bit more time to yourself at long last!*

How dare he! Uschi didn't want more time to herself. Uschi loved her job, her liver sausage with finest cayenne pepper, her mortadella with roasted pistachios, her cutlets – and her customers.

She was still shaken by her search for a smaller, cheaper flat, and the nightmare was nothing compared with the seven bedsits she'd visited. Teeny-tiny. The mere idea of spending the rest of her days in a flat like that brought tears to her eyes.

Then, two months ago, out of the blue, Mrs Kreuzer's son had stood there in the shop and offered her a room in a flatshare. An absolute godsend. She'd felt better ever since. Maybe her dream about the narrow coffin just represented a fear of being cooped up in a tiny apartment.

She tenderly wrapped the minced meat in special delicatessen paper.

Never mind. It could actually be a good thing. When you dreamed of something that was giving you grief, you could deal with it. She was sure of that. You could process it and even dream it away.

'Do you know *another* thing that dream could mean?' said Hedwig, giving Uschi a sly look. 'That you have to lose some weight beforehand.'

'Before what?' asked Uschi.

'You know, before you die,' Hedwig replied, looking pretty smug at her interpretation.

'In that case . . . ' Uschi giggled ' . . . pass me that cream slice!'

The women laughed, dispelling all those dark thoughts at once. The thing to do with bad dreams or omens was to put a good spin on them. That was the art of living, otherwise life made no sense.

The telephone rang shrilly.

'It's for you.' Hedwig handed Uschi the receiver. The long

telephone cable dangled over the lovingly decorated cold meats counter.

It was Ricarda. Uschi listened to her for a while with one eye on the Beckmann boy, who was gawping at the mortadella. Uschi lifted a slice from the pile with a small fork, rolled it up and passed it over the counter to him. Then she smiled and proudly interrupted Ricarda. 'Course I've kept my crockery.'

9

It was total chaos at Düsseldorf airport. Display boards, letters and numbers frantically flashing, people dashing in all directions, foreign languages, laughing, shouting; a flurry of activity. Eckart was completely out of his depth amid all the excitement. He had trouble keeping up with Christoph as his son lugged his two rucksacks straight towards check-in. Sydney was up on the departures board; Christoph was flying on from there to New Zealand.

Eckart tried to suppress a rising sense of what felt like panic. He would have liked simply to walk away. Walk away from a situation he didn't want to have to experience.

For thirty-five years his son had lived close at hand. Twenty years ago, when Lotte died, Eckart had tried to keep everything running smoothly, had conscientiously gone about his job as a bank clerk, never remarried, wouldn't board an aeroplane until Christoph turned eighteen, and had tried to be his father and mother all rolled into one.

Things had been harder since he'd retired a year ago. The days dragged by in the big, empty house. He had established certain little rituals such as going out to buy the newspaper every morning (and a croissant every other day), lingering over breakfast – breakfast was his favourite time of the day – reading the business pages, doing the crossword, listening to the news, keeping the garden neat, taking a nap, reading the features section, and shopping for a simple dinner, which he then ate alone on the corner seat at the kitchen table. Then he would watch television or an old film. He liked old films – good Westerns or classic *film noir* dramas and, increasingly, 'difficult' films by Bergman or Fassbinder. Being alone whetted his appetite for more challenging plots, for life was indeed a complex business. Then a small cognac and the eleven o'clock news on the radio before going to bed.

Of course this life was not particularly enjoyable, but Eckart had got used to it over time. He needed these rituals to keep him going. He never questioned their usefulness; he ticked them off, he completed them. He carried out his tasks, exactly as he'd done behind his bank counter before retirement. Eckart had settled into his loneliness. Once a week Christoph came to see him.

Then, a good two months ago, he had had a brief conversation with Mrs Kreuzer's son after her funeral. Eckart had taken care of Mrs Kreuzer's accounts. He liked the old lady. He had just found a buyer for his house and was starting to look for a small apartment. Philip Kreuzer had asked whether Eckart could recommend an estate agent to sell his mother's flat. They had talked on the phone a couple of times in the following days, and two weeks after the funeral Philip had suddenly asked him whether he could imagine joining a flatshare rather than moving into a small apartment.

At first Eckart couldn't imagine it at all, but, when he told his son, Christoph immediately urged him to at least take a look at the set-up. He said it would be ideal for Eckart; he needed people around him. How would he survive in a small flat? He himself would soon be gone, and Eckart had no one else. What would he do when he no longer enjoyed such good health? He'd go straight into an old people's home. If he wanted to change something, then he needed to do it *now*. Start all over again. Start all over again? As if that was so easy when you were sixty-four!

'Take care, Dad. I'm sure the flatshare will work out nicely. It'll do you a power of good, you'll see.' Christoph's voice interrupted Eckart's thoughts. Eckart hadn't noticed that they'd reached the security doors. Christoph gave him a hug. The time had come to say goodbye, the time when his son really would fly off to the other side of the globe. For good. At least right now it felt as if it was for good.

'The money should be in my account next week, and then I'll transfer ...' Eckart's words trailed off. He tried to fill the gaping void with formalities, but his words only dug the hole deeper. For weeks he had been dreading this moment, secretly hoping that it might never arrive. But here was Christoph, standing opposite him with his short blond hair, his earnest expression, his turquoise outdoor jacket and his grey rucksack. Eckart tried to memorise every detail, like the very last time he had seen Lotte at the mortuary.

The security officer was beckoning to them.

'I've got to go, Dad,' said Christoph. 'Look after yourself. Promise me you will?'

'Don't you worry about me,' said Eckart. 'And get in touch if you need anything, all right? I'll always be there for you. You know that, don't you? Whatever happens, you hear me?'

Christoph nodded, gave his father a last quick pat on the shoulder, placed his rucksack on the X-ray conveyor, removed his belt and strode through the metal detector. Eckart stared at the floor, fighting back the tears. By the time he looked up again his son had vanished into the crowd.

He was gone.

10

'You never know when you're going to run into someone again, Justus,' said Ricarda, gazing tenderly at the blind boy. Baskets were piled high around the small basket-weaving workshop. Five other weavers sat nearby. Justus drew a length of straw through a hole.

The fifteen-year-old boy had love trouble. His girlfriend Anna had moved to Munich the day before, with her parents. Justus and Anna had met at this workshop for the blind.

Ricarda had been holding a surgery here once a week for four years. She saw many cases of maladjusted children and teenagers at her practice. She worked closely with their parents and other family members. Although she had scored many successes, there had been a lot of setbacks too, many cases where she found herself ultimately powerless. Quite a few therapies were broken off because they weren't working. She could do very little if the parents didn't pull their weight, either from a lack of understanding or out of arrogance. It was as if the words she planted so cautiously had been swept away by the time the next appointment came around. Daily life and each family's particular circumstances were simply stronger than she was.

Ricarda enjoyed her appointments away from her practice all the more for these difficulties. She now held consultations in three centres for people with disabilities. The youngsters came to see her about sensitive issues and everyday troubles, and the conversations were always enriching and stimulating. She liked going to see the young basket-weavers most. The majority of them had been born blind, but they had such a clear vision of life, and such bravery and resilience that it occasionally brought tears to her eyes.

The charity's motto was 'Seeing with our hands', and Justus and Anna had obviously taken it literally. Their hands touched frequently as they learned to weave baskets. Ricarda had enjoyed watching the two of them gradually grow closer – they had even moved closer together physically – although being able to see made her feel like a voyeur. And now Justus was sitting there alone, drawing his length of straw indifferently through the small hole. She ran her fingers quickly through his dark blond curls.

'Can you guess how I came to be moving into a flat-share tomorrow?' she asked. Justus blinked with curiosity. 'Because I happened to run into a very old friend.'

'Really?'

'Philip studied medicine with my husband. The three of us were pretty inseparable.'

'And then?'

'Philip went to Africa and we lost touch. But . . . ' She left a dramatic pause. 'I suddenly bumped into him eight weeks ago and . . . he invited me to join his flatshare. Do you see, Justus? Sometimes fate makes sure that we meet a particular person again.'

She smiled. New memories had been bubbling to the surface every day since her path had crossed Philip's once more. It had been a very special time back then with Philip and Herbert – a student life of revolution, parties, and dreams of an exciting future. They had revised together, demonstrated together and gone on holiday together.

'Are you in love?' said Justus, looking up in surprise. His gaze was keen and clear, even though his eyes were focused on a point just to the right of her face.

'What nonsense!' said Ricarda, smiling and getting to her feet.

But there was a grain of truth to his words. Everything felt a little different since she'd decided to move into the flatshare – more alive. Suddenly that old feeling was back. It was bittersweet, because the past was at once both extremely tangible and irrevocably gone. It made her feel euphoric too, though, because that one word – 'flatshare' – made her feel as if she'd pressed a button marked 'Reboot your life'.

She'd never really wanted to acknowledge it, but various things in her life had worn out over time – and not just her body. She'd kept running away from the fact. After Herbert's death she had thrown herself even more passionately into her work, taking on extra cases from her colleague Berthe, who had been expecting a baby and wanted to ease up. She had started her consultations in centres for the disabled, joined a permaculture society, supported a 'Save the Bees' project and even kept three beehives for a year. Whenever there was a project to change the world, however minutely, she was on hand – and always had been. *Be the change you wish to see in the world.* She had carried Gandhi's adage around with her in her purse since she was thirteen, but in recent years she had pursued every project with such intensity that it was as though she were striving not only to join Gandhi on his march, but to overtake him. She ran and ran, and then suddenly, a little over a year ago, her sixtieth was upon her.

To be honest, it hadn't even really been on her radar. Or she hadn't wanted it to be. She just wanted to keep on running, as if none of this were happening. But Berthe had kept nagging her. 'Ricarda,' she'd said, 'either throw a huge party and face up to it, or run off to a desert island. But you have to decide what you're going to do on the big day, and, if it's the party, then you've got to organise it and you've got to get cracking.'

So she organised her sixtieth (organisation was of course

her strong suit), invited her friends and family to a restaurant by the Rhine, insisted throughout the evening that she didn't give a damn about her age and that everything would continue exactly as it had been before, gladly accepted everyone's compliments on her appearance and actually came out of the whole thing feeling very happy.

Yet, ever since she'd had this six in front of her age, things *hadn't* been exactly as they were before. The six had sucked some of the life out of her. Ricarda wouldn't fully acknowledge this feeling, but it had knocked her back. She'd never thought that she of all people would have a problem with ageing, but of course you always had to get stuck into something to know what it was like.

In short, she had suddenly been feeling almost as she had before, almost young again, since Philip had reappeared in her life with his flatshare.

'Were you already in love with him back then?' Justus enquired, undeterred.

Typical Justus. When he wanted to know something, he just went right ahead and asked.

'I'm not in love with him, and I never was,' she retorted.

'So why tell me that story?' he asked.

'Oh, Justus!' Ricarda reached for her bag with a laugh. 'You'd make quite a therapist, you would!' Sarcasm was always the best reply, to everything.

Justus grinned silently to himself and pulled his straw deftly through the next hole.

11

The World's Best Cold Meats Counter. The ten trophies, engraved with the respective years, stood in a harmonious line on the shelf. For ten years the delicatessen chain Flessen had awarded trophies to its fourteen branches in the Rhineland, and in those ten years Uschi had always come top, or near the top, of the rankings: five golds, three silvers and two bronzes. They were her pride and joy. One by one, she carefully wrapped the trophies in newspaper and placed them in her last packing case. It was almost midnight. Early tomorrow morning the adventure would finally get under way.

She did feel a bit queasy. She hardly knew the others. She'd seen Philip a couple of times at Mrs Kreuzer's. Ralf too, of course. Philip's mother had been a regular customer at Flessen, and, when Mrs Kreuzer's cancer had made it impossible for her to go out, Uschi would drop round once a week to deliver her special liver sausage. She'd done the odd bit of shopping for her too and occasionally taken Ralf for a walk. Mrs Kreuzer and she would then have a little chat together over a cup of coffee.

Uschi had liked Mrs Kreuzer. She was an elegant old lady. She'd often talked about her Philip, who ran a small health post out in the African bush. Mrs Kreuzer had missed him greatly during her final months. She had sensed that it would soon be all over for her, but she had never put any pressure on her son, of whom she was exceedingly proud.

Yet how overjoyed she had been when he'd phoned to say that he was coming back to Cologne to retire and take care of her. Mrs Kreuzer had been over the moon. The two ladies had even drunk a little glass of bubbly to celebrate.

Uschi had met Philip again at the funeral two and a half months ago, having earlier sent him the addresses of a few people who had supported his mother through her final months. At the funeral reception Uschi had happened to mention her search for a flat, and Philip had lent her a sympathetic ear. Uschi could see why Mrs Kreuzer had been proud of her son: he was an extremely distinguished man.

Two weeks later, he made her this amazing offer of a flat-share. Uschi had read about them in women's magazines. Vintage flatshares: the living arrangement of the future.

Sometimes, complete strangers would team up to organise joint activities and grow old together. Uschi had never imagined that she might be part of a 'living arrangement of the future'.

The other outsider in the flatshare was Eckart, a slim recent retiree with tortoiseshell-rimmed glasses and a melancholy look in his eyes. She had taken an immediate shine to Eckart on their first 'trial run' weekend on the North Sea island of Nordeney. His wife had died twenty years earlier and his son, having moved out of the family home ten years ago, had now jetted off to New Zealand. Eckart oozed loneliness, but he was a highly educated man, like the others; all of them had degrees.

Such people were called 'intellectuals' – Uschi knew that, and it put the wind up her. Uschi could show off about salami, but her knowledge was less sound when it came to politics and the economy, Europe, the recession and the various wars; those things were too complicated for her by far. If politicians couldn't deal with them, who was she to stick her oar in? But let no one take her for a fool regarding salami.

The weekend on Nordeney was very congenial. The sun smiled down from the sky, they went for long walks along the beach, chatted and told the others about their lives, shopped together, cooked together, drank wine and discussed a range of topics.

Ricarda had drawn up umpteen advance lists of questions

about what was important for whom, who needed how much space, and who was touchy on which subjects. She was a very meticulous woman. Uschi kept catching herself observing her. How did Ricarda manage to look so good for her age? She had a striking aura. She really came to life when she and Harry taunted each other, and her eyes would flash; it was clear that their squabbles were a habit from their student days. However, Ricarda's questionnaires did produce a few useful bits of information, for instance that Eckart didn't eat meat.

'Not even mincemeat?' laughed Harry, putting everyone in good spirits, but Uschi couldn't get this *vegetarianism* thing out of her mind. The next morning as they walked along the beach she explained to Eckart that battery farming was indeed an evil thing, but he should take a look at Flessen's private abattoir. Good animal husbandry – and Flessen only used the finest meat – had a positive effect on *taste* too; it didn't just make the animals' lives better before they—

Eckart interrupted her at this point: he didn't want any details.

That was the only slight note of discord. It was very pleasant overall, even the game when everyone had to stick a Post-it note on their forehead and guess who they were. Harry was Tolstoy. How was Uschi supposed to know who wrote *War and Peace*? Again she felt her nerves jangling; she hoped to goodness she would recognise her own character.

She was lucky: she was Marilyn Monroe. Things got a little tougher when Philip suggested that they play whist.

Whist. Never heard of it. Uschi found it hard to remember the rules. She got the black queens mixed up, but Eckart kindly helped her out. In any case, only four people could play at once: the dealer sat out.

They spent a second weekend on another island, Borkum, just to double-check. It thundered and rained the whole time, and they were trapped in the bungalow for three days solid; nobody felt like going outside. They heated up tinned food, drank wine and chatted as the shutters banged against the walls of the cottage. The others had another go at teaching her whist, and it rained and rained and rained.

By breakfast the next morning the storm had abated, but the clouds still hung low and the rain drummed quietly on the windowpanes. They said to themselves that, if they could make it through that weekend deluge without arguing, then they must be ready to share a flat.

Uschi smiled as she wrapped up her last trophy – *1999 Gold Medal for The World's Best Cold Meats Counter* – and laid it gently in the box. She gazed around her bare living room, which she had called her happy home for thirty-eight years. There were pale rectangles where the pictures had once hung.

She was ready.

12

Ralf sniffed his way across the empty flat's freshly polished floorboards. A scent of newly sanded wood lingered in the air; the smell was a bit similar to the park outside. The only objects left in his former owner's room were the flowery wingback chair and the old desk. Strong men had carried away all the other pieces of furniture. A new kitchen had been fitted, and Philip had moved into the master room, where he slept on a narrow day bed. The other rooms were empty.

The doorbell rang, and Philip went to answer it. Ralf wiggled out inquisitively on to the landing with him. A rumbling noise rose from the lower floors.

A naked woman edged her way up the stairs and banged her head on the side of the stairwell. Ouch! Philip's face twisted into a grimace of pain. Laden with a mannequin and five bags, with two cushions squashed under her arm, Ricarda climbed the last couple of stairs, her cheeks flushed red. She had put her hair up in a messy bun. Philip took a few steps towards her.

'Bitten off more than we can chew again?' He offered to relieve her of something. Ralf wagged his tail.

'No, don't,' said Ricarda, 'or you'll upset the balance.' All the same, Philip applied some light pressure and extracted the mannequin from under her arm. They smiled at each other.

'Ready?' he asked.

'Ready,' she replied with a nod.

They gave each other a kiss on both cheeks while contorting their bodies around the naked woman. The thuds from below grew louder, and deep male voices called out loud instructions.

'Well, friends, isn't this all very exciting!' Plump little Uschi came panting up the stairs. She too was weighed down, with bags and a plant. Ralf wagged his tail joyfully. He even considered jumping down a step to meet her and pawed at the air, but then opted to wait where he was. When Uschi reached the top, he sniffed nosily at her bag and jumped up happily against her legs. Not much, only about a half an inch, but that was a big deal for Ralf; he didn't do that for just anyone.

'Ralfie,' Uschi gasped, and tickled his floppy brown ears.

He yelped. He liked Uschi. Uschi smelled good. Uschi smelled of sausage.

'Crikey. How did Philip's mother ever get up here?' asked Harry, covered in sweat, as he went out on to the kitchen balcony for a smoke. He accidentally brushed the kitchen table as he went past. Uschi's pile of red stoneware plates with white polka dots sayed alarmingly. Ricarda had been unpacking the boxes for the kitchen, but she jumped to her feet to steady the teetering tower.

'You know what, Harry,' she said, 'those three floors are probably the very reason Philip's mother made it to ninety.'

'No, no – the oak wardrobe goes in the second room on the right. Yes, there.' Uschi's voice could be heard out in the hallway, conducting the removal men and redirecting at the last possible moment any packing cases that looked as if they might end up in the wrong room. Ralf was trying to stick close to Uschi, but it took all his agility to keep out of danger. Twice he received a light, unintentional kick, but he rolled nimbly aside and escaped into the nearest doorway.

'The dresser in the first room ... Yes, good. On the left there. What about this one?' Uschi inspected a box that another, slightly overweight removal man was hauling into the flat. It was unlabelled. She chatted away to the overweight man while she scratched the sticky tape off the packing case. 'No idea whose this is. I've only known them for two months, though Philip and Ricarda go way back ...'

Ricarda removed a red pressure cooker from a box and set it down beside four others.

'... since university, and Harry ... No, that little table goes in the first on the right. That's it. Anyway, Harry finished school with Philip, and ...'

A short removal man put another box down next to Ricarda and the kitchen table, causing Uschi's plates to wobble perilously again. Ralf toddled along the hallway.

'... no, Eckart and Philip didn't know each other, but Eckart's bank was in the same street as ...'

In his room, Eckart was instructing two movers to position his solid oak wardrobe one inch further to the left. Mind you ... He gauged the distance between it and the window, and shook his head. Back an inch to the right. Good. Or maybe a couple, if you'd be so kind. Perfect.

The overweight removal man stared at Uschi's fingers as if hypnotised. She had nearly finished scratching the tape off, but not quite.

'You see, Philip is very socially minded. He was in Africa, out in the bush, operating on people, in the middle of the wilderness. *Stop!* Put that box in the bathroom, please. Now, where was I?'

Oh, my— Uschi finally managed to open the box and fished out a *Playboy* magazine. A naked blonde beamed up at them. The mover directed a silent cry for help at Philip, who was lugging some tools into another room.

Philip glanced at the magazine cover on his way past. 'Harry,' he said drily.

'Which room?' the overweight mover begged breathlessly.

'Beautiful flat! Are you renting it?' asked one of Eckart's wardrobe-carriers. The overweight removal man rolled his eyes in horror, his expression saying, *Are you nuts?* Too late.

'Inherited,' Uschi continued. 'Philip's mother used to live here. She always bought her cooked sausage at our shop. She liked our liver sausage best. You should try—'

A terrible crash from the kitchen finally brought Uschi's stream of words to a halt. Ralf tucked his tail between his legs.

'Oh, *shit*!' hissed Harry. 'Who put those in such a stupid place?'

13

Paper plates. Paper plates on their first evening! Somewhat annoyed, Ricarda fetched her last three psychology books from the bottom of the box and slotted them into her bookcase. All because Harry couldn't look where he was going.

She pulled one of the books forward a tiny bit. She liked them to be perfectly aligned with the edge of the shelf. That way she could be sure no dust would settle there. She took a step back. Her new bookcase looked pretty good.

She folded the empty cardboard box and carried it to the front door. She couldn't help but smile as she passed the kitchen. Uschi was sitting at the kitchen table, absorbed with folding green napkins into fans to liven up the plain white paper plates. She was a real darling, that Uschi. And there were some nice smells coming from the stove, too.

Yet Ricarda's surge of contentment was immediately

dampened by the sight of the piles of pans, pots, chopping boards, kettles and cutlery trays next to Uschi's pasta sauce, which was bubbling away on the stove. Why had they only followed her instructions about the crockery? They'd ended up with three or four of everything else.

She put her folded box with the others by the entrance. She was just about to close the door of the small loo when her gaze fell on the toilet bowl. She put down the lid and called out: 'Friends, please shut the toilet lid. It really isn't—' Boom! Eckart rammed into her, muttered, 'Excuse me, please,' and backed a hand trolley into the flat.

'—feng shui,' Ricarda said, finishing her sentence with some bemusement. She stared at the unusual item Eckart was wheeling backwards along the passageway.

'A headstone?' whispered Philip.

'A headstone!' Ricarda nodded. She had taken refuge in Philip's room.

'His own?'

'No, Lotte's.'

'Who's Lotte?'

'His wife!'

'Oh, my God.'

'You can say that again.'

Philip took a deep breath to gather his wits. 'Ric, death is part of life. The Africans—'

'I don't want to sleep in this flat with a gravestone!'

'Dinner's ready!' came the call from the kitchen.

They tiptoed over to the door and watched Uschi make her way towards Eckart's room. She stopped outside Eckart's door. Ricarda and Philip held their breath. Uschi stood there for a while, staring into Eckart's room, before nodding slowly and turning on her heel. From the hallway she trilled, 'Everybody want some of my scrummy pasta?'

She caught sight of Ricarda and Philip hovering in the doorway before they could duck back inside.

'That includes you,' she said.

No reaction?

Admittedly, you had to be prepared for many things in a flatshare like this. But no reaction *whatsoever* to the discovery that one of them had furnished his room with a headstone? Ricarda swallowed hard. Hadn't the two weekends by the North Sea been long enough to check everything? Philip at first seemed equally stunned by Uschi's acceptance – but then, not by a bit of it.

'See,' he said, nodding. 'All part of life.'

Golly! Ricarda shook her head resignedly.

What had she let herself in for?

14

'And here we have ... the kitty.' Uschi placed a green, pot-bellied ceramic frog with boggling blue eyes and a wide mouth (with a slit for coins) on the kitchen windowsill.

It stopped Philip in his tracks as he cleared the table. It really was impressive how many things Uschi could conjure from her apparently bottomless box. Little home-made pots with ill-fitting lids; little wooden boards engraved with the likeness of animals; all manner of crocheted egg cosies – and Uschi's crochet skills seriously overstepped the boundaries of good taste. There were brightly coloured roosters, hens with blonde curls and cockerels that must have been cross-dressers, judging by their chic little feather miniskirts.

With a sly wink, Harry grabbed Philip's old photo album from the kitchen sideboard. He clearly found

Uschi's outlandish decorations highly amusing. Philip loaded the dirty salad bowls into the dishwasher, while Eckart, Ricarda and Harry studied the old snaps. Philip still felt a bit like the host, and he had therefore volunteered for washing-up duty. Uschi had cooked some delicious pasta with aubergines. Ricarda had got worked up once more over dinner about the lack of crockery and the surfeit of pressure cookers, but she soon calmed down again. Just like the old days.

It was their first evening together in his mother's apartment. She would have been happy to see them there. For years she had lived alone, and now all of a sudden there were all these guests, not to mention those splendid egg cosies.

Philip watched Ricarda examine a photo as he put the dirty cutlery into the machine. An anti-nuclear demo. She pushed back her hair and smiled.

'It was worth taking a stand back then. Remember those days, Philip?' Harry glanced up to catch Philip gazing at Ricarda. 'So? Are you happy, Philip?' said the old fox with a grin. 'That we're ... *all* here, I mean?'

Philip piled up the used paper plates. Was Harry alluding to how he'd rustled up these flatmates in record time? If only he hadn't taken Harry into his confidence.

'Absolutely, Harry, my dear. Absolutely,' he said, throwing him an unambiguous 'I'm-warning-you' glare.

'Why wouldn't Philip be happy?' said Ricarda, looking up.

'That's not at all what I meant,' said Harry. 'Our Philip just strikes me as being extremely shrewd.'

'Really?' asked Ricarda.

Philip stuffed the paper plates into the bin. 'Harry!' he said menacingly.

'What? What?' Harry gazed innocently at the paper plates. 'I'd have gladly washed up today too – that's all I wanted to say.'

Ha ha, very funny. *Screw you too*, thought Philip, grinning.

'Let's raise a glass,' called Uschi. 'I put a bottle of prosecco in the fridge.' And as if to mark the occasion she also produced five rust-red macramé napkin rings from her box.

'Look how young we were!' muttered Ricarda. The photo showed her standing at the seaside between Philip and Herbert, and the three of them were beaming into the camera with the reckless abandon of youth.

'When did you say your husband died?' asked Eckart.

'Five years ago.' Ricarda got up to give Philip a hand with the champagne glasses.

'And you didn't bring his gravestone with you?' teased Philip under his breath. Ricarda burst out laughing. She reached up to take the glasses out of the cupboard. Philip could smell her perfume, a scent of orange with a hint of Arabia, like a promise.

He fetched Uschi's prosecco out of the fridge and as he did so he accidentally brushed up against Ricarda's slim hips. He felt her give a slight start. 'You okay?' he asked.

'I – I'm okay,' she replied.

She took the fifth glass out of the cupboard and pushed it across the table to Philip, who popped the cork. Out of the corner of his eye he noticed Ricarda run her fingers distractedly through her hair.

'Wow, friends!' said Uschi as he filled the glasses. 'To think that I could have been sitting on my own in some teeny-weeny flat because of my part-time job. But no! Here I am, with you, all in one boat. Thank you, Philip.'

Eckart gulped. The idea of the boat seemed to alarm him.

Philip raised his glass. 'We're not what we say, but what we do. And therefore – I'm very happy that you're all here.'

They drank – a little emotionally perhaps.

'And remember,' Uschi continued, 'even when a storm is brewing, it doesn't matter which direction the wind's blowing, only how you set the sails.'

'Uh-oh,' said Harry, standing up and lighting his cigarette on the way out on to the balcony. 'Here's the first storm brewing! I call for a ban on Uschi's kitsch!'

They all laughed. Ricarda motioned to Harry to shut the balcony door. Uschi poured the last of the prosecco into Ricarda's glass. Eckart said that in France that meant that she'd be married before the year was out, and Uschi wondered who the bridesmaid would be. Interestingly, she didn't raise the issue of the groom.

*

Philip ran his eye over the lively little group.

The first thing that had struck him when he set foot in this apartment barely three months ago was the familiar smell. His mother had departed this life three days before he arrived, but the entire flat, its carpets and old furniture, had still exuded her life and her spirit. She had spent her whole life in this apartment, and he had grown up here.

And now here they were, five people life had pitched together, sitting in the refurbished kitchen, drinking prosecco. For a second, Philip felt as though they were only visiting, as if his mother might step through the door at any moment and marvel at the new fitted kitchen.

'I'm going to bed,' said Eckart, and stood up.

'What? How about another game of whist?' asked Ricarda disappointedly.

'No,' said Eckart with a shake of his head. He was tired.

'I'm in!' Harry came back into the kitchen from the balcony, full of enthusiasm.

'Hallelujah! Ric and Harry agree on something. We should drink to that!' said Philip, raising his glass a second time.

'Too true,' nodded Harry, and aimed a peck at Ricarda's cheek.

'Get away from me! You stink!' said Ricarda, waving her hand around to dispel Harry's cigarette fumes. Uschi fetched the playing cards.

'Goodnight,' said Eckart.

'Goodnight, Eckart,' they called cheerfully after him.

'Who wants to deal?' asked Philip, taking a bottle of red wine from the shelf.

'And make them squeal,' cried Harry, grabbing the notepad. The old repartee was still there. Philip glanced over at Ricarda again. Their eyes met. She looked away in slight confusion.

15

Eckart closed the door behind him, and stood for a while in the middle of the room. Peace at last. He was exhausted. He lit the small candle beside Lotte's headstone. He was glad the day was over. It was hard work having so many people around, all chattering incessantly. Eckart simply wasn't used to it. He was used to being alone. Now and then he would confide in Lotte, but that wasn't hard work: they generally agreed. He contemplated the gravestone. Was she truly comfortable here? Did she wonder where she'd ended up?

Tomorrow he would go to the cemetery where Lotte lay buried. Once a week he would take a stroll to her old grave as he always had, and place a small red candle on the mown lawn.

Twenty years ago, when the soil was shovelled on to her coffin and the dark, damp sods gradually filled the space between them, he had been sure that he would one day lie by her side. But the cemetery authorities had thwarted his plans. The cemetery had been forced to downsize, and the grave had been levelled. Lotte's headstone had stood in their garden ever since, next to the yellow rose bush that they had planted all those years ago and which still flowered every summer.

And now she lay here. That was a lot of moving within a short space of time.

'Sleep well, Eckart. The first night's dreams always come true,' said Uschi's muffled, friendly voice through the door.

Eckart looked up with a start, frantically racking his brains for a polite answer that would discourage Uschi from coming in, but then he heard her cross the creaking floorboards back to the kitchen. He breathed out in relief. Soon afterwards he heard the others' raucous laughter, and then the kitchen door closed softly.

Uschi had used his exquisite olive oil to fry onions, but apart from that Eckart probably liked her best of all. She was extremely considerate. And her egg cosies were something else.

Other than that, though? Had it been the right decision to move in here? He put on his pyjamas, blew out Lotte's candle, got into bed and switched off the light. He stared up into the darkness. Tomorrow he would go to the cemetery and talk it all through with Lotte.

16

Philip opened his eyes and blinked against the bright springtime sunlight. The sycamore leaves outside were swaying gently. The room faced east. Philip had instinctively chosen his parents' room when he moved in. Everything had still felt strange when he'd positioned his bed between his mother's wingback chair and his father's desk, despite the fact that it was in this very room that he had been born sixty-one years earlier.

He dangled his hand over the side of the bed, but nothing happened. Of course – Ralf wasn't there. Before the others moved in, Ralf would stretch out every night beside Philip's bed. Yesterday, however, he had trotted after Uschi without so much as a glance back at Philip. The tubby opportunist knew where there was salami to be had.

Philip got up and opened the window wide, letting the morning air stream in. He got back into bed, plumped up the pillow under his head and gazed out at the sycamore. He loved these early mornings; out in the bush they were the only time he'd had to himself. The sound of the wind rustling the big green leaves, and the twittering of the birds, were still unfamiliar to him; they were so unlike the noises of the savannah.

So now they had all moved in, and the adventure could begin. Their first evening together had felt completely natural. Philip smiled to himself. He thought of Uschi's scratchy macramé napkin rings, of Eckart's expression when Uschi had swamped the large frying pan with his exquisite olive oil, of Harry's reaction to Ricarda's suggestion that they draw up a cleaning rota. Harry had stuck a Post-it note on her forehead with the words 'I am obsessively tidy and thick'; and Ricarda had responded by whacking a Post-it on the fridge door that read 'If you've got anything heavy that needs carrying, just ask helpful Harry!' This in turn caused Uschi to declare it the flat's complaints box. Philip was eager to see how long it would be until the poor old fridge collapsed under the sheer weight of paper. They were a pretty mixed bunch, each with strong opinions, and none of them was a spring chicken any more. They'd have to close ranks, like rugby players, but even a winning team had the occasional wrangle.

What was new to Philip was the relatively trivial causes

of their arguments, and the luxury he'd observed since his return to Germany. No great luxury, no, but he found it disconcerting how people took it for granted that everything was available, everywhere and at all times.

From his time in the bush he was accustomed to getting by with very little. When something was lacking – and everything was always lacking – people would improvise. They would sit down together, think things over, tinker around, adapt objects, refine them and come up with a solution. Someone would always find a way of making up for what they lacked. And solving a problem was possibly the most enriching experience one could ever have.

He'd had to get used to the frugality of life when he'd first moved to Mali. He had assisted an old doctor in a health post. There were no modern appliances, and the whole set-up was nowhere near minimum medical standards. From that moment on, it had been all about basic medical provision.

The first few months were tough, but he gritted his teeth and learned to operate without electricity or running water – with next to nothing. When the old doctor died Philip took over the running of the health post, and eventually he no longer noticed that the working conditions verged on medieval.

There were setbacks, of course there were. Once, during an operation, the emergency generator broke down as well, and a fifteen-year-old boy whose parents had carried him for two days to the health post died in Philip's hands. All because of a power cut.

It had taken him weeks to get over that death. It was the only time that something had truly been lacking, because it had cost a person – a boy – his life.

Philip held his palm up to the wall. Was Ricarda awake? There was only this thin wall between them now.

They had played whist until four in the morning; they just couldn't stop. As in the old days. Philip hadn't been able to take his eyes off Ricarda, and every time the cards were dealt he had hoped that they would get to play together. Often his hopes had come true, but unfortunately each time one of them had had a weak hand. They'd still won a few games with their trumps, mind you. It had been magical, as if they were bound together by an invisible thread. Their hands had complemented each other's perfectly.

Philip swung his feet over the side of the bed. A promising clatter issued from the kitchen.

Their first breakfast together. Philip broke into a smile. New cards, a new stab at happiness.

17

There was something moving under the grey rug. A small, elongated bump, running back and forth. A mouse? Ricarda stared at it. It worked its way to the edge of the carpet, reached the fringe, paused for a second and then appeared. Ricarda recoiled. It was a hand. A slender old lady's hand.

Ricarda shrank back. The hand lay there on the floor, unmoving, then the little finger twitched, the hand reached out towards her and—

Ricarda woke with a start. She was bathed in sweat. Where was she? It took her a while to find her bearings in the new room.

She stared down at the rug. There was nothing there. No lump, no hand. She was breathing heavily. It was all a dream, all a bad dream. She sank back into her pillow in relief.

*

Ricarda slid her feet into her slippers and went into the bathroom. Sure, death was part of life, but was it acceptable to move in with a headstone? Not really, she thought, but on the other hand where was poor Eckart to put it otherwise? Why was she finding it so hard to deal with that stone? Because it reminded her of her own mortality?

Ricarda closed the bathroom door behind her and went over to the washbasin. Her crumpled face grimaced back at her. They'd stayed up late yesterday. They had played whist and drunk red wine through the night. Another hand, and then one more. Harry had been indefatigable, at the beginning of each new round Uschi had said, 'It's true, we'll never meet again this young,' and Philip had uncorked the next bottle. As luck would have it, he and she had played together quite a lot. They'd been on the same wavelength, not even needing to look at each other. It had been wonderful. Like the old days.

Only the next morning, right now, wasn't like the old days. You couldn't keep on drinking red wine until four in the morning and carry on as usual.

It didn't matter, though, and she didn't regret it.

She nodded politely to the crumpled lady in the mirror. 'I don't recognise you, but I'll wash you anyway,' she said, turning on the tap and immediately freezing. Directly in front of her on the ledge under the mirror was a glass with a set of dentures in it. A dental bridge with four false teeth. This was no dream. It was right under her nose.

Okay. Why not? Something new every day. Welcome to the vintage flatshare.

She picked up the glass and tidied it away next to the toothpaste-encrusted yellow plastic cup in Harry's compartment. A dirty shaving brush, a brown bar of curd soap, a splayed toothbrush: the false teeth were at home in Harry's compartment. Ricarda shook her head. Yep, you really did have to get stuck into something to know what it was like.

In her own compartment stood a tidy array of cosmetics. Ever since a pharmacist had first slipped a sample of anti-wrinkle cream *for very mature skin* into her bag, she had grown used to spending a lavish amount on creams and lotions to keep herself up to the mark. Not at that pharmacy, though. Somehow she hadn't appreciated the advice one bit. She ran her hand over the various little tubes.

'Going to be much longer?' said Harry with a knock on the door. The loo was obviously occupied.

'Are you desperate?' she asked innocently.

'Yeah! Get a move on!' said Harry, mumbling irritably that he would otherwise be forced to do a Gérard Depardieu, who had once relieved his bladder in an aeroplane aisle.

Ricarda wrinkled her nose. 'Grit your teeth, Gérard,' she muttered, savouring Harry's bladder trouble for a little longer before picking out a small tube of 'Relax', opening the door and shooting Harry a grin. 'Hi, Harry. How's the prostate this morning?'

'Working,' said Harry, slamming the bathroom door.

Ricarda smiled. She still loved teasing Harry more than anyone else in the world.

18

'Sorry, Uschi, but there's still no reason to haul that mutt around on a platter,' said Harry.

'Oh, yes, there is. The risk of a heart attack,' Uschi retorted, crowning the brown boiled eggs with her strange cockerel cosies. 'He's got such short legs.'

'Short legs?' Harry, who was rolling a cigarette at the table, glanced down at Ralf in bemusement. The fat dachshund wasn't budging from his position by Uschi's feet, hoping against hope that a slice of salami would fall his way.

'Exactly.' Uschi nodded. 'His legs are so short that his big belly scrapes on the floor the whole time. The continuous rubbing causes Ralf's heart to overheat, increasing his risk of a heart attack.'

Uschi seemed to have given the matter some serious thought. Harry found her theory incredibly simplistic, but very refreshing. In any case, Uschi had a clear world view, and he liked that. He reached for the empty tobacco tin and lobbed it towards the bin. Direct hit. A startled Ralf hopped to one side: the tin had caught him squarely on his chubby behind.

'Harry!' Uschi shouted indignantly.

'What? He needs exercise!'

'Do you know what I dreamed?' Ricarda came into the kitchen and absentmindedly scooped up the tobacco tin as it rolled towards her.

'I guess we'll soon find out,' grumbled Harry. He hadn't appreciated that prostate joke one bit. God knew he wasn't sensitive, but this constant urge to urinate was really getting him down. And Ricarda of all people, oh so proper Ricarda, had to rub it in childishly. It was very silly.

'A hand crawled out of my bedroom floor.'

'A hand?' Uschi, who was cutting a slice of crusty bread, turned round in shock.

'Was it Philip's mother's?' said Harry, looking up in astonishment. He wouldn't have credited Ricarda with such a subversive imagination.

Ricarda shook her head.

'I think it was Lotte's hand,' she whispered.

'Good grief!' gasped Uschi, staring wide-eyed at Ricarda.

'Hey, folks, it was like a youth hostel here last night. How often do you all have to go to the toilet?' Philip was in a good mood when he entered the kitchen – and was amazed to find himself confronted by three grave faces. 'Joke,' he added quickly. 'Forget it. When you gotta go, you gotta go. Something up?'

'It was a little shop of horrors here last night,' said Harry. 'We still have to identify the corpse.'

Ricarda opened the fridge and held her hand up to her nose. Harry grinned – he had been looking forward to this moment. He caught a whiff of smelly goat's cheese from his seat at the table. It had been entirely foreseeable that Eckart's taste in cheese wouldn't be the same as Ricarda's. Ricarda extracted the stinking cheese with her fingertips and reached for some Tupperware.

'I'm not really coping very well with having a headstone in the apart—'

'Good morning, Eckart!' said Philip at exaggerated volume. Ricarda looked round, caught with the stinking cheese in her hand. Eckart was standing in the doorway, gazing bashfully at it.

Why did oddballs always have such a hard time? Harry wondered. Eckart wouldn't hurt a fly, was the calmest of them all, and yet he had been cast out on to the margins after only one day.

'Come and sit down, Eckart.' He shunted up along the bench.

'Um, I always go for a little walk in the morning,' said Eckart, 'so don't bother waiting for me. I'm not really one for breakfast anyway. See you later.' He nodded and scuttled out of the flat; the latch snapped into place behind him.

'Damn,' said Ricarda. 'Did he hear me?'

Uschi shrugged.

'What if he did?' said Harry.

'Don't be so insensitive,' Ricarda retorted.

Come again? Harry couldn't believe his ears. 'Which one of us has a problem with that stone? Not me.'

19

'Did you see the look on Eckart's face?' said Ricarda, picking up a square blue and red striped plate.

'Well, Uschi did look pretty funky in that pink tracksuit and green sweatband of hers.'

'I didn't know Jane Fonda was still so trim.'

'I didn't even know she was still alive,' grinned Philip.

Ricarda put the plate down again. The china shop really had something for every taste. The five of them had set out to look for new crockery. Ricarda and Philip had gone ahead to check out what was on offer while Uschi, Harry and Eckart had a second coffee at the café opposite.

They'd been living together for three days now. Some things had clicked into place, others hadn't. No one had mentioned the stone again. Ricarda had chalked it up as a 'flatshare concession'. Eckart kept himself to himself; he needed time. Uschi was a dear, and you couldn't really hold anything against her – apart from, maybe, her constant stream of kitsch mottos, a somewhat eccentric taste in furnishings, her daily aerobics sessions with Jane Fonda, her slight fallibility when 'counting trumps' and ... No, she really was a dear.

It was funny too, how she had got up from the breakfast table the morning before and said to Eckart, 'I've got to work at the shop, Mr Eckart, but I'll be back at four. And I want you ready for gym at five p.m. sharp in the living room, okay?' And then she was gone.

Poor Eckart's shocked eyes stared at the doorway for several seconds until Uschi's face popped back into sight. 'Only joking!' she shrieked. Eckart let out an audible sigh of relief and smiled awkwardly, obviously out of practice. 'The aerobics lesson is optional,' Uschi had added mischievously, and a *genuine* smile had lit up Eckart's face.

She was a real sweetie, Uschi. She knew how to deal with people, how to loosen them up, or even get under their skin a bit – and she knew how to buck them up. That took generosity. Empathy and generosity. Not many people could do that, but Uschi definitely could.

Harry was the only one who got on Ricarda's nerves. Every evening he would thud his darts into his bloody dartboard, making Ricarda's mirror and nerves quiver. That too would click into place, though.

She looked at some branded china plates with a wreath of

hand-painted blue roses around the edges. They were pretty. Not exactly cheap, but they were understated and classic.

Ricarda looked around for Philip and found him in the entrance, inspecting a run-of-the-mill white dinner service that wouldn't have seemed out of place in a youth hostel. Special offer. Continuing to browse, she picked up a coffee cup decorated with a good old Friesian pattern. Timeless – and as easy on the eye as ever.

'To imagine we'd one day be choosing china together . . .' Philip murmured over her shoulder. She flinched. There was that feeling again. That look. Affectionate, and yet with a tiny spark of irony that always left room for a bit of ambiguity; it still tugged uneasily at her heartstrings, though.

There was undoubtedly something very romantic about choosing china together, however quintessentially middle class it was.

But Philip had nonetheless managed to plant a seed of doubt in her mind that this time his words might not be ironic.

'Yeah, who'd've thought it?' she said, a grin masking her uncertainty, but she was irritated by the sheer unimaginativeness of her answer, and pretended to be studying the various types of crockery *very closely indeed*. Philip wandered off in the other direction.

It wasn't the first time since their move that Philip had displayed that same sense of ambiguity. She was surprised to realise that she almost expected it of him. That was just as it had been at university, when she, Herbert and Philip had turned night into day, and each new day into an adventure. She'd often felt as if she were in Truffaut's film *Jules et Jim*, the only difference being that Philip hadn't been interested in her – not genuinely, in any case – nor she in him. Yet on some level they had loved each other. They got on well; they flirted with the ambiguity. She enjoyed the sense that they felt something for each other, but would never find out what. They were friends, nothing more. Ricarda was going out with Herbert – and the three of them had a feeling that together they ruled the world.

Now, over thirty-five years on, Ricarda suddenly felt that old between-the-lines feeling again. She didn't know what it meant, but it sent a tingle through her.

'What do you think of this?'

The plate Philip was waving in front of her nose was . . . Yes, it was a plate. A white plate. From the stack in the entrance. Ricarda groped for words.

'Almost as good as a paper plate,' she said.

'Except it's china.'

'Mm-hm.' Ricarda looked at the bottom of Philip's china paper plate: 5.99. 'It's not expensive,' she said with a nod.

Philip furrowed his brow. 'I'm not stingy.'

'You're not?'

'No,' said Philip, 'I just like to keep it plain. When I see the kinds of things that are important to you here—' indicating her delicate blue rosebuds '—they seem pointless to me.'

'Of course,' said Ricarda, running her finger gently over the hand-painted flowers.

'Sorry, Ric. Let's wait and see what the others say, but for my part I like to keep it plain.'

And tasteless, thought Ricarda.

The door opened, and Uschi, Harry, Eckart and Ralf came into the shop. Harry immediately picked up one of Philip's white plates from the stack in the entrance. 'Look at this,' he said, showing it to Eckart. 'Plain and tasteful.'

Ricarda's shoulders slumped. Why was she so keen on democracy? Why hadn't she just chosen the china herself? Why had she forced all her flatmates to make the all-important crockery decision together? Why? She should have anticipated that together Philip, Harry and Eckart would form an unassailable majority.

'So? What have you found?' Uschi came inquisitively over to them and her puzzled gaze shifted back and forth between Philip's white plate and Ricarda's 'pointless' little blue flowers. Eckart shrugged. 'Either's fine by me, to be honest. Although, come to think of it, I do perhaps prefer the plain ones,' he said, gesturing at Philip's white plates.

Uschi's eyes scoured the store and came to rest gleefully on a shelf containing some red stoneware plates with white polka dots. Ralf, by her side as always, wagged his tail.

Oh no, please, thought Ricarda, shaking her head. *Not the rustic-red stoneware with the white dots.*

'I'm so used to them,' Uschi sighed. She glanced again

at the two plates she had to choose from, and eventually pointed to Ricarda's blue flowers. 'Yep, that one's pretty.'

Ricarda flashed her a grateful smile.

One vote for white, one for flowers. A draw. Which meant: defeat. Because Harry's opting for the blue flowers was about as likely as hearing a vicar say, 'Now go forth and sin.'

Meanwhile Harry was looking at each plate in turn and shaking his head.

'Oh, boy, oh, boy! Really, couldn't you find anything better?'

Whoops! Ricarda had got Harry all wrong again. Her eyes ran quickly along the shelves. Time was of the essence if Harry were not to plump for 'plain'. There was still the . . .

She raced over to the Friesian set. 'Then how about this one? Timeless. A typical Friesian pattern!' She held up the plate. 'It's been a classic for at least eighty years, I'd say.'

'That's the one we had on Nordeney, isn't it?' beamed Uschi. 'Oh, yes! Wouldn't it be a lovely emblem for our flatshare?'

She nodded to Eckart and Philip, who both nodded back, their faces emotionless. *Yes, what a lovely emblem.*

'Eighty? Older than us? Crikey, let's get it.' Harry gave the saleswoman a cursory nod, brushed past the stack of plates in the entrance and disappeared through the door.

Phew. Okay, it was a compromise, but at least the china paper plates were off the table.

20

The red crazy-golf ball zipped along the track, sped into the
narrow entrance to the loop-the-loop, whipped around it
and shot out into the metal gutter on the far side. It banged
into the strip at the back of the roundabout and slid back,
rolling just past the hole and coming to a stop alongside it.
Ralf pricked up his ears.

'Good grief, Eckart!' said Uschi with a broad grin. 'Your
very first shot! I'll never get it into that loopy thing.'

Eckart gave a satisfied nod and strode off after his ball. 'A
fluke, Uschi. Pure luck.'

Ralf galloped off, overtook Eckart, picked up the red ball
with his teeth and set it down at Eckart's feet – on the near
side of the loop-the-loop.

'Oh, Ralf,' said Eckart. 'What did you do that for?'

Ralf looked up in surprise. For so many years his old

owner had bugged him to fetch balls and sticks, and now this. These new owners were strange.

Uschi burst out laughing, reached down and scratched his neck. 'Good boy, Ralfie. Good boy.' She stood up again and smiled innocently at Eckart. 'He doesn't know any better.'

Now Eckart also bent down to him and gave him a quick pat. 'You were a good boy, but leave them where they are next time, okay?'

Ralf didn't really find it okay, but he did as he was told. If they wanted to look a gift horse in the mouth, that was fine with him. He'd always found retrieving things stupid anyway. He trotted over to the old oak tree by the small clubhouse and stretched out, leaving the pair of them to get on with it. If they felt like retrieving each other's balls, then who was he to stand in their way? They had only themselves to blame.

It was a beautiful spring morning. After breakfast Uschi had suggested to Eckart that they go for a game of crazy golf. The others were already out and about. Eckart had initially turned her down as he sat at the table, hunched over the crossword puzzle with his magnifying glass, but Uschi had refused to take no for an answer. She didn't have to go to work that day, and she felt like having some fun.

So the three of them had set out for the little crazy-golf course in the park. They had attached Ralf to a long leash so that he could sniff around at his leisure, and for that he was extremely grateful. It made a welcome change.

A different person had taken him for a walk on each of the past four days. With Ricarda it had been frenetic, as she rushed from one house to the next, chattering into her phone the whole time. With Harry he'd had to wait for ages outside a corner pub, tied to a bike rack. Then Eckart had attached him directly to his bike and ridden around half the city with him. It had been a real challenge; Ralf had found himself longing, misty-eyed, for the bike rack outside Harry's pub. Luckily it was usually Philip who took him out. Philip would walk him to the park, sit down on a bench and give Ralf free rein while he read the newspaper. That was ideal.

Today Ralf had come out for the first time with Uschi and Eckart, and he regarded this cosy combination as a very good thing. They should do this more often. Definitely.

'Ralf?' Uschi was waving to him from the final hole. He clambered to his feet. A green ball was heading for the hole on the ramp nearest to him. He ran after it and pinched it.

'Come 'ere, you bloody mutt,' roared the wiry man who had hit the ball. Ralf was so terrified that he swallowed the ball and started to wheeze. It was lodged in his throat.

'Ralf!' Uschi and Eckart came rushing up to him.

'Can't you people keep control of your stupid mutt?' the wiry man grumbled. Ralf felt the air slowly seeping out of his lungs.

Suddenly Eckart grabbed him by the hind legs and

whirled him into the air upside down. Ralf coughed and spluttered. Eckart shook him high and low, and eventually the ball popped out on to the course.

Air. Saved. Eckart lowered him back to the ground.

'Eckart, you hero!' cried Uschi, cradling Ralf. 'As for you,' she said, pointing at the uneasy crazy-golfer, 'next time kindly keep control of your ball.'

The man was so taken aback that he couldn't think of a riposte.

Yes, all in all it had been a nice walk. Something a little different.

Uschi and Eckart handed in their equipment, and Eckart bought Uschi an ice cream before they set off home. The streets were busy. The mime artist who usually did a silent Charlie Chaplin impersonation was chatting to an Indian rose-seller and a clergyman. A group of Japanese tourists were taking snaps of a couple of Jehovah's Witnesses because they happened to be standing in front of a souvenir shop displaying huge sculptures of Cologne cathedral. A large lady was poised with her companion outside a carnival store, pointing in delight at a princess costume. A young couple were walking hand in hand in front of them.

'You can tell they haven't been going out together for very long, can't you?' said Uschi.

'Really?' asked Eckart.

'It still looks a bit awkward,' proclaimed Uschi.

'What does?' asked Eckart.

'Their happiness. It still looks awkward, the way they're holding hands. A bit stiff.'

'Stiff?' Eckart coughed. They ambled along for a while in silence. The young couple turned down a side street, but Eckart and Uschi were carried onwards by the stream of people. Ralf kept close to them. He was still aching with shock, and all that wheezing had quite worn him out.

'Did you use to walk along hand in hand with Lotte?' Uschi asked.

Eckart pondered this. 'No,' he said, 'but after she died I saw nothing but couples in the street. Couples everywhere, everywhere I looked.'

'Old couples?' she asked.

'Yes, that too,' he agreed. 'Young ones, old ones. Old couples are very endearing.'

'Because neither of them has wasted away yet and left the other behind,' she mumbled.

He nodded. 'What about your husband? Did he—'

'He didn't waste away. He ran away,' she said.

They continued walking and turned off into a quieter street. Ralf was fond of them both. Uschi, of course – for the salami. But Eckart too, and not just because he had saved his life in such spectacular fashion. That morning he too had let slip – from his fingertips – a piece of salami from the fridge.

In any case, it was worth sticking close to Eckart.

21

Uschi gazed with satisfaction at her three rabbits. Fine specimens, they were, raised free-range on south-facing slopes. She had skinned them at Flessen, and now here they lay, beautiful and naked, on the kitchen table. Harry was perched next to them. She had ordered him to peel some vegetables, and it was wonderful to see how ineptly he was going about it. The springtime sun was shining, so Ricarda was hanging out some washing on the balcony. Uschi loved these moments in the life of their little club.

'A thousand-star hotel?' asked Harry.

'With a pool!' Uschi announced proudly, and dried the salad leaves in a tea towel. 'Remember to bring your sleeping bag and swimming costume.'

Uschi was happy. She'd invited all her flatmates to spend

the weekend by a small lake, and the programme included a picnic, a campfire and a night under the stars. The work surface was covered with piles of brightly coloured Tupperware and aluminium foil packaging containing salads, sandwiches, crudités, dips and other treats.

Philip came into the kitchen, waving a piece of paper.

'Well?' Ricarda asked from outside on the balcony.

'Negative,' said Philip.

'Told you so,' said Ricarda with a smile.

'Is it compulsory to take the test when you come back from Africa?' asked Harry.

With a shake of his head, Philip leaned over Uschi's plastic boxes. 'It should be compulsory for you lot to go to Africa. Look at all this aluminium foil!'

'I've never taken an AIDS test. Maybe I should some time,' said Uschi, and shoved Philip away from her command centre.

'Uschi,' said Harry, 'the last time you had sex, AIDS wasn't even invented!'

'For God's sake, Harry! Can't you just *once in a while* spare us your stupid comments?' Ricarda called from the balcony, as she shook out a white vest.

'That one wasn't *so* bad,' laughed Philip, stealing a slice of red pepper from Uschi.

Hohoho, Harry chuckled.

That was the last straw! How dared they! Uschi grabbed the carving knife and, laughing, brandished it at Philip and

Harry. 'You men can count yourselves lucky I have to deal with the rabbits first, or else ... ' She paused.

Eckart was standing in the doorway, staring at the kitchen table.

Oh, dear – that vegetarianism thing!

Uschi gently lowered the knife. The rabbits were lying bare and dead on the table. Her laughter caught in her throat.

'Oh, hi, Eckart,' said Philip. 'We were just looking for—' He glanced anxiously at Uschi for something to cover the dead bodies.

She handed Philip some aluminium foil. He tore off a strip and awkwardly wrapped the rabbits in it. Their little heads flopped out of the end, so he shoved them back inside. Uschi pushed Philip with the package in his hands out on to the balcony to join Ricarda, and she blocked the doorway with her short, round body.

'Eckart, we—'

'That's for tomorrow, is it?' asked Eckart.

'For the barbecue ... ' she said sheepishly, nodding and trying her best to hide the carving knife behind her back.

'Don't take this the wrong way, Uschi, but ... I don't know yet whether I'm coming with you.'

She grasped for words. Poor Eckart was wrestling with himself, she knew; he obviously didn't want to be a spoil-sport again, but ... All of a sudden he was staring past her shoulder to the balcony, where Ricarda was vigorously shaking a large pair of men's underpants.

'Are those mine?' he asked.

'Um,' said Ricarda, holding up the pants with a puzzled expression, 'I just grabbed everything I could find.'

'You've been rummaging in my dirty washing?'

'No-o, well, only to fill the machine.'

Eckart walked stiffly out on to the balcony, tugged his underpants from Ricarda's hand and poked around for his other clothes in the basket full of Uschi's and Ricarda's knickers, bras and vests.

'I would ask you . . . to refrain from doing so in future.'

Tight-lipped, Eckart pushed past Philip and the rabbits on his way out of the kitchen. Ricarda cast Philip a look. One of the heads flopped out of the foil again.

'And yet *he* has a headstone,' giggled Ricarda.

Poor Eckart. Uschi followed him out into the hallway, still clutching her knife, and watched his back disappear into his room to the sound of stifled chuckles from the others.

'Time to set the sails, Uschi!' Harry called from the kitchen.

22

Eckart wondered what time it was right then in New Zealand. He asked himself the question at least once a day. Was it night-time there at the moment? Was Christoph asleep? Or was it daytime, and was Christoph awake? Like Eckart – except in Cologne it was the middle of the night.

He padded into the kitchen and went to turn on the light, but decided against it and gently drew the door shut behind him. *Just don't wake anyone up.* Beams of moonlight fell through the window. Ricarda's fifties kitchen clock read ten past three.

Even though they hadn't seen very much of each other since Christoph had left home years ago, he missed his son. It would be reassuring to have him nearby.

Christoph had been fifteen when his mother died. He suffered greatly from the loss; he'd always been a mummy's boy. He was a kind, affable lad: he really did justice to his surname, Fröhlich – 'cheerful'. Christoph had stared straight ahead during the funeral, his eyes blank; he didn't shed a single tear. And Eckart, who didn't know how to cope with his own grief, had had to shake hands, nod bravely and keep his composure, instead of taking his son in his arms and holing up with him somewhere – although Christoph would probably have preferred to hole up with his mother than with his father.

Their GP had put Christoph on pills to counter his bouts of depression, but within two months he had said that he was okay and didn't need to take the medication any more; he couldn't stay on medication for the rest of his life. Eckart took a while to grasp the brutal lucidity of his son's words: it was true that they would miss Lotte for the rest of their lives. Over and over again, whenever they least expected it.

They never directly broached the subject of her death. They arranged their lives around it; they appeared to have agreed to bracket it out. Speaking about it would only rub unnecessary salt in the wound. Christoph spent a lot of time in his bedroom, playing video games, devouring comics about violent superheroes and renting fantasy films from video stores. No, you couldn't say they were especially close, but they both knew what they had lost, and that united them without the need for much talk. And it put lots of things – not to say everything – into perspective. There were very few arguments. Christoph was average at school; only his chemistry and physics grades were good. He passed his exams without any fuss. Lotte would have been happy.

Eckart didn't really know what was on Christoph's mind. There was trouble with alcohol a couple of times, but on the whole the boy was low-maintenance. Handball certainly played a relatively important part in that: Christoph trained with his club twice a week, and he got on well with his teammates.

And thus they lived out the years – sometimes in tandem, sometimes in parallel – in a house from which the most important person was missing, the one person who really counted. Every morning Eckart went to the bank, and a little later Christoph went to university.

After finishing his studies the young man rented a small flat. He had a chemistry degree and had taken up a good job with a pharmaceutical company. He worked hard and continued to play handball. He was discreet regarding matters of the heart. He had the occasional girlfriend, but he never brought them home. Christoph was not forthcoming when Eckart enquired.

Then two years ago Christoph had met Elena, a bubbly New Zealander who worked for the same company as he did. Christoph had brought her round three months back, and the two of them had announced to Eckart that Elena was returning to New Zealand and Christoph wanted to go with her.

'What about your work?' Eckart had asked.

'My work's eating me up,' Christoph replied. He couldn't spend the rest of his life staring at a computer in a laboratory.

Couldn't he? Eckart asked.

'No,' Christoph had answered, bordering on insolent. Just because his father felt fine about having spent his whole life behind some stupid counter, it didn't mean that he, his son, had to adopt the same approach. Life was there to be lived, he'd said with a defiant grin at Elena.

She had given him a tense smile back. 'Cut it out, Christoph,' she'd mumbled in a placating tone.

'And what are you going to do in New Zealand?' Eckart had asked.

'Grow kiwis,' Christoph had replied. Elena and he were going to take over her parents' run-down kiwi plantation and fix the place up.

'Grow kiwis?' Eckart had repeated.

'Yes.' Elena had nodded enthusiastically. 'And you'll always be more than welcome.'

'That's kind of you,' Eckart had said. He couldn't think of anything else to say. It had felt as though he had learned more about his son in those five minutes than in the previous twenty years.

The monotonous ticking of Ricarda's kitchen clock cut through the silence. Eckart picked up the kettle and filled it with water. He put it on the gas ring and screwed up his eyes. He had to focus his attention on the strange automatic lighter. These new-fangled devices. He recalled with fondness the old electric stove back home.

Home.

Maybe he shouldn't have sold the house. Now he was standing here in the kitchen of someone else's flat, which he was supposed to call home.

He opened several cupboard doors, searching for the tea. He counted back through the hours. In New Zealand it was now—

'The tea's there on the right.'

He had a shock.

Uschi was sitting at the kitchen table in the dark. She was wearing a light-blue towelling dressing gown over her nightdress and had colourful foam rollers in her hair. She was holding a red stoneware cup with white polka dots.

'Uschi! What are you doing here?'

'Same as you, I guess.'

'Hmm?'

'I can't sleep.' She pointed to the second cupboard door from the right. Eckart opened it and took out the camomile tea.

'The cups are over there on the left,' said Uschi.

Even I know that, he thought. He grabbed a cup and dangled the teabag over the edge. He didn't really feel like talking right now. He adjusted the kettle until it was even more directly over the gas flame.

'I'm sorry about the rabbits, Eckart,' said Uschi.

'It's all right.' He shoved the kettle another quarter-inch to the right.

'All I have to offer are my sausages and my meat. I wanted to do my bit. You're all so educated and—'

'I said it's all right, Uschi.'

He joined her at the table. The hand of the kitchen clock continued to work its way through the night. It seemed to come into its own at this hour with an audible ticking. The kettle began to boil.

'But you will come tomorrow, won't you?' Uschi ventured cautiously.

Eckart had been dreading this question. It wasn't only about tomorrow, it was about . . . About what, exactly? About the skinned rabbits? About the sausage? No, of course not. About the members of the flatshare? Not that either. He liked the other four, he really did.

It was more about living together *per se*. After all, there were so many reasons *not* to move into a flatshare like this; if there weren't, everybody would share a flat.

There were so many things that made it difficult, like others rummaging in your dirty washing to fill the machine; like Uschi standing in front of that ageing Barbarella after breakfast in her garish aerobics outfit and scrambling around to the strains of unspeakable music; like having to push various packets of meat to one side with a long wooden spoon to get to his goat's cheese; like the disgusted looks he attracted on account of the aforementioned goat's cheese – the only cheese one could truly love; like Harry getting his hands on the crossword puzzle every day, leaving Eckart with only a few unsolved clues. And so on and so forth. There were a zillion reasons. It was tough to find common ground where none existed.

The kettle was whistling now. He got up and poured the steaming water over the teabag.

'To be completely honest with you, Uschi, this didn't feel right from the very start.' Cup in hand, he sat down at the table again. 'I liked the two weekends by the sea, but . . . it's all too close here, too much . . . too much company. Christoph talked me into it, to make sure I'd be with other people. But why? I've been living on my own for ten years. It's not that nice, but I've got used to it. And, ultimately, it's not so bad living on your own.'

'Without any rabbits,' Uschi murmured contritely.

He ignored her interjection. 'Nobody tells you what to do, no one solves the crossword, nobody plays music you don't want to hear, nobody . . .'

'But also nobody means – nobody,' said Uschi, sipping her tea.

'Certainly. Of course it's lonely, but . . . Uschi, I just don't think I'm made for crowding together like this. You have to be the right type of person.'

'Crowding together?'

He nodded silently.

The term didn't seem at all to Uschi's liking. 'Well, what can I say?'

He was silent.

'But where are you going to go?' asked Uschi. Her words cut cruelly through the silence. 'The house has been sold, your son's in New Zealand, and your bank doesn't need you any more. You haven't got anyone.'

Thanks for that, thought Eckart. *Very encouraging. With friends like that, who needs enemies?*

Uschi looked at him with an expression that suggested tough love.

Tick, tock: the clock hand marked the silence. *Ingmar Bergman would have taken sinister pleasure in this*, he brooded.

'Shit . . . ' He sighed. Uschi glanced up. Even Eckart was surprised at himself. He hadn't used that word in ages, but it was good to let the feeling out.

'You know what, Eckart, I've just remembered a wonderful saying.'

Oh, please, no kitsch slogans now! He gave Uschi's arm a quick squeeze. 'No offence, but I'm off to bed. And shouldn't you go and lie down too? Tomorrow's your big day.' He gave her a strained smile.

'Of course, Eckart. Sleep well.'

He picked up his mug of camomile tea and left the kitchen, but he nevertheless heard her whisper, 'Sleep on it.'

23

Little waves furled across the lake, and the sky above it was a blaze of blue. The grass was an alluring shade of green. There was a rustling in the bushes nearby. Philip peeked through the leaves: Ricarda was changing in the next-door 'bush cubicle'.

'I always thought he was borderline,' she said, 'but do you really think he'll move out?'

'Let's wait and see.' Philip pulled down his trousers. 'In any case, it's not a good sign that he didn't come along.' Through the branches he caught a glimpse of Ricarda's back as she thumbed the left strap of her swimming costume into place. The other strap snagged on a twig. Philip would have gladly helped her lift it on to her shoulder.

Ricarda ran her hand over her breasts and pushed them up slightly under her costume. Her nipples were poking through.

Philip held a small branch carefully to one side in order to peek, something he had last done aged fifteen on a class trip to southern Bavaria with their pretty maths teacher, Mrs Jung. He'd been madly in love with her. He had spied on her from the undergrowth beside the lake as she first stepped out of her dress before slipping into an outrageously skimpy bikini. That evening in bed he had imagined gently peeling that wet bikini from her body.

Ricarda bent down to touch her thigh and, as she did so, her breasts almost spilled out of her costume.

'Not looking too bad,' said Uschi as she walked up to Ricarda.

'Oh, my best days are behind me,' replied Ricarda. She straightened up and let out a little shriek.

Philip recoiled, thinking he had been caught in the act.

'Can't you swim?' Ricarda asked, aghast.

Philip had to grin. It was Uschi, rather than his silly teenage voyeurism, that had made Ricarda shriek: Uschi was wearing a pair of dazzling orange armbands.

'Sure I can swim! I'm only wearing these to distract attention from your cellulite,' Uschi replied sarcastically. 'Come on!' The two ladies ran screeching into the lake.

'Hey! Look at Uschi!' The garishly coloured rubber rings immediately fulfilled their unintended mission, lifting Harry's mood as he stood there up to his knees in water, holding a beer can and a cigarette.

Philip pulled up his tight black trunks, adjusted himself,

ran a critical eye over his body and then opted for his more modest (reserve) pair of swimming shorts in a neutral colour. He walked across the lush lawn to the small beach. A blue parasol with white dots was planted in the coarse sand, and next to it lay their towels – and Ralf. Ralf looked up, shut his eyes again and let out a long, deep sigh – the sigh of a contented dog.

Philip took a can of beer from the coolbox and joined Harry in the water. The two women's voices wafted over to them from the middle of the lake.

'Lost weight?' Uschi called to Ricarda. 'You must be joking. I've put on four pounds.'

'Four pounds?' Ricarda was paddling hard on her back.

'Yep, imagine that! That's eight packs of butter.'

'Oh, stop all that talk of packs of butter,' Ricarda protested with a laugh. 'It makes me feel sick.'

'That's just the point,' trilled Uschi. 'You get a much better idea, imagining them hanging from your hips. Even more motivation to lose weight.'

'One word: pilates,' Ricarda called back. 'You should try it.'

'I've heard an awful lot about your pilots,' groaned Uschi, 'but I've kind of got used to my Jane.'

'Oh, boy, oh, boy.' Harry could only shake his head at the two women's conversation out in the lake.

'Do you think Eckart will stay?' asked Philip.

Harry shrugged and took another swig of beer.

'You know what I was thinking this morning?' shouted Uschi as she splashed towards the bank in her orange armbands. 'At some point we'll share one of those Polish women.'

'A Polish woman?' Ricarda was now swimming ten yards away to Uschi's left.

'Yes,' called Uschi, 'we can afford one if we all chip in. She can do the cleaning and anything else that arises.'

'*If* anything still does rise,' shouted Harry, nudging Philip in the ribs with a smirk.

'Ugh, Harry!' shouted Ricarda. 'A euro in Uschi's frog for every stupid remark you make from now on!'

'Pardon me, Ricarda,' Harry yelled back, 'but it's a serious issue for men of my age.'

'I just thought,' Uschi interjected, as she trod water, 'that she could lend a hand when we're no longer quite up to it.'

'I'm all for that,' hooted Harry. Philip couldn't help but smile.

A bicycle bell rang out behind them.

'Well, I never, it's Eckart!' shouted Philip.

It was indeed Eckart who came cycling up. He vaulted off his bike, and waded towards them through the shallow water, waving a large piece of paper.

'Respect!' Harry broke into a broad grin and fetched the prodigal flatmate a can of beer from the coolbox.

'Well, I wouldn't have bet on this, quite frankly. It's great!' said Philip.

Eckart handed him the piece of paper. 'There are some arguments against which one is helpless, Philip.' It was a colourful hand-painted chart, a sort of treasure map. Emblazoned across the top in the finest cursive handwriting was the message:

What I meant to tell you last night, dear Eckart,
was not to give up, because 'today's shit is
tomorrow's fertiliser'. So come and join us.
Yours, Uschi.

'Today's *what*?'

Harry tore the piece of paper from Eckart's hand as he went back into the water with a can of beer, and read the last sentence with amazement. 'Ooh, Eckart, ever the ladies' man.' He grinned and gazed out to where the lady with the orange armbands and the world's most devastating proverbs was paddling away.

'Eckaaaart!' The two women had spotted him now and waved gleefully.

Eckart shyly raised one hand and struggled with the ring-pull. Ralf stretched out and came waddling over. The three men banged their cans together and stared out happily across the water. Philip felt something like emotion welling up inside him: they appeared to have weathered their first storm.

'Philip?' Harry said.

'Yes?'

'What's going on between you and Ricarda?'

'Nothing. What do you mean?'

The other two nodded, then Harry chuckled. Eckart winked coyly at Philip.

Uschi's words about fertiliser were bearing their first fruit. Their community was growing; they really were growing together.

24

Harry did up his fly. Ah, was there anything nicer than relieving oneself in the open air? he thought. He stepped out of the bushes.

The sun was already low in the sky, bathing the meadow in warm light. Ricarda and Uschi spread out Uschi's picnic on the tartan blankets. They shoved Ralf insistently to one side. He kept getting in the way when there was food in sight; of course he did.

Eckart served some sparkling wine and spoke of young people's trouble finding a permanent job. Philip turned his back on Eckart and sought to lay the delicious marinated rabbits on the barbecue as discreetly as possible.

'It was the same in our day,' said Harry. 'I couldn't find anything after my studies either.'

'Harry,' Ricarda butted in, as she unpacked Uschi's cheesy nibbles from their aluminium foil, 'you never finished your studies.'

'You always were a pedant,' he muttered.

Philip tried to break a thick branch in half. Harry grabbed hold of the piece of wood and gave it a quick, hard kick. The branch shattered. Eckart cast Harry an appreciative glance.

'I spent seven years in the middle of nowhere,' nodded Harry.

'Sorry?' said Eckart.

'Seven years in Canada.' Harry laughed. 'And not like your son. I was a lumberjack! Far out in the forests!' *Growing kiwis, tsk*, thought Harry and shook his head.

'Has Christoph been in touch?' Philip asked Eckart, flipping the rabbit over.

'One text,' Eckart said as he handed Ricarda and Uschi their glasses of sparkling wine.

'He's alive!' called Harry.

'Harry,' Philip warned him with a laugh.

'You've got *us* now, Eckart,' said Ricarda. 'It's good that you came.' She gave him an affectionate kiss on the cheek that made his head spin, and they clinked their glasses.

'Cheese!' Philip took a photo of them all, including the dachshund, on self-timer, and Eckart lit the torches. Night was falling.

*

Harry took care of the fire. The food had been delicious, and they'd drunk a fair amount too. He felt better than he had in a long time. The trip out to the lake surrounded by dense forest, the fragrances of the countryside, the campfire: the whole thing brought memories of his years in Canada flooding back.

If Eileen hadn't broken his heart he would have stayed out there; he would have run that small saloon in the backwoods of Saskatchewan with her. But she'd chosen Hank, his best friend.

He'd tried to get over it, kept his sadness at bay, as always, with witticisms, rammed his chainsaw deep into tree trunks during the daytime and knocked back a bottle of whisky each night in his room. A 'love coma' was what he'd named his condition in a moment of lucidity.

It had worked – for a while. He *was* in a coma, drowning his gloomy feelings and thoughts in alcohol. One day, though, as some clever person had once said, those damned things learn to swim. And that was exactly what happened: his grief came bubbling up to the surface.

Three months passed and he couldn't stand those bloody forests any longer. He screamed and cursed them, all those bloody trees rooted so sturdily and so unshakeably in the soil. He didn't know what to do. Everything he had come here to find – the feeling of freedom, the wide, open spaces, the sense of adventure . . . everything he had found there – by day an honest job and good friends, by night the bar where *that* woman served – those entire seven years were all suddenly worthless. Worthless. Dead. Moments of happiness lay scattered around him like useless woodchips.

So he packed his belongings and got on the long-distance bus to Edmonton. He didn't say goodbye to anyone and he didn't look back. In Edmonton he bought a plane ticket, and two days later he landed in Cologne – with three lumberjack shirts that he still wore to this day, and this broken heart that just wouldn't heal.

He married Gisela, a girl he had known since school, and a year later Britta was born. For a time things went well, but after only two years they couldn't stand each other any longer. It wasn't her fault: it was just that Gisela wasn't *that* woman behind the counter in a small Canadian lumber outpost far from civilisation. Gisela was Gisela. From Wuppertal.

They argued every single day, Britta whined and Harry worked as a taxi driver. Gisela started to hit the bottle, and they got drunk together in the evenings to be able to stand each other's presence, or else they watched television. After seven years Gisela was a confirmed alcoholic. She went into rehab too many times to count. He looked after Britta. A neighbour stepped into the breach while he drove his taxi.

No, it hadn't been easy. For the past three years Gisela had been teetotal, and lived with her new man in Mallorca.

Harry tossed some new branches on the fire, and the sparks flew. Uschi's small transistor radio played 'Dreams Are My Reality' from the French film *La Boum*. Shitty music, thought

Harry, but somehow appropriate. He observed his new friends – this club they had formed – and felt his heart sing.

'Take early retirement? You?' said Philip to Ricarda. 'There's no way that's a good move.' They were sitting on a tree trunk beside the fire, sharing a blanket.

'Why not?' replied Ricarda. 'Being free, having time, doing whatever I like. Once I've let out my flat and I've got a bit of money coming in—'

'But what it also means is "I've entered the final phase of my life, and there's no turning back",' commented Eckart, who was an early retiree.

'Aw, lay off that kind of chatter,' complained Uschi. She stood up and invited Eckart to dance, but he declined. 'You, then,' Uschi said to Harry.

'Uschi! This is a slow dance,' he protested.

'Perfect.' She was quite obviously a little tipsy, which was her only excuse.

'No way,' he said.

'Oh, go on,' she pleaded.

Harry nodded. He stood up, the short woman melded herself to him, and they really did dance to a lousy tune from a French teen flick . . . All right, one slow dance, then. *His* only excuse was that he was a bit tipsy too. The others laughed and sang along: *Dre-e-eams are my-y re-e-e-a-li-ty-y-y . . .*

*

That night had a magical charge. It felt as if mortality were on hold. Yes, anything was possible with these new-found friends, in this brand-new club.

'Look,' called Uschi, pointing up at the starry sky. The five of them were lying there in their sleeping bags, under the vaulted ceiling of Uschi's 'Thousand-Star Hotel'. Wow – she hadn't over-promised!

Harry rolled himself another cigarette and noted how Philip's sleeping bag was creeping slowly – infinitely slowly – towards Ricarda's. Harry wondered how long it would take the two of them to get together.

'Heard this one before?' he asked. 'What do cannibals call a wheelchair-user?'

'Oh, God, what's he going to come out with this time?' came a murmur from Ricarda's sleeping bag.

'Well?' he probed as he lit his cigarette.

'Go on, then, tell us,' called Uschi.

'Meals on wheels.' Harry chuckled.

There was silence from the other bags. Then there was a gradual swell of giggling. The giggling was coming from Eckart's bag and then Eckart suddenly broke out into gales of laughter – of a kind no one had ever heard from him before.

This was funnier than the original joke, and it proved infectious. Their combined laughter rose into the night, right up to the stars, and perhaps beyond, thought Harry.

25

The sun was tickling Uschi's nose. The air smelled of dew, the green, woody fragrance one caught only in the early morning. Uschi blinked and opened her eyes. The blue of the sky was tinged with pink, and the sun was rising slowly behind the trees. Uschi sat up. A fine mist hung over the lake, and a heron flapped into the air.

The barbecue was cold and black. Scattered around it were colourful sleeping bags with the heads of Uschi's new family poking out of them. Ralf was snoring away next to her. His ears twitched. He was fast asleep.

Ricarda and Philip lay side by side, he in his bag, she in hers. A hand suddenly emerged from Harry's sleeping bag and groped for tobacco and cigarette papers. He rolled his morning cigarette without opening his eyes. The first wonderful smoke of the day, in his own fine words. Quite a character, that Harry.

Now Eckart sat up. His hair was dishevelled, and he had that unbeatable 'only-just-woken-up' look on his face – that childlike look that adults had when they first woke up and not a single care had yet burrowed its way into their thoughts.

They gave each other a quick nod, then sat and savoured this peaceful moment amid the morning dew. Uschi gazed out over the lake and wondered what she had done to be so lucky.

26

There was a loud crash, followed by a resounding thud. Ralf's barks startled Ricarda from her sleep. Since when did Ralf bark? He'd never barked before.

She swung her feet over the side of the bed, opened the door and went out into the hallway. The noise was coming from the kitchen. She ran down the hall and tore open the kitchen door. Ralf was standing on his own in the middle of the room, howling. Her gaze ran over the breakfast table; Barry Manilow's 'Mandy' was tinkling away on the radio in the background. It was then that Ricarda spotted the shattered glass teapot on the tiles, and two legs sticking out from behind the kitchen table.

'Uschi!' Uschi was lying spreadeagled on the floor amid shards of crockery and slices of salami.

'Uschi, what's wrong?' Ricarda shook her gently, but

Uschi didn't react. 'Philip,' Ricarda cried. 'Philip! Come quickly!'

Philip came running into the kitchen in his pyjamas. He bent over Uschi and softly patted her on one cheek. 'Uschi! Hey, can you hear me?' Slowly she opened her eyes. 'Give me a smile! Come on, Uschi, give me a smile!'

'What's going on?' Harry and Eckart joined them by the table.

Uschi attempted to smile. Her face was lopsided. Ricarda shoved Ralf aside as the dachshund tried to force his way through the broken plates and glass to the sausage.

'Stretch out your arms in front of you! Come on, both of them in front of you. Both at the same time. Go on, do it, Uschi!' cried Philip. Uschi raised her left arm, but her right arm hung limply by her side.

'Ric! Call an ambulance!' shouted Philip. 'Quick! It looks as if she's had a stroke. *Quick!*'

Ricarda raced to the telephone and rang 999. She got a ringing tone. 'Someone pick up, for God's sake. Come on, pick up will you!' she hissed. Every second counted. Literally every second counted when someone had had a stroke.

'My name is Uschi Müller,' she heard Philip say in the kitchen. 'Come on, Uschi, say "my – name – is – Uschi Müller"!'

'Damn you, Uschi, just say it!' grumbled Harry. 'My name is Uschi Müller!'

Someone finally answered the phone.

'Hello, Uschi Mü— Oh, no! Ricarda Busch here. This is an emergency, a suspected stroke!'

Philip glanced up as Ricarda came back into the kitchen. 'Five minutes,' she said. She stood helplessly alongside Harry and Eckart while Philip tried to get Uschi to speak. The five minutes crawled past. Why weren't they here yet? Uschi gazed up at them and she didn't seem to know what was happening to her either.

Then, at long last, the doorbell rang.

Two paramedics carried Uschi down the stairs on a stretcher and loaded her into the ambulance. Philip clambered in alongside her. Standing outside the front door with Eckart and Harry, Ricarda pulled her dressing gown more tightly around herself and stared at the ambulance as it sped off under the majestic plane trees.

Even without blaring sirens, the blue emergency lights sliced through the sleepy morning.

27

Philip stepped out of the lift, balancing four paper cups of hot coffee in his hands. Ricarda, Harry and Eckart were sitting on some grey plastic chairs screwed to the otherwise bare wall of the intensive care unit.

Eckart had dozed off with his mouth half open and his head lolling on Harry's shoulder, while Harry stared stoically straight ahead. It was now a quarter past three; they'd been waiting here for a good six hours.

Philip had talked to the doctor when Uschi was first admitted, and discussed the main details. They suspected a stroke caused by a blocked artery. The others had turned up shortly afterwards, having thrown on some clothes and jumped into Harry's taxi. Philip had urged them to return home, but to no avail. Contrast medium imaging, MRI scanner, thrombolytic therapy. The tests and treatment would take quite a while, but none of them wanted to leave now. The hours dragged on, grinding them down, like a glimpse of eternity. Nurses constantly scurried past, but none stopped to give them any information.

Philip handed the steaming coffees to Ricarda and Harry. Eckart's head rolled off Harry's shoulder and he woke with a snort. Philip passed him his cup and shook his head to signal that no, still no news.

After another quarter of an hour the heavy automatic doors of the intensive care unit finally whirred open, and the doctor stepped into the room. He nodded reassuringly.

'We've dissolved the clot. It's a good job you acted so fast.'

'Any serious damage?' Philip asked.

'The area of the brain responsible for speech has been affected, and her right side is currently paralysed.'

'But . . . will she pull through?' asked Ricarda.

The doctor's expression was non-committal.

'Can the damage be repaired?' Harry said hesitantly.

'First we have to wait for a few days and keep an eye on how her brain recovers, then we'll see. According to my records,' he said, flicking through his file, 'Mrs Müller has no family, no relatives. Are you her doctor?' he asked Philip.

Not until now, thought Philip. 'Yes,' he said.

The doctor nodded and switched his attention to Ricarda, Harry and Eckart.

'And who are you?'

28

'If you're ill, you're out!' said Harry.

Eckart winced. The two of them were sitting around the kitchen table with Ricarda and Philip for an emergency meeting. The kitchen table was strewn with crumbs and still covered with plates and three muesli bowls, coffee cups and a bag of sliced bread from breakfast.

Ricarda had paid an early visit to the clinic, and Harry, who was actually on kitchen-cleaning duty, had done the shopping. They'd been getting by as best they could since Uschi had been in rehabilitation.

Seven weeks earlier Uschi had lain on the tiles beside this very table. She had been in convalescence for a good five of those weeks, during which time they had paid her regular visits. It had been extremely depressing at first: Uschi was a shadow of her former self, a little bundle of misery. Her hemiplegia and impaired speech had made her a different person.

They didn't know what to say or how to react. Uschi seemed utterly disconsolate, and it was particularly tough to see such a natural optimist looking so down. Eckart felt more helpless than he had in a long while.

On his third visit Eckart had waved a piece of paper under her nose. It was the note Uschi had written weeks ago, suggesting that today's shit was tomorrow's fertiliser; well, now she should kindly follow her own advice. She stared at the piece of paper in silence, then looked Eckart in the eye with a crooked grin. 'Right you are,' she mumbled.

She had been valiantly undergoing her physiotherapy and speech exercises ever since, putting in the effort without complaint. The therapists praised her discipline, and she made a little progress every week, but she was a long way from being the Uschi of old.

Eckart pushed Harry's dirty Peace and Love mug to one side of the kitchen table.

Ricarda was incensed. 'Harry,' she said, 'this is community living. If one of us is not so well then the others take care of him or her. That's what a community like this is all about.'

'There's a bit of a difference between "not so well" and a stroke.' Harry groped for his tobacco. 'She's been in rehab for five weeks now and she can just about lift her little finger.'

'She can speak again!' Ricarda protested.

'But she can't walk!' said Harry, extracting a cigarette paper from its packet.

'Which is why she's staying in for a bit longer!'

'Yeah, right. Three weeks from now Uschi'll be skipping around the flat to Jane Fonda again, will she?'

It was a typical Ricarda–Harry tussle. Eckart felt uncomfortable: he didn't know what to think. Thus far they'd simply done their best to ignore the topic; they lived from day to day and celebrated any little sign of improvement. Yet now that Uschi was doing a bit better, and her rehabilitation was coming to an end, the subject was creeping relentlessly back on to the table: where was Uschi to go *after* rehab?

Eckart could understand where Harry was coming from. He'd cared for Lotte at home, and accompanied her through her final weeks when it became clear that she'd lost her battle with cancer. Caring for someone was no walk in the park. Did he want to put himself through the same thing all over again?

The day before had been the anniversary of Lotte's death. Twenty years. He had gone to the cemetery, laid a bouquet of salmon-coloured roses on the levelled lawn, and lit a candle. The young cemetery gardener came by a few minutes later. They knew each other by sight; he was a good lad.

'Mr Fröhlich,' the gardener said falteringly, 'they're going to put a tool shed here soon.'

'A tool shed?' Eckart had no idea what the kid was talking about at first.

'Yes.' The gardener hemmed and hawed. He was sorry, but the cemetery administration had issued new instructions.

They were going to put a tool shed on top of Lotte's grave? Eckart took a moment to grasp the meaning of the gardener's words; he felt a stab of pain in his chest. The boy asked him if he needed help, but Eckart waved him away and thanked him for the news. What else could he do? Soon he wouldn't even have the cemetery left – and Lotte would have a tool shed over her head.

Eckart lingered by her side and then walked slowly home. He'd had quite a shock, but hey, he would get over it. He didn't really have any choice, did he? The dust would soon settle on this too.

Suddenly – he had no idea how it happened – he found himself outside their former house. He was so lost in thought that he'd automatically taken his old route home, and it was the first time he'd been back since he'd moved out.

The kitchen light was on. A young woman was cooking at the stove; she lifted a little boy with blond curly hair on to the kitchen table; a man joined them and gave the boy a slice of apple; the boy laughed; the man set the table . . .

*

117

Eckart was torn from his musings by Ricarda's voice. 'What on earth did you expect?' she asked the assembled faces. 'Why are we doing this? Of course it's earlier than we'd like, but shunting Uschi off to a home . . .'

Eckart avoided her gaze. Philip got up and walked over to the window.

'Over my dead body,' Ricarda announced resolutely.

No one said anything for a while.

'How does it look financially?' asked Eckart. He needed to bring things back to the realm of facts; moral arguments were too close to the bone for him. Obviously he liked Uschi, and the mere thought of shunting her off anywhere was unbearable in the extreme, but he too had only one life – and he wanted to continue and end it in peace.

'Friends can apply for a carer's allowance too,' said Ricarda, 'and she's still on sick leave.'

'We can't stick our heads in the sand, Ric,' said Philip. 'We don't know what the results of her extended rehabilitation will be; Harry's right there. We're on the third floor with no lift. Our apartment is not at all disability-friendly. Uschi needs dressing and undressing. And washing. Plus she'll have to do physiotherapy, speech therapy and occupational therapy as an outpatient. Taking care of Uschi would be—'

'There are ambulances,' Ricarda interrupted. 'And the little physiotherapy she's getting isn't enough for a stroke victim – you know that. She has to exercise, and keep exercising. She doesn't have anyone else,' she added quietly.

She doesn't have anyone else. Ricarda's words echoed in Eckart's ears, awakening a sudden feeling that he hadn't experienced since moving into this flat: a feeling of loneliness.

'Up and down,' Philip continued, 'lifting her into the bath, washing her, every day. Every day, Ricarda. Bringing Uschi back here isn't just . . . It's a full-time job!'

'You've devoted half your life to the sick,' Ricarda shot back.

'Exactly.' Philip nodded. His voice was very calm and grave.

For a while there was silence.

'If you shunt her off somewhere, I'm moving out,' said Ricarda.

Now that was unfair, thought Eckart. Blackmail was unfair. Nasty. You didn't do that. Philip stared helplessly at her.

'Let's at least give it a go,' said Ricarda, relenting. 'She can move her little finger already. Soon it'll be her big toe. There's a chance she'll walk again! But only with us. She'll wither away in a home. She'd never stand on her own two feet again. I was planning to give up my practice and work less next year anyway. I'll do it now instead. I'll take care of her. I – I cannot farm Uschi out. Sorry, I just can't.'

Her voice quavered. She was fighting as though her life depended on it, and Eckart admired her for that. He admired her determination and her intransigence – two qualities he'd appreciated in Ricarda several times already in recent weeks.

She was right. They couldn't farm Uschi out somewhere. They would be confronted with the thought of her each and every day; they would have to live with their decision every day. He had read an article about the brain's plasticity, which said that stroke victims could make significant progress with sufficient training.

'If it really doesn't work out, then we can always . . . ' said Ricarda. 'But we'll get Uschi back on her own two feet! I'm sure we will.'

'Fine.' Philip looked at everyone in turn. 'Who's in favour of bringing Uschi home?'

Ricarda held up her hand. Eckart nodded and also raised his hand. Harry demonstratively crossed his arms. All eyes were now on Philip.

'She looked after your mother,' said Ricarda softly.

'That's unfair, Ric,' Harry interjected. 'She brought Philip's mother some sausage from time to time! That's not the same thing.'

'She was there.' Ricarda didn't take her eyes off Philip for a second. 'We're not what we say, but what we do,' she continued, repeating Philip's own words.

He wrestled with his conscience, then nodded. 'Okay. Let's give it a go.'

'Oh, boy!' Harry buried his face in his hands.

Ricarda gave Eckart's arm a quick squeeze and thanked him for his support. Eckart nodded. They had come to the right decision, of that he was sure. And yet . . . He cleared his throat.

'I was simply wondering whether the vote didn't have to be unanimous in a case like this.' He hated it when things didn't follow the rulebook.

'Huh?' said Harry, slowly raising his head from his hands. He stared at Eckart in puzzlement for a second before breaking into a smile. 'You're quite something, Eckart, but really, it's fine. Democracy is democracy. I'll just have to live with it.' He stood up and took his cigarette out on to the balcony.

Re-spect, thought Eckart, imitating Harry's tone of voice in his mind. Respect. His flatmates were truly proving to be a compassionate bunch.

'But let's get one thing straight,' Harry called from the balcony. 'I'm not wiping her backside!'

29

Stella hadn't seen her mother for three months. Ricarda had texted her to say that she was going to share a flat with her old student friends Harry and Philip because her own apartment needed a complete overhaul. She was accustomed to her mother's surprises, but to think that all it took were a couple of workmen to convince her to move in with other people?

Stella had got back from Granada the day before. As beautiful as southern Spain was, she was glad it was over. A German screw manufacturer had hired her on a three-month contract to translate for some Spanish screw specialists what a German screw specialist was trying to teach them. Three months of screws. Small screws, large screws, small threads, large threads ... Whatever spin you put on it, there were more exciting translating and interpreting jobs to be had. In any case, Stella's mind had been on an entirely different matter for the past four weeks. She needed some advice.

She brushed her short blonde curls away from her face and ran her fingers down to a set of buzzers on the outside of the pretty Art Nouveau building. One of the nameplates was covered with writing, five names in all. This must be the one. She pressed the buzzer and put her shoulder to the carved wooden door, which was on the latch.

Under the letterboxes stood a gigantic box containing a bath seat. A bath seat? How old were her mother's new flatmates? she wondered. She climbed the dark wooden steps. She heard a commotion ahead: two men were dragging an unwieldy nursing bed upstairs.

'Still moving in?' she asked. She wanted to give them a hand, but the men set the bed down for a second. They were short of breath.

'You're one of Ricarda's flatmates, right? I'm her daughter, Stella.'

'Oh, so *you're* Stella. I'm Philip,' said one of the two men with a smile and offered her his hand. 'Nice to meet you. I met your mother at university.'

'I know,' nodded Stella, 'and you were a friend of my father's too.'

'Oh, yes,' he chuckled. 'Your mother and Herbert and I were pretty . . .'

'. . . close.' She grinned.

'That's one way of putting it.' He discreetly sized her up. 'You take after him a little.'

'I would hope so,' she said with a hint of indignation in her laughter. She'd taken an immediate liking to him.

'I'm Eckart,' the other man said, wiping his sweaty hands on his trousers and offering one to her.

'Your mother's up on the third floor,' said Philip. 'And send Harry down! He was supposed—'

'I'm coming,' muttered a voice upstairs. Harry came trotting down, but he stopped short when he caught sight of Stella.

'Yes,' she said,' it's me. Stella, the little brat.' The last time she'd seen Harry was at a party her mother had thrown about a hundred years ago. She reached out her hand. He waved her away with a casual flick of his wrist, and his eyes drifted down her bare brown legs. She was wearing a pair of apricot-coloured shorts.

'You didn't turn out too bad after all,' he said.

'Oh. Thanks,' she said. 'As for you ... You haven't changed a bit.'

'Oh, yeah?' muttered Harry, running his hand nervously over his head to his grey ponytail. For a second, as Philip and Eckart cast him a sideways glance, he actually appeared to be weighing up whether her words might somehow be true.

'I was joking.' She grinned and walked off up the stairs. Eckart couldn't suppress a chuckle.

'Just like her mother!' said Philip with a laugh. 'You should have known better, Harry!'

'Hilarious,' snapped Harry. 'Now get lifting!'

Full of curiosity, Stella stepped through the open door into the flat. Her mother was hastily touching up her lipstick in front of the hall mirror.

'Hi, Mum.'

'Stella! You're home! How was it?' Ricarda hugged her.

'Exhausting. I—'

'Hey, tell me all about it when we've got more time. I've got to nip out now, but come in and take a look around our kingdom.' She invited Stella into the flat with an expansive gesture and hurried off along the hall.

'How lovely to have you back,' she called from her room. 'You must tell me all about it! Absolutely everything ... Now where did I ...?'

Stella was standing undecidedly in the hallway as the nursing bed came rumbling into the flat. When the men had stamped back down the staircase to fetch the bath seat, Stella sauntered after her mother. A fat, sleepy dachshund came waddling out of the kitchen towards her and wagged its tail a little half-heartedly.

'And who are you?' She crouched down and ruffled the dog's coat.

'That's Ralf,' called Ricarda. 'Philip inherited him from his mother.'

Her mother's bedroom was furnished exactly the same way as in her former flat. Bookshelves along the right-hand wall; her designer friend Nico's old mannequin, which she hung her clothes on, by the window; the mauve gossamer curtains; the slender, elegant coconut palm; her white, glass-topped desk; above the bed her beloved red and yellow Rothko print; the grey rug on the wooden floorboards. Stella stood in the doorway for a moment in the hope that her mother might look around and turn her attention away from her pile of papers.

'Where's that form?' said Ricarda as she sifted through the documents. 'Reimbursement for care products. Reimbursement for nursing aids. You wouldn't believe how much health insurance paperwork there is to do.'

Stella wondered whether these words were directed at her and required a response. She swallowed hard. It was back: the old sensation was back, not even five minutes after she'd stepped through the door. They hadn't seen each other for three months, yet they still hadn't exchanged so much as two full sentences. As usual, her mother wasn't really 'there'; her mind was elsewhere. And now she had to rush off again.

Like the time Stella's best friend Regine had smashed her Barbie doll to bits and snapped the left hind leg off her Barbie's horse at kindergarten.

Like the time Peter had poked fun at her in front of the whole class because she'd suddenly got her period and had red stains on her trousers.

Like the time she'd blacked out in the chemistry exam and didn't know whether she'd pass the damn thing.

Like all the other times. Her mother had to run off; yet again she had to take care of something for someone else.

Stella had occasionally even gone as far as to ask herself whether her mother actually loved her – 'truly and deeply', that was. She knew that Ricarda would do anything for her. Because she always did anything for anyone. She wanted to be loved by everyone. As if her husband's and her daughter's love wasn't enough for her. Yet wasn't this constant concern for other people an escape from them – from her own family?

Her parents' relationship hadn't been an especially loving one from her perspective; if they did get on well, they did a brilliant job of concealing it. It wasn't as if they'd argued at home, though. No, there hadn't even been any arguments.

Her mother had taken it on the chin when Stella's father was diagnosed with cancer five years ago and died soon after. Ricarda had stayed in control throughout, as always, and thrown herself even more passionately into her work.

Stella had coped too; she'd had no option. She'd just been starting at the translation agency and was sent to Barcelona not long afterwards. There she had met Xavi. Living in the Catalonian city had been good for her and it had helped her get over her grief. She had even considered upping sticks from Germany and moving in with Xavi, but pragmatism had prevailed: she didn't want to lose her job.

So they'd had a four-year long-distance relationship. He'd finished with her a year back; he'd met someone else. So she no longer flew to Barcelona every other weekend and had suddenly noticed that she'd lost virtually all contact with her friends in Cologne.

Ralf shuffled around her feet. Stella glared at him, then set out to explore the rest of the flat. The furnishings were all very nice and appealing. One got the distinct impression of several strong personalities at work, but it was cosy. A cosy, harmonious chaos.

She took a peek into another room and gasped. There was a headstone under the window. A genuine headstone, flanked by two bonsai trees, a pink salt lamp, a nice, colourful bunch of flowers in a vase, and a small red grave candle. Ralf rolled on to his back next to Stella and waved his stubby little legs in the air.

'Eckart's wife,' Ricarda whispered in her ear, and quietly told her Eckart's story as she pulled on her jacket.

How deeply this man must have loved his wife, thought Stella, as she tickled Ralf's fat belly. Ricarda flicked through the documents in her bag. One quick final check – how typical of her mum.

'Mum, I'd really like a short—'

'Oh, drat, I forgot . . .' said Ricarda, and darted back into her room.

'—chat,' sighed Stella, peeping into the room opposite. A room decorated in various shades of blue with all kinds of

128

knick-knacks on the windowsill and kitsch figurines on the shelves. Countless trophies were lined up on a sideboard. So one of her mother's flatmates was a champion athlete, no less. Stella studied the trophies. *The World's Best Cold Meats Counter 2003, 2004, 2005* ... Gold, silver, bronze. Wow.

'Uschi. Our stroke victim,' Ricarda remarked from out in the hallway.

'*Stroke* victim?'

'That's why I'm rushing out. I'm already late. Uschi's being discharged in two weeks' time.' Her mother kissed her on the forehead and ran her fingers gently over her cheek. 'You look really pretty with that light tan. I've got to go. I'll tell you all about it when we've got more time. You won't hold it against me, will you? We'll talk later, okay?' When she reached the door, she turned around again to whisper, 'Love you.' Then she was gone.

Stella stood there helplessly in the sky-blue room of the woman who had had a stroke. Her eyes came to rest on the sausage trophies again.

'Hi, Mum,' she said. 'I just wanted to tell you that I'm pregnant and I don't know whether to keep it, because the father's an arsehole. But no-o-o! We've got time. No hurry.'

There were some thuds out in the hallway. The bath seat had moved in.

30

Ricarda pulled the blue and green checked pyjama bottoms over her hand. 'Okay ... I'll use my arm to help pull it on and ...'

Philip nodded, took her wrist and guided it carefully to the leg. 'Perfect. Take hold of the heel. Pull up the trousers, ye-es ... No, only to the knee to begin with. Perfect.' Ricarda was doing really well. Philip was surprised by her dexterity.

'Everything okay, old man?' asked Harry, while tapping on Eckart's stomach.

'Ouch,' Eckart groaned.

Eckart was lying on Uschi's new nursing bed. Philip shot Harry a stern look. He was trying to teach the three of them how to put a pair of pyjamas on a hemiplegic woman without overtaxing their own joints.

By now Ricarda had inched the bottoms up to Eckart's left knee. Philip watched her push the trousers over his right knee. Her movements were fluent and decisive, and in her concentration her tongue flickered from the right corner of her mouth to the left. Philip caught himself imagining it was *his* knee.

She'd given him no sign in the time since they'd moved in together that there was anything more than friendship between them. He respected that: he didn't want to ruin things. And yet . . . however much he told himself that they were only good friends, he felt more than that for Ricarda. It had been some time since he'd felt more for a woman – since Malu had died seven years before, to be precise.

Malu had been sent to him as a nurse twenty-five years back when he was working in Africa. She was a beautiful woman, gentle and intelligent. A year later they were married. They wanted children, but it didn't work out. Malu sent her sister to Philip's bedroom, then her cousin, then a different cousin, but Philip had scruples about polygamy; it wasn't his thing.

So they made their lives without kids. They devoted all their love and attention to their patients, the children and the elderly. They worked hand in hand. They enjoyed being there for others. The health post was their family. They were happy together. It was only when he saw how compassionately and skilfully Malu dealt with the children at the health post that he realised their loss. Malu would have made a good mother. Seven years ago she had been infected with an incurable virus, and, despite doing everything in his power, Philip had lost the toughest battle of his life. Her death tore a hole in his world, in his very existence. It was as though someone had chopped off his arm. Or a leg. Or ripped out his kidney.

Day after day he struggled because Malu was no longer there: no longer passing him the instruments; no longer leaving him little notes decorated with tiny drawings in the medical records; no longer running her hands over his back when he didn't manage to heal someone; no longer pouring him a whisky on the terrace when the day's work was done and they sat listening to the African night.

It was a good three years before Philip ceased to feel the emptiness Malu had left behind every day, every morning, every evening and every night. His only solace was his work and his patients. The village elders presented other women to him, but Philip politely declined. He didn't want to lose someone again. Nor did he feel any need, either emotional or sexual.

Harry had visited him twice during this period, and it had been good to talk about anything and everything with an old friend, a friend who always called a spade a spade, even if it was painful sometimes. Yet this candour and this uncompromising openness were perhaps Harry's most wonderful and most precious qualities.

Harry had been nursing his own worries when he came

out to visit Philip. Gisela was in detox again; she simply couldn't wean herself off the bottle. The two men had consoled each other.

'Harry, you've got to turn me over *here*!' said Ricarda, who had taken Eckart's place on the nursing bed. The pyjama trousers were just below her bottom and she had to force herself not to intervene. There were limits to her sensitivity in certain situations, thought Philip, and chuckled at this new team: Ricarda the victim, Harry the aggressor.

'There! Now turn me over,' Ricarda insisted, and guided Harry's hand around her hips.

'Cripes, Ricarda,' Harry said. 'Take your arm away. You're paralysed there!'

Eckart chortled. Harry grabbed hold of Ricarda by the part of the hip she had indicated and rolled her none too gently on to her side.

'Ow! Don't be so rough,' she yelled.

'See! That's the advantage of being paralysed!' Harry returned. He pulled the pyjamas up over Ricarda's backside from behind and, aiming a wink at Philip and Eckart, said, 'You're a bit rounder in the hips too, eh, Ric?'

Oh, Harry. He never passed up an opportunity. Philip tried to keep a straight face, and even the corners of Eckart's mouth were twitching. Ricarda glared over her shoulder at the three men behaving so insolently behind her back. If looks could kill.

Come on, Ricarda, he thought. *Don't be so stupid. You're so beautiful, there's no need.*

'Nobody would say that to a man,' she snapped petulantly.

'Course not, Ricarda,' the three men said with one voice.

Time to switch positions.

Philip looked out into the street while Ricarda pulled off the pyjama bottoms with a grunt, and vacated Uschi's bed for Harry to take her place. The old man on the far side of the road was standing at his window again. The afternoon sun was shining into his flat, turning its spotlight on the grime and loneliness inside his bare, run-down apartment. Still dressed in his yellowing ribbed vest, the man was shaking out his tattered burgundy and black striped dressing gown.

Philip had spotted him as soon as he'd moved in. Hardly a day went by that he didn't glimpse the old man at his window and note his solitude. It was as if the mere fact that another human being noticed him at least once a day rendered the old man less lonely. He was almost part of Philip's life by now; Philip was gripped by anxiety if he didn't see him there.

'Philip?' Eckart's voice came to him from far away. Philip looked around. Eckart had pulled the pyjama trousers over one half of Harry's bottom.

'That's it,' said Philip. 'Now turn him over here and . . .

pull. That's right . . . up that way. Perfect. Yes, up to the base of the pelvis.'

'Ouch!' groaned the man with the pelvis.

'Hurts, doesn't it?' said Ricarda with a certain degree of satisfaction and, with a little nudge, urged Eckart not to show any mercy.

Why could most people not resist the urge to be silly at some point during exercises like these? Philip tried to concentrate on the matter at hand.

'Eckart, now you have to check that the seam is properly in the middle of his backside.'

'You what?' snorted Harry. 'The middle of his backside? Call it a bum crack!'

Eckart seemed to be finding this imposed proximity unpleasant, but Harry's comment sent him into gales of laughter and even Ricarda had to giggle. 'Bum crack? I haven't heard that in ages.'

Oh, boy, things might really hot up now.

All four of them laughed heartily, setting each other off again and again until tears ran down Eckart's cheeks. It was silly, damn silly, and deep down it wasn't even funny, but it felt good.

They had little idea what was in store for them. Uschi was coming home from rehab the next day.

31

Ralf padded impatiently on the spot. Something was up. He didn't yet know what, but there was a vague uneasiness in the air. Ricarda and his three other owners were standing in a group outside the front door, peering down the street at an approaching ambulance. The driver got out, gave them a quick nod and opened the sliding door.

A wheelchair was placed on the pavement. Ralf wagged his tail. Uschi! The lady with the delicious sausage aroma was back. She looked a little bothered, but she managed a tentative smile.

'Hello,' she said.

'Oh, Uschi,' Harry said warmly. He looked genuinely moved, and Ralf barely recognised his voice. He waddled towards Uschi, tail wagging, but he was wary of her chair's huge wheels.

'Ralfie!' She leaned down slightly to him, but she didn't even reach out to tickle him.

She looked up at Harry with a crooked grin and mumbled, 'Meawls on wheewls.'

Ralf followed the others into the hallway.

'Don't stop to think, Harry!' was Philip's response to Harry's scowl. They were standing with the wheelchair at the bottom of the long, steep staircase.

Ralf was familiar with this problem.

Harry and Philip bent down and got ready to heave the wheelchair into the air – with Uschi in it. Ralf glanced around, searching for Ricarda and Eckart. Would one of them carry him upstairs? Or should he try to hitch a lift on the chair with the big wheels? He shuffled towards the wheelchair.

'For crying out loud, Ralf, get out of here.' Harry shoved the dog to one side, sending him sliding across the floor on his belly.

'Ready? One and two a-a-and ... go,' came the command from Philip. They lifted the chair and wobbled with great difficulty up the stairs, Harry in front, Philip behind, and Eckart stabilising it. Ricarda anxiously observed the action from below.

'Urrgh! A bit higher, Philip,' groaned Harry.

'I can't,' Philip squawked. 'My back ...'

The wheelchair tilted and tipped slightly, making Uschi screech.

'Uschi!' cried Ricarda, running up the stairs.

Uschi slid halfway out of her chair, Eckart braced himself against it, and Ricarda braced herself against Eckart. The group fought their way up to the first landing and set the wheelchair down to have a discussion. Ralf was keeping a close eye on proceedings. They had forgotten him at the bottom, just as he had expected.

'I told you the third floor was shit!' said Harry, drawing his sleeve across his sweat-soaked brow.

'I'm *sho* heavy,' Uschi's words came out in slur.

'Nonsense!' said Ricarda, patting Uschi's arm. 'It's the wheelchair. It's too awkward.'

'There's no way all four of us can show up here every time,' Eckart remarked.

'Cripes, let's get rid of this crappy wheelchair!' moaned Harry. 'You don't carry an elephant upstairs in a cage!'

Philip had to laugh.

'That's not funny!' Ricarda snarled.

'I know,' laughed Philip.

'What now? With or without the wheelchair?' said Ricarda, hands on hips.

'But someone might nick it from downstairs,' Eckart pointed out.

'Who'd nick a wheelchair?' asked Ricarda.

'Without!' said Philip, concluding their discussion. 'Ready, Uschi?'

Uschi nodded. Philip and Harry each grabbed her by

a leg and an arm, and hoisted her gently out of the chair. They climbed the stairs carefully, with Ricarda and Eckart following on behind.

'Drat! Ralf!' Ricarda dashed back down the stairs.

Better late than never, thought Ralf.

32

Philip and Harry laid Uschi down on the nursing bed with loud groans. They were breathing heavily, but both affected a smile, as if they'd actually enjoyed hauling her upstairs. Harry patted her on the shoulder again and left the room, while Ricarda and Philip gently began to undress her. They went about it differently from the carers in rehab – more clumsily.

Uschi wanted to help out, but couldn't: she was incapable of helping out. Her two friends touched parts of her body she didn't even feel. She raised her eyes to the ceiling so that she wouldn't have to watch.

She realised that a tear was trickling very slowly down her cheek. Ricarda gave Philip a discreet signal to leave the room. She pulled up the bedcovers and tucked Uschi in. Ricarda sat down on the edge of the bed and stroked

Uschi's cheek. Uschi felt the tear continue down her face, with the next one close behind. Ricarda tugged a tissue from the box on the bedside table and dabbed at Uschi's tears, then wiped away her own. 'Get some rest, all right?' she said before walking to the door and pulling it shut behind her.

Uschi stared at the ceiling. She had had a tough time in rehab. A thousand strange hands had touched, kneaded and pawed at her body. Helping hands, but still. She had been happy – so happy – when the doctor told her that she was free to go home. But now, back at the flat, back in her room, surrounded by the four people who had to care for her, her throat suddenly felt tight.

33

Ricarda, Eckart and Philip were waving their arms wildly. Harry was leaning against the window with a grin on his face, for the spectacle unfolding before his eyes was too good to be true.

Uschi was sitting in an armchair in the middle of the living room. Facing her was a cool young man in black leather trousers with a file propped on his knees. Behind him stood Eckart, Ricarda and Philip, giving their all, commenting on Uschi's answers in pantomime – not to say, panicky – fashion. For Uschi too was giving her all: her dignity was at stake.

A fatal mistake. The young man in the leather trousers had been sent by the health insurance. It was cash that was actually at stake: this was about the level of care Uschi required.

'Getting up and getting dressed?' the assessor asked.

'It's still a bit fiddicult ... I mean, difficult,' said Uschi, receiving, at long last, appreciative nods from her three friends standing behind the assessor. 'But I'll get,' Uschi continued, 'I'll get.'

'There?' asked the assessor.

Yes, Uschi nodded.

Nooooo! mouthed Phil and co., shaking their heads.

The assessor noted Uschi's answer on his questionnaire.

'Help with washing: how long each morning? How long does someone help you with your morning wash?' he asked kindly.

Uschi considered this. Eckart and Ricarda held up ten fingers each and punched the air with their hands. Philip made a two with one hand and a zero with the other. Harry deciphered this as 20 – twenty minutes – and, though he wasn't a hundred per cent certain, he preferred Philip's method of illustration. Uschi, however, was either totally unsure or else didn't even bother to interpret the others' hand movements. She looked rather stressed and anxious, and her brain was obviously whirring with the effort.

'Um, well … a few minutes,' she said eventually. 'I do many things by myself.'

What??!?!? What do you do by yourself? Harry heard the question screech through the heads of his comrades-in-arms, who were all busting a gut to care for Uschi. Philip crossed his arms behind his head and gazed up at the ceiling in disbelief.

This was a disaster; there was no other word for it. Uschi wanted to make do; she didn't want to be a burden on anyone.

Whatever the assessor asked, Uschi got it – sometimes better, sometimes worse, but she got it. There. Oh, yeah.

'Five minutes?' she followed up in a daze when the assessor asked her about putting her shoes on. He nodded and the three people behind him held their breath and got their hopes up, but then . . .

'At the *very* most,' she conceded, 'and almost certainly only to start with. I don't want to urine anyone, you know.'

The assessor squinted at her for a second, then slowly nodded.

'Ruin?' he suggested.

'Absolutely,' nodded Uschi. 'Quite honestly, everything'll soon be working perfectly.'

'Working' – *just like my kidneys*, thought Harry. If the whole thing hadn't been so tragic, he'd have been rolling around on the floor in hysterics.

'Oh, you bet,' said Uschi, 'I'll get.'

It continued this way for some time. The assessor asked and took notes, the trio gesticulated, and Uschi worked.

Then the young man asked how long it took to put Uschi to bed at night. And while Uschi was thinking, and Ricarda was preparing to waggle all ten fingers to indicate sixty minutes, the assessor said, without turning around, 'Save your energy back there.'

Ricarda let her hands sink to her sides in bemusement.

Blimey! thought Harry. *Pretty cool, this young man in the leather trousers. Really pretty cool.*

34

Fabian was relieved that it was all over. He hated these assessments. He'd been doing this for a year now: going to families, listening to what people had to say as they went prattling on; trying to distinguish what was true from what was false; and witnessing people's pain and unhappiness at their sudden helplessness, unhappy that nothing was as easy as it used to be, that nothing worked as it had worked their whole lives, and that they needed help to take care of even the tiniest of details.

There were some really tough cases, which hit him like a punch to the solar plexus. There were others where he felt that the person's relatives unnecessarily exaggerated the invalid's neediness. And then from time to time there were cases like this, when invalids strained every sinew, much to their family's despair, as if they were taking an all-deciding test, as if they had to prove that they could cope all by themselves. Maybe they were trying to prove that they weren't in such a bad state after all.

'It takes at least thirty minutes. And dressing and undressing,' said Ricarda as she walked Fabian to the door, glanced at her watch and put on her jacket.

'I'm going to recommend Level Two,' he interrupted her.

'You are?' Ricarda paused, taken aback.

Mrs Müller had certainly turned in an admirable performance, but Fabian knew the consequences of stroke-induced hemiplegia. He had also been moved, from the very beginning of the examination, by the realisation that this ragtag bunch were clearly determined to care for this woman. In a day and age when children were inclined to farm their own parents out somewhere, here were four people bent on putting this woman back on her feet. It was great.

'I was a carer myself for many years,' he said with a smile. 'Some patients turn in Oscar-winning performances during the assessment. I'll file my report later today.'

Ricarda looked at him. 'Thank you,' she said quietly.

No worries, thought Fabian.

'I've got to go,' she said apologetically. She picked up her bag and ran her finger over the forms inside. Just then the doorbell rang. A pretty woman with short blonde curls and long brown legs was standing outside the door.

'Stella! Damn!' Ricarda said inadvertently.

Now there's a warm welcome, thought Fabian.

The look on the pretty woman's face spoke volumes, but, before she could say a word, Ricarda's mobile rang.

'I'm sorry. Just a sec.' She took the call. 'Mr Bose! I'm on my way! Yes ... Yes ... See you in a few minutes!' She hung up. 'He's taking over the practice from me,' she said to Stella by way of explanation, then stopped short. 'Didn't we say next week?'

'No,' said Stella, 'we didn't say anything. I was merely paying my mother a brave, impromptu visit. But okay then: I hereby apply for an official appointment.' She turned to Fabian and said, 'And *you* are my witness.'

Okay, he nodded. He liked her.

'Stella, I—' Ricarda began.

'Who are you anyway?' asked Stella.

'Your witness,' he said.

He really liked her.

35

Stella flushed the toilet. Another bout of sickness. She rinsed her mouth, washed her hands, drank a second glass of water in the kitchen and pulled the front door shut as she left the shared flat.

As she walked down the stairs she tried to suppress her anger. Where had she got the crazy idea of visiting her mother unannounced? It had been so predictable that Ricarda would have no time.

Stella had decided to keep the baby. She had stopped by to ask her mother whether she could at least count on a little support. But, if her mother couldn't spare even two minutes to hear that she was going to have a grandchild, how on earth was she ever going to find an hour to look after the little squirt from time to time?

Stella stepped out into dazzling sunlight. She checked her mobile, uncertain what to do next.

'Fancy a brave, impromptu beer?' asked the man she'd met upstairs. He was bending over his moped, fiddling with the lock.

Ha ha, very funny. She grinned.

'It's on me,' he said without looking up. He had dark hair and freckles – a strange combination, thought Stella. She couldn't help noticing that he looked good in those black leather trousers.

'Got something to celebrate?'

'That was my last report. I passed my exam yesterday.'

'Your exam?'

'Physiotherapy,' he said, grabbing his helmet.

'Second career?'

'Ooh, if I count the various other things I've done . . .' he weighed it up sarcastically '. . . then it's probably . . . the tenth?'

A grin spread over her face. She liked him. 'A physiotherapist? Well, you may as well leave them your business card right now,' she said, thinking, *And give me one too.*

He nodded appreciatively. 'Now that's what I call on the ball. Can I hire you as my manager?'

'I'll take you up on that beer first,' she said and thought, *Alcohol-free – damn!*

He held out his spare helmet. 'I'm Fabian.'

'Stella,' she said, taking the helmet.

Yep, she liked him.

36

At least her digestive system was working properly again. She could even flush the toilet on her own. That hadn't been easy to begin with because she couldn't turn around. Now she could do it 'hands down – or rather, one hand down', as she sometimes joked. As for many other things, she'd developed a special technique. She wedged a book – the whopping toilet read *1000 Places to See Before You Die* – between her left buttock and the toilet seat, and from this slightly raised position she was able to press the flush button with her left elbow. This way she didn't need to embarrass anyone by asking for help. She also always waited for at least twenty minutes before calling 'Ready!' to allow the smell to disappear.

Sometimes it felt weird to see the lengths the others would go to on her behalf. She had physiotherapy twice a week, occupational therapy twice, and speech therapy once. Two men from the ambulance service picked her up and brought her home again. That was fine; they were paid to do it. It was their job. However, the brunt of her other outings was borne entirely by her friends – with the emphasis firmly on 'borne'.

Harry had installed a steel pole at the bottom of the stairs, to which they locked an outdoor wheelchair. Then at least two people would carry her upstairs and set her down in her indoor wheelchair, which she could drive with one hand. At least two people, every time. That had to be agreed and organised. Sometimes she would hear the others whispering, debating and negotiating who had to be where for what and when. Occasionally voices were raised, but the others made sure that Uschi didn't get wind of their organisational arrangements.

The men also tried their best to hide from Uschi how strenuous it was to lug her up and down three floors. Of course they didn't succeed. Of course she noticed. She was quite a lump, and she felt every single stair. They set off fairly quickly, but from the first floor onwards their tread would grow heavier with every step. Uschi could read the pulse of each of her carriers like a seismographer: Eckart's arm muscles would begin to shake after the second floor, Harry would break out in a sweat at two and a half, and Philip would start to tremble and pant shortly before they reached the door of their flat.

In short: she was a burden. She was a big, fat, heavy burden.

She hated the times when she was being carried up and down – maybe even more than she hated toilet time. She always held her breath in the hope that it would make her lighter, which was of course ludicrous. But then everything was ludicrous at the moment. The way down was, incidentally, even harder than the way up. Eckart seemed particularly unsteady, scared of missing a step.

Ricarda had taken on the responsibility for planning. There was a calendar on the kitchen wall on which Uschi's physio, occupational and speech therapy appointments were marked. On Sunday evenings Ricarda used different coloured pens to indicate when each of them was on duty. On Monday everything was still there in neat and tidy writing, but by the time Sunday came around again, and Ricarda set about planning the next week, the previous week was nothing but a mess of colourful whirls and arrows pointing in all directions. Things didn't always work out as Ricarda had planned; there were alterations and rearrangements, as well as all the health insurance paperwork.

It was a huge amount of work, and not only for Ricarda. All because she, Uschi Müller, had had that bloody stroke and couldn't recover any sensation in the right half of her body.

Uschi gazed out of the toilet window. A robin was perched on the wrought-iron railing, wagging its head.

Uschi let out a long sigh. A good long sigh every now and again, and you felt a whole lot better.

Quite apart from the fact that it pained her to be such a burden on the others, inside her something had shattered. Depending on the day, her mood swung between unspeakable sadness and all-out rage. She found it completely unfair. How cruel of fate to strike her. Why? She'd never done anyone any harm; she'd tried to go through life being healthy, and kind and friendly to those around her. So why was she being punished so harshly all of a sudden? Why?

She knew that these feelings and thoughts were stupid, but she simply couldn't come to terms with the unfairness of it. She constantly tried to pep herself up, she berated herself, but she just couldn't get used to it. She still had so many plans.

Why? Why her?

Uschi sniffed. It was hard to judge when the smell had disappeared, but the air seemed clear to her. She coughed and called out the word, the joyless word, 'Ready.'

It came out as a croak. No response. Uschi cleared her throat again.

'Reeaady!' This time her voice carried. The door opened, and Ricarda came in.

'Everything okay?' she asked fondly, looking at Uschi as she would at a little child. Uschi nodded. *Yes, thanks, everything's fine.*

She knew that Ricarda meant well, but it still cut her to

153

the quick. Uschi always dreaded that look, which she was obliged to return with good grace. It was humiliating, and it was really none of Ricarda's business whether she had had a good bowel movement, a less good one or none at all. Yet, given that the others bore some of the responsibility for her wellbeing, and given that she was completely dependent on them, they had every right – and maybe even a duty – to know how she felt.

Yes, she deserved that look.

37

Uschi had almost slithered out of her arms. Uschi's good leg had slipped on the bathmat, and her full weight came crashing down on Ricarda. Ricarda stumbled, groped for something to hold, clutched at the bathroom cupboard and wedged her leg under Uschi's buttocks. The cupboard handle bored into her upper arm, but she pushed upwards, grabbed Uschi around the hips and dumped her with a practised movement on to the bath seat.

'Phew! Got away with it again, eh?' she panted. Shaken, Uschi nodded.

Heaving Uschi over from the toilet to the bath seat was one of the trickiest moments of the day. Philip had shown her how to do this as well. Initially they'd done it together, but Ricarda had quickly learned the ropes. It was amazing what you could do with a few smart grips. It was only when one of the holds wasn't right that you felt, and realised, how much strain you were putting on your body.

Ricarda soaped Uschi's back and rubbed her skin with gentle circular movements of the large natural sponge. 'Is the temperature all right?' she asked.

Uschi nodded and hung her head. She didn't seem in a good way today. Sometimes they would chat, as Ricarda sought to lend an air of normality to these situations, trying to take Uschi's mind off the fact that she was sitting naked in the bathtub. Naked and dependent.

Sometimes it worked, sometimes it didn't. Ricarda knew how hard it was for Uschi to accept and tolerate all this help and support. She was obviously still in shock from the close call earlier.

Ricarda passed Uschi the sponge so she could wash her front, which she could reach with her good arm. Uschi took the sponge and briefly glanced up at Ricarda. *None of this is easy for me*, said her eyes. *I know*, Ricarda nodded. She looked out the window, exhaling noiselessly. The near-fall had scared her too. The effect was always delayed. When it happened – and it wasn't the first time – instinct took over; you carried on, you went through with it. But the cumulative effect was both physically and emotionally draining.

A key turned in the front door.

'I'm back,' called Philip cheerfully. Ricarda smiled, picked up the bottle of shampoo and lathered Uschi's hair. The doorsill creaked behind her. She looked around

156

and nodded to Philip: *all okay, everything's going fine.* They avoided subjecting Uschi to the presence of too many people.

Ricarda turned on the tap, sending water spurting into the bathtub. She checked the temperature and rinsed Uschi's hair. Suddenly she felt a hand on the back of her neck – Philip's hand. Her body contracted, even though his hand was merely resting softly on her skin. The water ran over Uschi's head, sending foam scooting down her back. Slowly Ricarda relaxed and breathed out. Philip's hand was practically forcing her to release the tension from her shoulders. She was breathing more calmly now. Her fingers glided through Uschi's hair, and her movements slowed down.

She glanced tentatively up at him. He winked and ran his fingers quickly and affectionately down her cheek and then left her alone with Uschi again.

In a daze, Ricarda turned off the tap, picked up the towel, gently rubbed Uschi's hair dry and wound the towel around her friend's head.

Once again Philip had succeeded in knocking her momentarily off balance. A silent conversation had taken place between them – a thrilling second that didn't lead anywhere, nor could it.

Something similar had occurred yesterday. Ricarda was standing by the wall calendar with a glass of red wine, crossing out Harry's Tuesday shift because he had a doctor's appointment of his own. She was wondering who might be able to step in for him, and which shift Harry should do in exchange. All of a sudden, Philip had encircled her hips from behind, taken her pen and crossed out his name next to speech therapy on Thursday. Their faces were very close.

'What's going on?' she whispered.

He grinned and replaced his own name with Harry's next to speech therapy. She had to laugh. Harry and speech exercises? Nothing could be more far-fetched. Harry never missed a chance to tell everyone in what low esteem he held these 'chatter therapies'.

'Bravo,' she said. 'And what are *you* going to do instead?'

'I've got an idea.'

'Oh, yeah?' she asked.

'Uh-huh,' he said.

She pulled back her head a little, partly because of her eyesight – he was too close up.

'Do you have to move away that far to see me clearly?' he said with an enigmatic grin. But, before she could react, Eckart came into the kitchen. Philip winked at her and left the room.

Such ambiguous moments were becoming a bit of a habit. She glanced in the bathroom mirror and, touching her cheek, ran her fingers over the spot Philip's had just so lovingly caressed.

38

The wheelchair glinted in the rays of the setting sun. His swimming trunks were too tight around the crotch. He'd need a new pair if they were going to make a habit of coming to this lake, thought Eckart, tugging the checked shorts down a little.

At breakfast the day before, Ricarda had suggested that they make another outing to the lake. Eckart had panicked a bit at first: after all, their previous trip, the night before Uschi's stroke, had been the last place and time they had been truly carefree.

However, now that they were here by the lakeside, in the soothing light of the late-afternoon sun, everyone appeared to be enjoying themselves. Whichever way you looked at it, they simply had to get away from time to time. They were shattered. It was more draining than they had imagined.

Emotionally too. Uschi spoke little and seemed despondent. She found it hard to accept her flatmates' help. The various therapies were not having the desired effect or inspiring the rapid progress they had hoped for. The whole situation demanded extraordinary patience – and effort. And the harder they worked, the more their patience dwindled. Harry grumbled a great deal; every now and then he forgot an appointment. Even he, Eckart, had recently dozed off during Uschi's physiotherapy.

Still, there was the odd burst from Harry that livened up the place. Each time Eckart was about to give up, Harry would come out with one of his remarks. Take yesterday evening for example, when they had finally got around to playing another game of whist, and Uschi – poor old Uschi! – had mixed up the black queens *again*. Who could blame her? Good grief, there were far more important things at the moment than being able to tell the queen of spades and the queen of clubs apart! But Harry was having none of that and showed her no mercy.

'You bloody nincompoop, Uschi! It can't be that difficult! This is a club,' he'd said, grabbing Uschi's cards and slamming the queens down on the table, 'and this is a spade. Or an upside-down heart, if you prefer!'

'Harry . . . ' Ricarda had laid a placating hand on Harry's arm.

'What? That's the way it is,' moaned Harry.

Uschi had looked around contritely.

'No need to act like that, Uschi my dear!' said Harry. 'Your brain's working just fine. Pull yourself together.'

Uschi had nervously picked up the queen of spades and turned it around to make a black 'queen of hearts'. Eckart's and Philip's eyes had met. It might have been a bit cruel, but, when it came down to it, Harry's was the healthiest way of dealing with the situation. He was a force of nature.

Eckart emerged from the bushes and headed down to the lake. Harry lay sprawled on the grass, dozing, with Ralf. Ricarda was crouching in her swimming costume beside the wheelchair. She took off Uschi's socks and dangled her flatmate's feet in the water. Eckart couldn't see whether Uschi was enjoying this because her head was concealed by an enormous straw sunhat that Philip had bought her that morning. Philip blew up one of Uschi's orange armbands and handed it to her.

'Want to try it on?'

The enormous straw hat wiggled from side to side to signal no.

'Maybe it's a bit too soon,' said Ricarda, and stood up. 'Shall we?' she said to Philip with a charming tilt of her head. Philip nodded, and they waded into the water. Eckart sat down next to Uschi's chair and leaned against one of the big wheels.

Ricarda and Philip swam out into the middle of the lake. Their voices faded into the distance, and their laughter drifted over to the couple on the shore. Eckart enjoyed watching the two of them. It was fairly obvious that they more than liked each other, but for some reason they weren't managing to take that step beyond friendship. Eckart wondered whether it was due to age.

Suddenly a shadow fell on his face. It was cast by the enormous straw hat, which was bending down to him.

'They're sweet together, aren't they?' remarked Uschi from her straw camouflage. Her nose was puckered. She was smiling; Uschi was actually smiling. It was as if the sun had risen anew. The birds were atwitter, the turtle doves were afloat, Harry and Ralf were snoring, and his trunks were pinching him, but Uschi had smiled. Things couldn't get much better than they were right then.

Eckart took Uschi's hand, but she didn't react: it was her right hand.

'That was a good tip about the upside-down heart yesterday,' she muttered.

Thank goodness for Harry, thought Eckart. Whatever would they do without him?

39

Harry couldn't be bothered any more. He couldn't be bothered one jot. He was sitting with Uschi in the speech therapist's waiting room, although he actually wanted to be at the racetrack. A fellow taxi driver had given him a tip, and the tide was currently out in Harry's wallet.

However, Ricarda had suddenly slapped an extra shift on him the day before at the lake. Harry didn't appreciate that. And Harry appreciated the fact that it was the speech therapist slot even less. Plus she had given him a telling-off that morning for not putting out the rubbish; that he appreciated even *even* less.

Earlier that morning he'd decided on the spur of the moment to round up Uschi and Ralf and take them for a walk in the park. He had barely lugged the two meatballs back up the three flights of stairs – Uschi was gradually taking her toll on his back! – when Ricarda had laid into him. She'd come storming down the hallway with her stupid vacuum cleaner. Eckart had obviously been sentenced to mop the kitchen, Philip had pushed past Harry with a crate of empties and a look on his face that indicated trouble was brewing, and Ricarda had given Harry a good and proper telling-off because he hadn't put out the rubbish! He wouldn't take it. He just wouldn't take it. He. Would. Not. Take. It.

Trouble was brewing. In fact that was a massive understatement.

Harry was doing his level best. He didn't like to see Uschi looking so down. He didn't like it when Eckart lowered his eyes in embarrassment when he, Harry, snapped yet again. But neither could he change his spots overnight. He'd arranged his whole life to ensure nobody could boss him around, and then along came Madam Ricarda, laying down the law. The whole thing stuck in his craw.

Even as a boy, he had rebelled when Aunt Matilda had moved in with them after her husband's death, and started reprimanding him and trying to educate him. No one educated Harry Markwand. If he was going to care for Uschi, then it was because he wanted to – not because Madam 'The-Situation's-Serious-But-We-Can-Tough-It-Out-Together' wanted him to. No, it was because he, Harry Markwand, wanted to. Because he had taken the decision, or because he agreed with someone else's suggestion.

Take yesterday at the lake, for example, when Eckart – Eckart! – had got into his head the crackpot idea of practising aerobics with Uschi. Harry a) didn't fancy aerobics, and b) didn't have the faintest idea what had suddenly driven Eckart to take up aerobics. There was no rhyme nor reason to it. None. It had cost Harry a lot, but he'd joined in for Eckart's sake. And it was good. Damn good, in fact, because after a few beats Uschi had started to bob around with her upper body and smiled.

How dared she smile? No more than just *smile*? Harry would have burst out laughing at the scene! Jane Fonda was squawking instructions from the smartphone to a backdrop of dreadful disco music, and Eckart, Ricarda, Philip and he obeyed her every command. Yes, they did whatever Jane Fonda screeched at them from that small device. They lifted their legs, punched the air with their fists and twisted their bodies as though it were the most natural thing in the world for a sixty-year-old to stand in his swimming trunks facing a wheelchair by a lake and shake his backside to the strains of Jane Fonda.

It was a hit. Even chubby old Ralf started hopping around on the spot like an idiot – and boy, did he need the exercise! It was all so borderline absurd that it seemed normal again. Eckart – every now and then he just blew them all away.

But, as already mentioned, Harry had volunteered for that; he'd done it of his own accord.

*

The door opened. 'Do come in,' announced the speech therapist's voice. Harry sighed and wheeled Uschi into the treatment room.

He definitely hadn't volunteered for *this*.

Harry didn't think much of speech therapists. His grandson Timmy had also been to see one because words came out of his cheeks with a strange hiss. So many sessions and no progress. It had finally sorted itself out when Harry had told Timmy that he didn't have to talk like Clint Eastwood to be a cool cowboy. It was all in the mind.

Uschi seemed tense, and after the first exercise Harry understood why.

'Six thick thistle sticks,' said the lady to Uschi.

Six thick WHAT? Six thick WHAT THE HELL? Six thick thistle sticks? Harry ran this bizarre phrase through his bullshit-detection programme, and felt a grudging sense of admiration. Crikey! It took some imagination to come up with rubbish words like that!

'Sick thick thistle schticks,' said Uschi, slurring and faltering.

'Sticks,' the speech therapist pronounced slowly, mouthing every syllable. She was about thirty and wore her blonde hair in a plait.

Uschi concentrated on her lips, then took a deep breath and imitated the woman's friendly singsong: 'S-ti-cks.'

'Don't cheat, Mrs Müller. The whole word. Go on.'

Uschi nodded. 'Sick ... thwick ... '

That's right, Uschi, thought Harry. *You've seen through it. The only possible comment on nonsense like this is 'sick'.*

Uschi hung her head despondently.

'Mrs Müller,' said the therapist, refusing to back down, 'you can do this. All right?' She gave Uschi an encouraging nod.

Uschi looked up and gulped, her eyes wide with alarm. She tried to start again, took a deep breath (Harry breathed in with her) and another (Harry could feel the emptiness in his own throat) and then she broke down. Instead of the intended word, all she could produce was a tear.

'Mrs Müller ...' said the therapist, introducing a gentle undercurrent of severity into her voice. Harry noticed that his blood was slowly beginning to boil. What was the point of this? Did she have to torment and humiliate this little woman with these absurd exercises, all so that Uschi could pronounce a few words more clearly? Just let her mumble. And, if the aim was to cure her mumbling, then there must be a better method than using six thick thistle sticks.

His thoughts were promptly turned against him. He felt the therapist's friendly gaze on his face.

'Why don't you lend your friend a helping hand?'

'With six thick thistle sticks?' Harry shot back.

'Uh-huh,' she said, as cheerfully as ever.

Uh-huh, thought Harry.

He glanced at Uschi. The poor dear looked utterly dejected. Her eyes welled up with tears, and she was struggling bravely to hold them back. *Okay*, he thought, *let's go along with this crazy, shitty game.*

'Ready?' he asked.

Uschi nodded. One of the tears rolled out and ran down her cheek. He leaned towards her, spread his index and middle fingers into a V, pointed them at his eyes, then hers, then back at his. *Watch me, Uschi. Watch me closely.*

He pursed his lips and pronounced the first three syllables loudly and clearly. 'Cry-Ba-By.'

The therapist's eyebrows shot up. Uschi snivelled even more loudly. Harry didn't take his eyes off her, offering her no mercy and leaving her no way out.

Uschi was battling with her emotions. He could sense her inner turmoil as she sought to counter his gentle insult. Then she leaned forward, pursed one side of her lips and formed the three syllables: 'Screw-Zou-Too.'

'You,' Harry corrected her, pushing his lips forward as far as they would go. 'You.'

'You,' Uschi answered.

'She did it!' laughed Harry, leaning back. The therapist grinned.

And Uschi? She thanked him for his wonderful therapy session with a crooked smile.

40

'Do you think he ever cheated on you?' asked Philip, as he hammered a nail into the narrow wooden board lying across his knees. Ralf had made himself comfortable by Philip's feet on the lushly planted balcony, but now he toddled off into the kitchen. His ears couldn't stand the banging.

Ricarda passed her watering can slowly over the flowers. Drops of water trickled off the leaves.

Philip examined his board. The nail had gone in perfectly straight, protruding exactly one inch from the other side of the piece of wood. He picked up the second nail.

'I think so,' said Ricarda after a while. 'Herbert was quite a charmer.' She twisted a shrivelled leaf off a red gerbera daisy. Philip let his eyes wander down her back. He hammered in the second nail half an inch to the left of the first.

'How could anyone cheat on you?' He tried to phrase the

question as winningly as possible, but he regretted saying it the moment it had crossed his lips.

She said nothing and, with her back still to him, she shook the watering can, only to establish that it was empty. Why wasn't she reacting?

After what seemed like an eternity she turned to face him. 'Are you trying to tell me something?'

'What if I am?' Unfortunately his voice didn't come out as forcefully as he'd have liked.

'Hmm . . .' She nodded slowly, a smile playing on her lips and then . . . a piercing scream erupted from the bathroom, accompanied by an unholy din.

Uschi! Oh, no! They'd totally forgotten her!

Philip tripped over Ralf as he ran to the bathroom, and the dog let out a terrified howl. Philip flung the door open to find Uschi spluttering, her legs thrashing in the water alongside the collapsed bath seat. He grabbed her under the armpits, but her arms were beating the air and they slipped from his grasp. Ricarda came to his assistance, and together they managed to pull Uschi out of the water. She was gasping for air; her face had gone bright red, and her eyes were wide and staring.

Philip sank down on to the toilet seat, and Ricarda slumped against the wall. They took several deep breaths. That was a close shave. They'd put Uschi in the bathtub and then forgotten all about her. Clean forgotten her.

41

'She can't swim! She can't walk! She can't sit! Oh, boy, oh, boy, oh, boy! This isn't over by a long way!'

Eckart jumped. Once again Harry was voicing the thoughts that everyone else had been keeping to themselves. They were gathered around the kitchen table. It was time for an emergency meeting.

'We bear a huge responsibility,' Eckart said in agreement.

Ricarda came into the kitchen. 'I've given her a sedative and she's asleep now.' For the first time Eckart sensed that Ricarda was extremely tense, at the very limit of her capabilities. 'If only she'd show some progress.' She sighed and began to unload the dishwasher.

'Physiotherapy twice a week just isn't enough,' Philip

added. 'I'm going to prescribe her daily sessions at home. I'll get it past the insurance somehow or other.' He pondered the matter for a second. 'We could ask that guy Fabian.'

'Fabian?' Eckart chose a red apple from the fruit bowl.

'The assessor,' said Philip.

'What's the assessor got to do with this?' Ralf had made himself at home on Harry's right shoe, but he shoved the dog to one side.

'Actually, he's no longer an assessor. He's a qualified physiotherapist now,' said Philip with a quick sideways glance at Ricarda, who was absentmindedly putting away the glasses in the cupboard.

'How the hell do you know *that*?' asked Harry.

'From Stella.' Philip glanced over at Ricarda again.

'Are they shagging or something?' asked Harry.

Philip wiggled his head. 'Ric?'

'Hmm?' She turned around to face the group with a bowl in one hand and a surprised expression on her face.

'Don't you have something to tell us?' grinned Philip.

Ricarda had no idea what he meant.

'I bumped into Stella in the park just now as I was walking Ralf and ... we had a little chat.' He paused for dramatic effect, but Ricarda was still staring blankly at him. 'Granny.'

'What do you mean, Granny?' asked Ricarda.

'Er ...' Philip arched his eyebrows. 'If *your* daughter's pregnant, then *you're* going to be a *granny*? Right?'

Harry was a picture of curiosity.

Granny – the word hung sad and lonely in the kitchen air. Ricarda looked at Philip, her face empty of all emotion. Granny?

Oh, dear. Eckart lowered his gaze and stared at the apple. This wasn't going to plan. For a while no one in the kitchen made a sound except for Ralf, who yawned and stretched. Eckart raised his eyes cautiously. Ricarda put the bowls very deliberately into the cupboard. She stared at the half-empty dishwasher as though one of the compartments might hold the answer.

'Fine,' she said calmly and headed towards the door. 'Let's ask that guy . . . Fabian. Good idea!'

They heard her go into her room and quietly close the door. Philip studied the table top and adjusted the position of a candle.

'Out with it!' said Harry. 'The assessor's got Stella pregnant? Within a few days?'

'Don't be stupid,' said Philip with a shake of the head. Harry grabbed his tobacco pouch and began to roll himself a cigarette. The pouch was virtually empty, and some of the dried-out remnants spilled on to the table. He stood up and went out on to the balcony.

'Don't smoke so much,' Philip warned him distractedly. 'It's not good for you.'

'Lots of things aren't good around here,' snapped Harry as he pulled the balcony door shut behind him. Philip walked out of the kitchen too, leaving Eckart alone at the table, where he declared the meeting closed.

Poor Ricarda. He wondered whether Christoph would let *him* know if he became a father. He put the apple back in the fruit bowl.

42

There was a knock on the door, startling Philip and making him blink in the darkness. The African statue stood in a pool of moonlight. His door opened quietly, and Ricarda crept into the room in her nightdress.

'Uschi?' he asked sleepily. 'Has something happened to Uschi?'

Ricarda shook her head. She walked over to the window and looked out. He sat up. Her body shimmered through the fine white fabric. She didn't say a word and didn't move, just gazed out at the moon.

'I thought you knew,' he said softly. He had felt guilty all afternoon. Never in his wildest dreams could he have imagined that Stella hadn't told her mother that she was pregnant. He had tapped on Ricarda's door several times, but there was no response.

He got out of bed and came to stand behind her. He could smell her floral skin cream and the scent of her hair.

'Did you fall out, or why else would she not tell you?' he asked.

'She's been wanting to talk to me ever since she got back from Spain. I just don't understand. By whom?'

'One of those screw specialists. A Spaniard. A four-night stand, at most. Not a potential father anyway.'

Ricarda nodded silently. Philip felt an urge to take her in his arms. He raised one hand. He wanted to comfort her. He wanted to touch the white fabric and pass his hand through to her skin, to her body.

She turned around, her eyes brimming with sadness. He wanted to kiss those eyes. He wanted to run his lips over their lids and kiss away the sadness. For a few seconds they stood facing each other, a mere matter of inches between their bodies – and all those years apart. He longed to slip the straps from her shoulders, see her naked body in the moonlight, touch her breasts and feel them against him.

Her mouth opened slightly and her breathing deepened. He could feel her chest rising and falling, brushing ever so slightly against him. The wooden floorboards creaked.

She lowered her eyes, laid her hand for a brief instant on his shoulder, sighed and left the room. Philip watched the door close behind her. He took a deep breath and, perching on the edge of his desk, poured himself a whisky, feeling the agreeable burning sensation on his tongue.

He shut his eyes. He could feel the rise and fall of Ricarda's breasts. He could feel her gaze on his face.

43

Fabian oiled his hands, the same hands that Uschi loved for their strength and the calm and relaxation they radiated. He rubbed his palms together and wiped some oil on to the backs of his hands too. He looked very dapper in his white linen trousers and white T-shirt.

Today was Fabian's first session with her, but from now on he would come five times a week, as Philip had agreed with the health insurance. Fabian had suggested that they begin with a massage so that he could get to know Uschi and familiarise himself with her nerve fibres and muscle groups. He had explained to her in advance what he was going to do.

Ready, he asked with his eyes. Ready, Uschi nodded.

She felt his hands on her good leg, and it was wonderful. Stella came into the room and shot her a smile. She and

Fabian had arrived together, though Uschi wasn't quite clear about the status of their relationship.

'Are you two an item?' she asked.

'I'm only making sure he does his job properly,' Stella grinned, 'because after all I was the one who set this up.' That wasn't an answer, but Fabian was smiling.

'And *I*'ve set her up with a swimming class for pregnant women.' He worked his way up Uschi's leg. How lovely, thought Uschi. The two of them seemed to like each other a lot.

There was the sound of a key in the front door. 'And,' Stella continued with a laugh, 'he's even volunteered to come with me. What's more, he's offered to fix my crooked ba—'

She broke off and stared coolly at the door. 'Hi, Mum.'

'There you are, Stella.' Ricarda smiled as she went over to her daughter, but Stella sidestepped her and sat down demonstratively on the chair on the far side of Uschi's bed.

'I tried to call you,' said Ricarda.

Uschi glanced back and forth from left to right, from Ricarda to Stella, who merely shrugged. Fabian was working attentively on her leg – the one she couldn't feel.

'Why didn't you say anything to me?' Ricarda asked.

'When?' Stella's icy courteousness was harder than any slap.

'And who's the—'

'An arsehole.'

'Oh. And ...' Ricarda looked uneasily at Uschi and Fabian, but Stella stayed where she was.

'How many weeks?' Stella asked pointedly. 'Too late to get rid of it. Your advice? Yes, I could've done with it.'

Uschi closed her eyes. She felt for Ricarda. Stella was being too hard on her mother – it wasn't fair. In any case, Uschi didn't want to be party to this conversation; it made her uncomfortable. She'd never liked it when people argued, settled scores and hurt each other in her presence. Even if it wasn't vicious. Simply because people's feelings, or – even worse – their pride took a battering. No, she didn't want to witness this exchange of blows, but nobody had asked her opinion, and she couldn't get away.

This wasn't the first time. It was funny how invisible she'd become since her stroke. People ignored her. Generally it was no big deal, because she often fancied erasing herself from the room on account of the half of her that was no longer good for anything, but still caused everyone a whole bunch of problems.

And yet: even if she was only 'half' there, she was still there. She wasn't deaf, and her feelings and her heart still worked as well as they'd always done. Her antennae were possibly keener than before – for other people's feelings too. She was no longer an actor; against her will she had become an observer.

There was quite a lot to observe. People fought their battles and brooded over their problems right under her nose.

It was insignificant whether she was there or not; she didn't exist. At moments like this she was just a lump – a sickly, insignificant lump.

But then there were the other moments when everyone was completely focused on *her*. *She* was the problem. *She* had to be dealt with. She was a lump that needed organising.

She looked up at Fabian. He didn't want to be here either. He winked at her. She liked this freckly lad. She might not have been able to feel his beautiful, strong hands – they were somewhere on her left arm by now – but his eyes were tender and kind.

Uschi sensed Ricarda's gaze on her.

'Stella, could we discuss this outside?' Ricarda said.

'I can't right now,' Stella answered frostily. 'As you can see, I'm chatting!'

Well, *I* could have done without this particular chat, thought Uschi. Crikey, this girl was tough! She must be deeply stung.

Ricarda gasped and left the room. Fabian knitted his brow. Uschi wondered whether he was going to say something, comment on Stella's untoward behaviour.

'*What?*' Stella said grouchily.

Well, thought Uschi, at least she realised that she'd overstepped the mark.

44

Why was Stella being so hard on her? thought Ricarda. The naked mannequin stared at her without a trace of emotion. Ricarda fiddled with the turquoise scarf hanging around the plastic dummy's neck.

Whichever way she looked at it, Stella was right: she hadn't listened to her daughter. Ricarda had been completely absorbed with the flatshare since Stella had got back from Granada. Their days revolved around Uschi, and she had to keep a tight rein on things. She knew that she got on the others' nerves. Still, someone had to do this job; someone had to play the bad guy; someone had to keep things in order and remind Harry of his duties and his appointments.

Exhausted, Ricarda placed her hands on the mannequin's shoulders. Now she was seeking reassurance from a plastic display dummy.

She thought of Philip. What had that all been about the other night? She had barely resisted the urge to kiss him, and, once back in bed, she had imagined him touching her.

It had been their game, back when she was with Herbert. They'd flirted with fantasies of what might have been, under different circumstances, in another life. Their old game had resumed since she'd moved into the flatshare. Except: now they were in that other life, and the former rules were no longer so strict.

But seriously, was it a good idea to start a relationship here in the flat to add to all her other worries? No, it wasn't. It was far from a good idea.

She sighed. The mannequin's right shoulder groaned and the arm fell to the floor. Ricarda picked it up and tried in vain to screw it back into place, but the damned arm wouldn't obey her. She wiggled it around, but it was no use, part of the mechanism was broken. Just like Uschi. Great. The symbolism wasn't lost on her.

She thought of all the work, all the effort, all the tension. Still, how could she have neglected and ignored her own daughter like that? What was she trying to prove, and to whom? Was she overlooking the most important things as she tried to make everything else work out?

BANG!

BANG!

The mirror on the wall trembled. Again. That did it!

Ricarda tore the door open, barged into the adjacent room without knocking and levelled the plastic arm at Harry.

'You do realise it's me you're aiming those darts at, don't you?'

Harry was standing in front of his dartboard in nothing but a pair of baggy, washed-out blue underpants. He was balancing a dart in his hand and squinting down the shaft at the bull's eye.

'Oh, boy, Ricarda,' he said in a cool voice, without looking round, 'I'd completely forgotten that people's character traits become *more* rather than *less* pronounced with age, and they grow—' pulling his hand back to launch the dart '—increasingly fractious.'

The dart sailed through the air. BANG! Bingo – triple twenty!

'You really ought to calm down,' he said with a nod of his head, and furrowed his brow for dramatic effect.

Ricarda couldn't think of a comeback. She turned on her heel and slammed Harry's door behind her. When was the last time she had slammed a door? She hated to lose control, but that damned Harry never failed to get her goat. The door opened again.

'Take cover! Three-armed Ricarda on the warpath!' Harry called for all their flatmates to hear.

'You bloody nincompoop,' she shouted. Had she really just used Harry's expression? 'Stop winding me up!'

Harry stood still, adjusted his baggy blue underpants and arched an eyebrow.

'What?' she said.

'You do realise you're standing in the middle of our beloved flat threatening me with a plastic arm?' he said.

No, she hadn't realised.

She lowered her arm – or rather, her arm holding a plastic arm.

If it hadn't been so pathetic it would have been hilarious.

45

The old woman in the wheelchair was sawing away with her left hand at a carrot that had been fastened to a chopping board. Timmy had never seen a chopping board with two nails in it for holding down a carrot.

Grandpa Harry had explained to him in advance that Auntie Uschi's right side didn't work any more. There was something wrong with it. Maybe it was a bit like his Luke Skywalker figurine, which had lost an arm. These things happen.

In any case, Auntie Uschi could slice carrots on that board. He didn't really understand why Auntie Uschi *had* to slice carrots, but grown-ups always came up with a solution for everything.

Timmy was sitting at the kitchen table with her. Grandpa Harry had laid out a few sheets of paper and some coloured pens and asked whether Timmy could look after Auntie Uschi for an hour or so while he popped out.

'Of course,' Timmy had said. He was almost seven after all. He grabbed a red pen and started to draw.

'Everything okay?' said Grandpa Harry, poking his head around the door. Timmy nodded.

'Auntie Uschi?' asked Harry. It was as if they were sitting in a spaceship and ground control was checking if they were ready for take-off.

'Everything's okay,' said Auntie Uschi. She was ready for take-off. She had a bit of a wonky smile, but Timmy liked her. She had kind eyes. He considered for a second which colour he should use for the second coffin. He plumped for green, and drew another coffin next to the red one he'd marked 'Granpa' and wrote 'Filip' on it. That was the name of the man who'd made the carrot board.

Timmy had learned to write a month before and ever since he'd been drawing things to which he could add letters. Yesterday he'd drawn the Cologne FC kit. Today it was coffins for the members of the flatshare, as Grandpa had told him to draw something nice for them.

Timmy took the blue pen for the third coffin and wrote 'Uschi' on it, marked 'Rikada' in purple on the fourth, and then coloured the fifth coffin yellow.

'What's the thin man with the sad eyes called again?' he asked Uschi, who was still carving away at her carrots.

'Eckart.' She leaned inquisitively over his drawing, and

Timmy turned it proudly towards her. Oddly, though, this wasn't followed by the usual cry of 'good work'; Auntie Uschi didn't much seem to like his drawing. Well, of course the picture wasn't finished yet. He spun the sheet of paper around again and wrote 'Ekkaat' on the yellow coffin.

'I need a wee,' said Auntie Uschi. Timmy picked up the brown pen and started work on the next little coffin. Auntie Uschi was rocking back and forth. He wondered whether he should add a little cross to each coffin, but decided against it. The little coffin was too little for that, and he still had to write a name on it.

Auntie Uschi continued to rock back and forth. Why didn't she go to the loo if she needed a wee so badly? he wondered, and looked up. She was looking strangely at him. *Oh, pooh*, he thought, *Auntie Uschi can't walk*. Grandpa had not told him what to do if she needed to go to the loo.

'Can't you hold it in?' he asked. She nodded, her face pinched. *That's all right, then*, he thought, and wrote 'Timmy' on his little coffin. 'But you're going to die first!' he explained as he dotted the 'i'.

'How come?' Auntie Uschi asked, her face now even more pinched.

What a stupid question. 'Because you're the oldest.'

She was giving him that strange look again. Had he said something wrong? Didn't old people always die first? He thought it over, then something occurred to him. 'And because half of you is already broken.' Yep, that's what he'd forgotten.

Now she was looking *really* strangely at him. She was holding herself where you weren't supposed to hold yourself. He suddenly had a fright. Auntie Uschi wasn't going to pee in her pants, was she?

46

Philip unlocked the door to the apartment just in time to hear Ricarda shout in the bathroom, 'At the races?! I can't believe my ears!'

What was it now? Philip closed the door behind him, put the key on the little shelf, and took a few steps along the hallway. Harry was standing in the bathroom doorway, ready to blow his top. He nodded and said, 'Hi, Philip.'

Stella was pottering about in the kitchen.

'What's wrong?' asked Philip, peering beyond Harry into the bathroom. Ricarda was leaning over the bathtub, rinsing soapsuds from Uschi's back. His eyes came to rest involuntarily on Ricarda's chest.

'What's *wrong*?' she said, rounding on him. Her breasts moved up and down as she washed Uschi. 'Harry left Uschi all on her own,' she cried. 'And he had the fantastic idea of leaving Timmy here too. With Uschi of all people.' She noticed the direction of his gaze and pulled her blouse up a touch. She stared at him, eyes blazing.

'So?' said Philip, giving an embarrassed little cough at having been caught out. He always found Ricarda especially beautiful when she was angry. Factor in her jiggling cleavage and for a second he'd been completely unreceptive to the stern tone of her words.

'So?' Ricarda shot back. 'Timmy's six years old! And he tried to put Uschi on the loo.'

'Okay, okay, calm down a bit,' snapped Harry with a wink at Uschi. 'Hey, Uschi, you didn't mean to urine us.'

Worth a try, thought Philip. He would have laughed, but Ricarda wasn't at all in the mood for jokes.

'Listen, Philip. When I got home Uschi was lying next to the bath in a sopping wet dress and Timmy was wailing on the floor. Thank God she didn't break anything. If this carries on, sooner or later we're going to have a serious problem.'

'Where's the boy?' he broke in.

'His mother picked him up a few minutes ago,' replied Ricarda. 'He was totally shell-shocked. You have to look after a child, Harry. You can't just—'

'Oh, now *that's* news to me,' Stella interrupted, as she joined them.

Ricarda's hand fell to her side with the sponge in it. 'What's the big idea, Stella?'

'I was just saying.'

'Just saying? I'm getting tired of this, Stella. If you want to talk to me, let's talk, but not like this!' Ricarda's tone was extremely sharp and, unaccustomed to that, Stella flinched. She nodded slowly, turned around and put on her jacket.

'Oh, shit. Stella!' Ricarda got to her feet. 'Stella, wait ... let's ... Wait, my love!' She made to chase after her daughter, but she was suddenly brought up short in the doorway.

'*I* told Harry he could go out. *I* wanted to look after Timmy,' said a faint voice from the bathtub.

'Sorry?' Ricarda looked around in disbelief. 'You wanted to look after ...?'

Uschi nodded sheepishly, as soap ran down her wrinkled neck.

'I don't believe this,' said Ricarda. The front door slammed, and Stella was gone. Ricarda slumped on to the toilet seat. 'Have you all gone completely—'

'What do you mean?' Harry shouted. 'We can't treat her as if she's handicapped the whole time.' He was really fuming now, shaking his head and staring at Philip. 'Christ! She's totally unhinged at the minute!' he spluttered. He strode out of the bathroom and slammed his bedroom door.

Ralf came trotting out of the kitchen. Philip crouched down and scratched the dog's neck. This was a tricky situation. Everyone meant well, but they kept saying the wrong thing.

Ricarda raised herself wearily from the toilet seat, reached for the blue towel and wrapped it around Uschi's upper body. Philip lifted her out of the tub and helped her into the wheelchair. Uschi hung her head, but Ricarda ran her fingers through her flatmate's hair. Philip went into the kitchen to refill Ralf's water bowl and to make himself a cup of tea. Walking over to the window as the kettle began to wheeze, he spotted an elderly woman in the old man's flat opposite. She opened the window and hung out a 'To Let' sign.

47

Her bag rang, and Stella fished out her mobile; it was her mother. She hesitated, but Eckart cocked his head at her. *Take the call*, he seemed to say with his eyes. Ralf cast them a bored look from under the table.

'Not now.' Stella pressed Ricarda away. She was sitting on a café terrace at Baudriplatz with Eckart, who had called her to ask whether they could meet. And here they were, drinking cappuccinos and gazing out over the square. The sun was shining, and a few kids were playing while their mothers chatted on a bench. Peaceful sounds floated over to Stella and Eckart. Stella suddenly pictured herself sitting on one of these benches, watching her child playing with others. She smiled at the thought.

She was glad that Eckart had called. He'd witnessed the whole ruckus, and now here he was staring at her and offering to mediate. Sweet of him, she thought. The five of them had bonded and become quite a little family.

Eckart, like Fabian before him, had told her how much Ricarda did for the flatshare and how caring for Uschi was now weighing on them all. He could understand that she was cross with her mother, but she should try not to take it personally. Ricarda had chided herself before, but their clash yesterday had really finished her off. 'She's stretched to the limit, but she loves you, Stella.'

'Hmm,' said Stella. It wasn't exactly clear to Stella herself why she was suddenly reacting so strongly to her mother. Might it be the hormones? Or some age-old pattern of behaviour?

A funny thing had happened to her the day before. She and Fabian had gone to the movies and then to the CineBar next door. She'd had to go the toilet and, when she'd pushed open the door to the washrooms, there were two faces looking out at her: from the left-hand toilet door Sissy Spacek's freckled, mousy features in Brian de Palma's horror film *Carrie*; from the right-hand door the cool gaze of Faye Dunaway as beret-wearing, gun-toting Bonnie. Just as Stella was about to step through the left-hand door, she paused and asked herself, *Why do I always choose the victim's door, and not the door with the beautiful woman who blasts her way through life?*

She hadn't been able to help but smile at herself. Her thoughts took off in very odd directions sometimes. Then she had indeed opted for Bonnie, and wow, it had changed the whole experience!

Fabian had laughed his head off when she told him.

Eckart took another sip of his cappuccino, and the foam stuck to his upper lip. 'Try your best, Stella, all right?'

One of the mothers sitting on the bench ran over to her child who was whining.

'It's just that I sometimes wonder whether she really loves me. You know ... truly,' she mumbled.

'Of course she does. All parents love their children.'

'Yes, but deeply. Not just because she's my mother.'

He was silent, but then he said, 'Maybe you're asking too much?'

'You think so?'

Eckart took the unopened sugar sachet and squeezed it between his index finger and thumb. 'Christoph's only written to me twice so far. A text to say he'd arrived okay, and a short email with a photo of the kiwi plantation.'

'Did you fall out?'

'No. He just suddenly had something against bank clerks.'

'Against bank clerks?' she asked with a grin.

Eckart nodded.

'That can't be the only reason, can it?'

'No, that can't be the only reason.' He nodded again. 'Same as with you.'

Ralf picked himself up off the floor, and Stella tousled

the hair on his head. Maybe parents and children didn't actually need to like each other.

'You know what happened one time?' she said.

'No.'

'We were sitting in the kitchen one evening, having dinner, and Mum was taking care of some paperwork while she ate. She was reading and making notes. She always carried her patients' records around with her. When she'd finished eating, she picked up her files, stood up, and turned out the light on her way out of the room.'

'Oh!' exclaimed Eckart.

'Uh-huh,' said Stella. Her own mother. The woman everyone always admired and defended.

'She didn't!' Eckart said in disbelief.

'Oh, yes, she did. She was concentrating so hard and was so lost in her thoughts that she left the room and switched the light off. She forgot about me. She forgot I was sitting there.'

'Ouch. That's tough.' Eckart tried not to laugh out loud.

'Yep,' she said, and his sweet chuckle made her join in with his laughter. She liked him and it was good to talk to him – to 'Uncle' Eckart from the flatshare.

'Have you got an hour or so?' he asked.

Stella nodded.

'Fancy a game of crazy golf?'

Crazy golf? She hadn't played in ages.

'I used to play it a lot with Christoph. It's fun.' He leaned under the table. 'Isn't that right, Ralf?'

'All right, then,' she said. 'Why not? Let's go crazy golfing.'

They paid and strolled slowly to the park. Ralf sniffed about as if his nose had to make an inventory of every smell along the street. Every smell, and all the other odd things the creatures of this planet were capable of producing.

'I love her,' she said.

'I know,' Eckart replied.

48

Someone unlocked the front door. 'At last,' groaned Eckart through clenched teeth. It must be Ricarda and Philip. Uschi grunted under him, and he wondered whether she was getting enough air.

'Do you know what the thyroid gland actually does?' he heard Philip ask. 'Any disorder can have a significant effect on a person's temper, and that—'

'Philip, I don't have thyroid trouble; I have Harry trouble,' Ricarda interrupted.

'And Granny trouble,' Philip teased her. Their two voices came closer.

'She could give me a bit of a break,' said Ricarda. 'I don't know what more I can—'

She broke off and stared at the living room armchair, on

which Eckart was contorted into a suspicious position over Uschi.

'Eckart!' Philip walked over to him, and gently lifted him from the chair on to the sofa. Eckart groaned again. Harry hadn't turned up, as had been agreed, to help him carry Uschi, so he had humped her up the stairs on his own. It had been torture. He had just about got her into the arm-chair when a stabbing pain in his shoulder and back had left him sprawled on top of her. He couldn't move an inch. He'd dislocated something, and he must have been lying on the unfortunate Uschi for a quarter of an hour or so.

'Aahh! No, Philip, don't!' A flash of lightning coursed through his back like an electric shock. Philip turned him cautiously on to his side on the sofa. He was in a great deal of pain.

'Where's Harry?' asked Ricarda. 'Did he fail to show up again?'

An infernal jolt ran through Eckart's body when Philip grabbed his arm and tugged it to the side. There was an audible crack, but Philip had obviously relocated the dislocated limb.

'What's up, Eckart?' Harry suddenly appeared in the doorway.

'Where *were* you?' cried Ricarda.

Harry looked past her at Eckart.

'Harry,' said Philip, glancing up, 'we could really do with a bit of discipline around here.'

'You all right, Eckart?' asked Harry.

Eckart nodded. Of course he wasn't, but like hell was he going to pour more oil on this fire.

Ricarda sat down in the armchair. 'Harry,' she said, reining in her temper, 'I'm trying my best to handle all of this. I make an enormous effort. I respect your freedom. You've got the fewest shifts of any of us, but *when* it's your turn, you have to—'

'*You* were the one who wanted all of this,' Harry calmly interrupted her. '*You.*'

He walked over to the window. Ricarda gasped. Uschi wiggled her left arm uneasily, and Philip massaged the aching areas of Eckart's back.

'That's all you have to say for yourself?' Ricarda said quietly.

Harry continued to stare out the window. He didn't react; he didn't say anything. Not a good sign: Harry *always* reacted. Eckart feared the worst and considered what he might say to defuse the situation.

'It's all right now.' His voice was scratchier than he would have liked. Speaking was painful.

Harry turned slowly to face him. *No, it's not all right*, he said with his gaze. Eckart wanted to add something, wanted to stop Harry saying what was obviously on the tip of his tongue, but Harry's eyes had moved on to Ricarda.

'Now listen here, Ricarda,' he said. 'I didn't win this flat-share in a prize draw, and God knows I didn't go looking for it. Well, I've made up my mind. I've had it up to here! As soon as I find somewhere, I'm moving out.'

No, please don't, thought Eckart. *Don't move out, Harry; don't leave us alone here.* He took a peek at Ricarda. She needed to back down and placate the troops. But Ricarda didn't back down.

Slowly she stood up and looked directly at Harry. Her voice wavered as she said, 'Fine. Great. Then at least we won't have to put up with your cigarette butts in the flowers, your darts in the wall and your bloody teeth in the bathroom any more!'

'You know what, Ricarda,' Harry retorted, 'we've been living together for well over four months, and you still can't tell mine from Eckart's!'

'Huh?' What did his teeth have to do with any of this?

'See, Eckart!' said Harry, nodding. 'Welcome to the mean old men's club!'

'Come on, Harry.' Philip got up and took Harry's arm in an attempt at reconciliation. But Harry didn't want reconciliation.

'Nope,' he said. 'No more Harry. Harry doesn't want this any more! Harry didn't want this from the start. Sorry, Uschi. And, if I may briefly remind you, Philip, nor did you. But otherwise your Ricarda would have jumped ship.' His stare was unrelenting. 'So, you two? Have you done it yet? Or you still haven't? It's taking an *age*.'

'What are you talking about, Harry?' Ricarda snapped.

202

'There's nothing going on between us. We're friends! We're flatmates, we . . . ' Philip looked at her in surprise.

Even Harry raised an astonished eyebrow. 'Friends?' he chuckled cynically. His gaze shifted from Philip to Ricarda, then back to Philip.

'Oh, boy, Philip. I didn't realise do-gooders didn't even fuck!' Still shaking his head, he left the room. The door clicked shut.

Silence.

'This is all my fault,' Uschi burst out.

'Oh, stop blubbing!' roared Philip.

Talk about adding insult to injury. Eckart didn't know what hurt more right now – his back or his sympathy for Philip. Or for Uschi. Or Harry. Or Ricarda.

Who cared? It was all going to shit.

49

Harry slid his old friend Theo's vinyl out of its sleeve and laid it on the record player. He lowered the needle and, as it bumped over the grooves, guitar chords began to crackle.

Last night I woke up with tears in my eyes,
Kind of a strange dream, had a drink, smelled the lies . . .

Any time he felt down he would put on this record. During his studies he'd hung out a lot with Theo, who was a singer in a rock band that had scored a minor hit with 'Free Drinks at My Funeral'. They'd played the song at Theo's funeral too.

Am I the person I wanted to be?
Am I the hero a child wants to see?

He had sung this song during their wonderful campfire evening together, and at the words *'Please don't miss me, there'll be drinks when we die'* Uschi had asked the four of them whether they were scared of death.

'Not scared, exactly,' was Ricarda's shrewd reply, 'but I'm happy it's not around.'

Eckart had said, 'The bad thing is that you've *no* idea what's coming.' Typical Eckart.

'Oh, Eckart,' was Harry's immediate comeback, 'we've been through it all before. Before we were even born, we were already dead.'

The others had laughed. And so had Harry, even though the thought of death did put the wind up him. But what business was that of anyone else's? *Where would we be if everyone let their fears run loose?* he thought. And yet: he did have a problem with this damned mortality. It wasn't easy if you didn't believe in God. He was scared even now that he would change his mind when it came to the end, and give the big man in the sky another chance after all. He'd have nothing left to lose except his cool – and he'd have no use for that in the emptiness to come anyway.

And if you're crying, it's just tears in the rain.

Harry stared indecisively at his shelf. He didn't have many belongings, but was he really going to pack everything up again, and move back in with his daughter? He couldn't afford a place of his own. It wasn't a pretty prospect, but it would be the most practical option.

He thought of Uschi. On that starry night during their slow dance she had quietly revealed to him why she'd never wanted to have kids. She had said it was because she'd lost her mother when she was young, and she hadn't wanted to take on the role of a figure she herself had missed so badly. To Harry that had sounded like the worst kind of home-spun psychology, but that was just how Uschi was. She had her own definite, clear – some would say simple – philoso-phy. She still had the soul of a child, and now she was living with the consequences. She wasn't a child any more – and she was alone.

He rang Britta. He asked whether the granny flat was still available. There was a short silence on the other end of the line before she said, 'Of course, Dad, of course. When do you want to come?'

Her voice was friendly. Not warm, but friendly. It was the voice of a daughter who wouldn't let her father down, even if he had screwed up yet again.

He slotted the records into the cardboard box.

The same old refrain.

Please don't miss me, there'll be drinks when we die . . .

Harry sang along under his breath. It comforted him to sing the refrain with his dead friend.

50

Ricarda tapped tentatively on Philip's door. There was no answer. She tapped again. What was going on? Her world was out of kilter: Harry had triggered a system error.

She was in Uschi mode, in 'we've-got-to-stick-together' mode, in 'we'll-get-everything-under-control' mode, and with a single sentence Harry had brought the whole operation to a standstill. She'd reckoned with many possibilities, but not with Harry's direct threat to move out. He had knocked her completely off balance with his simple 'I've had it up to here!' *Error.* She'd been in control neither of the system nor of the software.

His reproaches were as unfair as they were ungrateful, but ultimately he had the upper hand, and he had declared the experiment in its current form a flop. They had failed. *She* had failed.

But that wasn't enough for Harry. He had then had the audacity to expose her feelings for all to see. What did he know about how she felt? Even she didn't know how she felt! *Error.*

'Yes?' she heard Philip murmur. She pushed down the door handle and entered. Philip was standing by the window in exactly the same pose Harry had struck a few minutes earlier. Why did people always stand by the window when they were seized by smouldering emotions? In melodramas too, an unrequited lover would stand staring out of the window. And the other person would stand behind him or her.

She shut the door. For a while they stood in Philip's room. He looked out, and she stood behind him.

Her eyes came to rest on his desk with the beautiful African female figure, the photo of his mother and the photo of his deceased wife Malu.

'I thought we were more than friends,' he said.

'Phil, please. Let's not get everything mixed up.'

He stepped out of his melodramatic pose at the window, walked over to the shelves and poured himself a whisky.

'I imagined it was going to be relaxed,' he said, 'the way we used to picture it. Remember?'

There was a sadness in his grey eyes that she'd never seen there before. Of course she remembered. '*When we're old,*' she said, quoting her own words, *'we'll move in together and smoke cigars and drink whisky.'*

'Want one?' Without waiting for her reply he poured her a glass and nodded. 'We never mentioned wiping each other's backsides. You overlook that kind of detail when you're young. Cheers!' They clinked glasses, and the whisky burned their throats.

'We'll get things under control again, Philip.'

'Oh, yeah?' he said bitterly.

'Phil, you wanted to give this living arrangement a go, and now we have to—'

'How was I to guess that we'd have a stroke victim right at the *start*?' he erupted. He knocked back the whisky and refilled his glass.

Ricarda tried to organise her thoughts and feelings. 'I don't understand why you're suddenly so ...' What was going on? After all, the flatshare had been *his* idea. What had got into him all of a sudden?

Philip swirled the amber whisky around his glass. He studied the drink as if it might contain an answer then looked up abruptly, his eyes sparkling.

'Ricarda, I wanted to be with you. I wanted to grow old with *you* and pick up from the old days, with our ... *friendship.*'

She felt her heart contract slightly. Friendship. Yes, that was precisely what bound them together – the reason she woke each morning with a smile on her lips. Because she knew that he was lying in the next room, and that if there were a problem, he was there and she could talk things through with him and count on his unconditional support.

'Except,' Philip continued haltingly, 'now that we're living here together, so close, day after day, I ... I've noticed how strong my feelings for you really are.'

He looked at her with something verging on helplessness. Ricarda had a little too much saliva in her mouth, as if she were watching a rom-com and the lovers were about to kiss.

'And *always have been*,' he said. 'Ever since I first saw you in the Park Café.'

She gasped. Ever since he'd first seen her? Hundreds of images shot through her head.

'Ric, I love you,' he said.

His words were a bolt to her heart; it tightened again. Philip loved her? Ever since they first met?

Instead of simply letting the force of his words act upon her, her neurons sent questions whizzing around her mind, as if his words were far too potent and impossible for her to process just then.

That was why he'd set up the flatshare? That was why they were struggling with all these unforeseen circumstances, caring for poor Uschi, fighting a running battle with Harry? Was that why?

'Well, you couldn't really have made it any more complicated if you'd tried,' she mumbled.

Philip's eyelids twitched.

Her mind whirred. 'First I've got to ... I ... I've got to put Uschi to bed first, okay?'

'Of course,' nodded Philip. 'Of course.'

'See you later,' she said, and went out.

Of course. She had to put Uschi to bed first.

Put Uschi to bed.

51

Soon this would all be over. Soon she would put an end to the whole thing, thought Uschi. There was no point any more. The earlier argument had made everything crystal clear. The bother with Timmy had been bad enough, but now Harry was moving out. Because of her. Uschi was finding it hard to think straight, but she had to do something.

The bedside lamp cast only a dim light over the room. It was shortly after ten. Bedtime. Ricarda tugged at her arm a bit roughly, then pulled on Uschi's nightdress and tucked her into bed. She seemed absent.

'Is Harry moving out?' asked Uschi.

'He's moving back to his daughter's,' replied Ricarda, adding curtly, 'A ground-floor granny flat.' She turned off the bedside lamp and distractedly stroked Uschi's cheek.

'*I* should go, not Harry,' said Uschi.

'Don't be so stupid.'

'And Philip and you should . . .'

'Go to sleep now, Uschi. Everything'll be fine, don't you worry.' Ricarda made for the door, lost in her thoughts.

Uschi didn't like being fobbed off like this. Okay, she was the cause of all their troubles, but she was still entitled to speak – and she was entitled to a reasonable answer. And she just couldn't watch Ricarda refuse to recognise her own good fortune. She just couldn't.

She gathered up her courage. It took her a huge effort because she was so exhausted by the whole business, but, if there was one loose end she had to tie up here, this was it. Her left hand groped for the switch on the bedside lamp. She knocked the massage oil over, but located the button and pushed it. The light was dazzling.

Ricarda looked around. 'Need to go to the loo again?' she asked guiltily.

Uschi shook her head. 'You belong together.'

'Uschi,' said Ricarda, 'Philip and I are friends, nothing more. We just happen to know each other very well. Sometimes we get a few emotional wires crossed.'

'But Harry said . . .'

'Harry's stirring up trouble, that's all. Wherever he goes, Harry always has to stir up trouble. You've seen that.'

Uschi couldn't make head nor tail of this. Why didn't Ricarda want to accept that she and Philip belonged together?

'I'm sorry to disappoint you,' said Ricarda, shaking her head, 'but this isn't a romantic comedy. Got that? Now go to sleep.' She glowered at the bedside lamp.

No, Uschi didn't want to turn out the light. She didn't want to sleep. She didn't want to be dismissed with sarcastic remarks. She didn't take her eyes off Ricarda. She wanted to sort this out, once and for all.

Ricarda shook her head. *Nothing's going on*, her expression said, but there was the tiniest hint of a smile. The veneer was cracking, thought Uschi. She held Ricarda's gaze, outstaring her.

'Uschi!' grinned Ricarda.

'So I'm right.'

'No! For the last time, nothing's going on. That's it. Now go to sleep.' Ricarda laughed briefly before pulling the door shut behind her.

Uschi stared at the ceiling. She knew Ricarda was lying. Her thoughts wandered until suddenly a terrible suspicion bored its way into her mind. Might it be on *her* account that Ricarda wouldn't give in? Was *this* her fault too?

She thought back to the day before. For the first time in a long while, she had been enjoying a nice moment of peace. She'd been lying on the exercise mat in her room, while Fabian massaged her good leg. Dressed in his white outfit, which set off his shock of dark hair, he was running his oiled fingers over her skin. She loved it when he worked on her good leg. She felt a tweak every now and then, not much else – but still, it was heavenly. As they chatted, Fabian told her about the time he'd worked in a tattoo parlour. His story about a woman who wanted a kangaroo inscribed on her left buttock made Uschi giggle. She enjoyed her sessions with Fabian. He came, gave her a massage, and took her through her exercises – and he was paid for it. Their relationship was professional; she didn't owe him anything. He wasn't doing it out of friendship, though she was growing fonder of him by the day. He did it to earn a living. It was an unbelievably relaxing arrangement.

Then the doorbell had rung. Fabian had run his fingers gently along her arm, as he always did when he went away, and got up to answer the door. It was Stella.

'Isn't Mum here?' Stella had asked. Uschi could hear her voice from out in the hall, and she sounded disappointed. 'We arranged to meet.'

She was right. The two of them had agreed on an appointment so that they could finally have an undisturbed conversation. Eckart must have played the go-between. So why wasn't Ricarda here? Uschi felt extremely anxious.

'Don't be so hard on her,' said Fabian. He had lowered his voice, but she'd still caught his words. 'None of this is easy to handle. Your mother's doing her very best and—'

'She always does her best for *other* people,' Stella had answered sadly. 'Her main concern is to spread the love. A blind person here, a stroke victim there.' She was speaking quietly now, Fabian having obviously signalled to her that

215

Uschi was lying nearby on the exercise mat and might over-hear them. 'That's why she became a therapist – to solve other people's problems,' Uschi had heard Stella whisper before – thank God – Ricarda had arrived and the two women had gone out for lunch.

To solve other people's problems. Uschi kept replaying Stella's words from the day before in her mind. Every day a new sentence added a new piece to the puzzle.

It was clear: wherever she was, she was in the way. She was disrupting other people's lives. None of the therapies was having much effect, the flatshare was prey to con-stant tension, and there were arguments – argument after argument. Stella wasn't getting enough attention from her mother, Philip couldn't get his hands on Ricarda, Eckart had hurt his back, and now Harry was moving out. All because of her.

She glanced at the clock. It was already half-past ten.

Half-past ten. And tomorrow morning it would be half-past seven again. Half-past twelve next time, then half-past ten. Uschi felt the familiar weariness suffusing her, taking hold of her limbs, streaming into her head, occupying her whole body and paralysing those fibres she could still feel. This unfathomable weariness. This emptiness. This non-presence.

Some days ago, as the others were drawing up the week's timetable, she had secretly rung up the advice centre to order a few brochures about care homes. She would barely be able to afford more than a charity-run home, but in any case the catalogues hadn't arrived. Ricarda had probably intercepted them and thrown them in the bin. Ricarda would never agree to put Uschi in a home; it was incompatible with her philosophy. And, if Uschi was honest, she didn't want to go into one either.

One thing was obvious, though: there was no way she was going to continue to be a burden on these four dear people, ruining their lives all because she, Uschi Müller, had a problem. She clicked off the light.

She had to put an end to this whole situation.

52

'Ric, I love you.'

Ricarda couldn't get his voice out of her mind. His words – and, even more, his voice – ran through her thoughts like a mantra. She had mulled over the details of their conversation as she tried to fall asleep the night before, attempting to comprehend the situation and to analyse it. Philip had set up the flatshare to be with *her*? She couldn't get her head around it. Eventually she had fallen asleep.

Ricarda threw back the covers, sat up and swung her feet to the floor. She sat there for a while on the edge of the bed. The sun was shining into her room, small specks of dust were floating through the air, and outside an excavator was at work.

Now that she was fully awake, it took her a moment to recall all of yesterday's events and to realise that everything looked different today. Completely different. Harry was moving out – and Philip loved her.

'Ric, I love you,' his voice echoed inside her. She stood up and watered her coconut palm.

'Since I first saw you.'

Since he first saw her.

Why had he never said anything? Why hadn't they – potentially – spent over thirty years of their lives together when he'd known way back then that he . . . ? And why had he had to set up this flatshare before he could tell her? The man had worked in a disaster zone for thirty-five years, but hadn't had the guts to tell her that . . .

She set down the watering can. She knew that she was being unfair right then. He hadn't set up the flatshare to . . .

But nonetheless.

She pulled her dressing gown over her nightdress and looked in the mirror. She suddenly felt nervous. In a minute their paths would cross. How did you cross paths with someone who'd told you the night before that he had loved you for decades? She took a deep breath, tidied her hair and stepped out into the hallway.

She could hear Harry's and Eckart's muffled voices in the kitchen. She went over to the bathroom. She was about to knock and ask whether it was free when the door opened and Philip appeared. He was just putting on his shirt.

'Hey,' he said.

'Hey,' she said.

'Everything okay?' He stuffed his second arm into the shirt and began to do up the buttons. His expression was apologetic, and he grinned shyly.

'Fine. Everything's fine,' she said, and pulled her dressing gown more tightly around herself. 'Nice shirt.'

'You think so?'

She nodded. She didn't know what to say. There was a lump in her throat and she could only manage a silly smile. Philip furrowed his brow.

'Ricarda, maybe today we should . . .'

'Ralfie!' she cried as Ralf came waddling out of the kitchen. She crouched down and scratched his back. 'Oh, there you are, there you are!' she shrieked, and gave a happy little laugh when he flopped on to his back and wiggled his legs in the air. 'Ooh, what a nice doggie you are. Such a sweet little doggie!'

Was she really doing this? She looked up, smiling. Philip gazed down at her, attempting to muster a smile too.

'What a rascal, eh?' she said.

'Yes,' offered Philip, doing up the last button. 'Well, see you later, then.' He gave a final quick nod and went along the hall to his room. She watched him go, but he didn't look around again before pulling the door quietly shut behind him.

She couldn't understand what had just happened. A total emotional blackout. Philip was her best friend, and suddenly she couldn't talk to him, let alone look him in the eye. She headed towards the low, narrow building that housed the workshop for the blind.

She had arranged to see Justus. She didn't really do consultations any more, but she still paid the occasional visit to her old workplace. She said hello to the man doing his community service and walked through to find Justus all alone in the workshop at the back.

'Hi, Justus.'

'Ricarda.' He beamed.

She ran her hand quickly through his hair. 'Everything okay, comrade?'

Yes, he was feeling better, he said. Anna had phoned to say that she was coming the following weekend with her parents, and they had a date to go for ice cream. He smiled at a point beyond her ear.

'How long is she staying for?' asked Ricarda.

'Three days,' he said, and resumed weaving his basket. 'Better than nothing.'

'Of course it's better than nothing.'

'Is something up?' asked Justus.

'No. Why?'

'Your voice sounds weird.'

'Oh, yeah?'

'Sad.'

'Um . . .'

'Did something happen?'

'Nah,' she said unconvincingly.

'So something did.' He tipped his head to the side. 'Is it that man?'

She studied the pattern of his half-woven basket. 'Yes,' she said in a small voice.

Justus's attention didn't waver. 'Have you already . . .' He cleared his throat. 'Have you already slept with each other?'

'Justus!' She stared at him in amazement.

'I'd like to kiss Anna this weekend,' he said softly.

Ricarda smiled. 'Are you afraid?'

'Sure.'

'I can understand,' she replied.

'So you haven't yet?'

'Hm?'

'So you haven't slept with him yet,' Justus stated. 'Are you afraid too?'

Yes, a little bit, she thought.

'That he won't find you attractive?' he insisted.

'You and your questions,' she mumbled. He wasn't entirely wrong: she didn't even like getting undressed in front of herself these days.

'I'm afraid she won't like me,' he said.

'Rubbish! You're a very good-looking boy.'

'Are you good-looking?' he asked.

'Oh, sadly that becomes more and more relative with age.'

'I could have a look,' he said.

'What?'

'May I?' He put a hand on her face and ran his fingers over her eyelids and lips.

'What are you doing?'

'I want to see how well preserved you are,' he said.

Great, she thought with a grin. 'You're used to lots of little bumps from reading Braille, right?' She felt his fingers run over her skin, and wondered whether she should give him some more advice about Anna.

He smiled. 'Nothing – like a new leaf.'

'You see, Justus, autumn has its fine days too.'

He giggled.

She tousled his hair again, wished him luck for his rendezvous with Anna, and set off back to her own unfinished business.

53

'Bye, then,' said Harry as he stood by the front door with his last packing case.

'Bye, Harry,' said Ricarda.

'If you happen to be nearby . . .' Eckart swallowed the rest of his sentence.

'I'll come down with you,' said Philip.

They had all assembled in the hall, lined up like a set of organ pipes: tall Philip, slender Eckart, Ricarda, Uschi in her wheelchair, and Ralf. Even the tubby little dachshund had felt duty-bound to bid Harry farewell.

Harry gazed at Uschi. She was the only one who was yet to say something. If there'd been a trophy for the saddest eyes, she'd have won it. With distinction. It wasn't only her eyes, though. She looked utterly lost.

Get out of here quick, he told himself. Farewells were

always bad news, but this one beat all the others hands down.

'I'm sorry, but it's better this way,' he said to them all. He even managed to instil some of the usual grumpiness into his tone.

The one-arm drive wheelchair squeaked as Uschi manoeuvred herself into her room. As she turned around to close the door, their eyes met for a second.

Oh, Uschi, he thought.

She shut the door.

'Come on.' Philip brought the wretched scene to a close, caught Harry by the arm and walked out the door. Harry bowed his head to the others and followed Philip. The three flights took their toll on his joints, and his arms began to tremble: the box was heavier than he'd thought. Damn records.

The two men stepped out into the street, where the sun was shining and the birds were warbling as though they were being paid to do so. Philip opened the boot of Eckart's estate car, and Harry hoisted the box inside, next to the hazard warning triangle and the pallet with the red grave candles. Philip slammed the hatchback shut.

'Say thanks to Eckart again,' said Harry. 'I'll bring it back tomorrow.' Eckart had kindly lent him the car, as Harry's taxi was in for repairs. Sometimes, everything broke down at once.

'Will do,' said Philip.

They looked at each other.

'Wasn't meant to be,' said Harry, nodding, and thought how stupid these words sounded.

'We'll be in touch.'

'Of course ... and make things clear to Ricarda, will you? She's not so bad.'

Harry didn't have a clue where the urge had come from, but he had felt a real need to sign off with a friendly farewell comment. Was he going soft in his old age?

Philip gave a little chuckle, but it didn't sound very convincing. They gave each other a brisk pat on the back. A manly farewell, quick and painless. Exactly the way it should be.

Harry got into the car, put the key in the ignition and started the engine. *Quick and painless, that's the way it should be*, he thought to himself again, and drove off. He didn't intend to glance in the rear-view mirror. He did anyway. He saw Eckart emerge from the house and stand next to Philip. They gazed after him, dwindling in size.

Harry swallowed the lump in his throat, flicked the indicator on and turned right.

54

'Nothing?' asked Philip.

Lying in front of him on the exercise mat, Uschi shook her head. He pushed the sole of her right foot upwards to stretch the ligaments, but Uschi couldn't feel a thing. The radio was playing the song 'Operator, Give Me Jesus on the Line'. The exaggerated happy-clappy Jesus message got on his nerves, so Philip switched it off, muttering, 'Save your breath, he's not going to pick up.'

He took hold of Uschi's right leg.

Why was Ricarda avoiding him? He could understand why she had run away yesterday night when he'd confessed his love for her. But this morning? That business with Ralf? What had got into Ricarda? Their encounter outside the bathroom had completely thrown him; he felt like a schoolboy.

When Harry had gone and he'd reached the top of the stairs, her door had been closed. He'd put Ralf on his leash and taken him out for a walk. Later, when she got back from shopping, it was *he* who stayed in his room. He'd said what he had to say; now it was her turn to share her feelings. But she said nothing.

Had he ruined everything? Had he lost Ricarda by over-stepping the boundaries of friendship? Harry had laid the bomb, torpedoing the status quo, and he, Philip, had detonated it. He'd had to go and detonate it.

He set down Uschi's right leg and lifted up her good left leg, carrying out the same exercise by pushing against the sole of her foot.

'Philip?' Uschi said.

Did Ricarda feel the same way about him? Or didn't she, and therefore didn't know what to say to him now?

'You were against my moving back in too,' said Uschi.

'What?' He hadn't been listening.

'My moving back in: you were against the idea too.'

'Uschi, I was simply considering the practical consequences.' He set down her leg and bent it at the knee.

'Why didn't you get your way?'

He pushed her bent leg outwards. 'We'll make it work, Uschi.'

'Because of your mother?'

'Don't be stupid.'

He put down her leg and repeated the exercise with its paralysed counterpart.

'If you really want to do me a favour, Philip . . . to pay me back for delivering your mother's liver sausage once a week, then . . . let me move into a home.'

He lowered her leg and sat down beside her. 'Why, Uschi? Why?'

She studied him for a long time. 'Would you prefer to have your backside wiped by someone you know, or by someone you don't know?'

He hung his head. As arguments went, it was a clincher.

'Have a think about it,' said Uschi.

He stretched out on the floor alongside her. And so they lay there together, with no idea what to do.

Ralf came trotting up, settled himself down and laid his head on Philip's stomach. Philip scratched the dog absent-mindedly. He was at a loss. For the very first time since he'd set up the flatshare, he had no idea what to do. Harry had left, Uschi wanted to leave, and Ricarda . . . Well, what *did* Ricarda want?

'Philip?' said Uschi.

'Yes?'

'Our heart is like a little reservoir. And, when the dam breaks, it hurts a bit, but the river can take its rightful course.'

He stared at the ceiling. What did Uschi, purveyor of kitsch sayings, mean by that?

'She needs time,' whispered Uschi, 'but she loves you. Of that I'm sure.'

He turned his head to look at his flatmate and friend. She nodded.

55

Ricarda lay, arms outstretched, on the floor of her room with a piece of blue paper in her hand, a smile on her face, and a heart that was beating as if it had been fitted with a new motor.

Five minutes ago she'd been kneeling beside a box of old photos – her treasure trove – like a little girl, sorting through pictures of yesteryear, rummaging back and forth through time. She'd let the photos slip through her fingers along with their associated years; the snapshots exuded so many memories. Herself with Philip and Herbert in the mountains on top of the Zugspitze; her and Herbert holding beer bottles at a party on the terrace of the Park Café; her wedding photo with Herbert; umpteen pictures of the wedding reception with friends, her parents, her parents-in-law. And with Philip, again and again. Her and Philip and Herbert at the protest against a nuclear power station.

She was suddenly overwhelmed by a strange yearning: a yearning for youth's refusal to compromise, for the determination to do things better than your elders, but also for the beautiful, unbeatable feeling of having your whole life in front of you, the feeling that every decision was still to be made.

No longer. It was all over. Irrevocably. It was over, and there was nothing to be done about it, not even with the utmost determination. That time was gone.

She had lingered over the photo of the Zugspitze. She was standing between Herbert and Philip, both of them with an arm around her. Philip had long hair and a cheeky grin on his face. He was incredibly good-looking then – and still was now.

Then she picked up the photo of herself and Stella, who must have been five at the time, laughing into the camera on a beach on the North Sea island of Amrum. Stella's eyes were narrowed from laughing. Ricarda was standing behind her, holding her daughter's hand as Stella snuggled against her legs. The photo was a picture of unadulterated happiness. Ricarda ran her fingers over Stella's blonde curls, which straggled from the sailor's cap with the red bobble on it.

That evening – she remembered this clearly – they had bought a bag of unpeeled shrimps from a fisherman in the harbour, made themselves comfortable on a heap of fishing nets, and peeled the shrimps. Stella had sworn that she would never ever again buy 'ready' shrimps because she liked peeling them so much. Stella had always been a lovely, happy child.

Yet, now that Stella was pregnant, something between them had broken, even though their relationship had been nice and amicable until then – or at least she'd thought it was until they'd gone out together for lunch three days ago and Stella had suddenly given her both barrels. She had accused Ricarda of only ever spreading love among strangers and causes, and never truly engaging. What was she afraid of?

Afraid? Ricarda had had no idea what Stella was talking about. She wasn't afraid. She was simply doing what had to be done. *Be the change you wish to see in the world*; that wasn't always easy.

'Will *you* look after me when I no longer can?' she'd asked Stella. 'That's not what this is about,' Stella had answered. But Ricarda's follow-up question – 'Well, what is it about then?' – had put Stella's back up.

Her daughter had nonetheless acknowledged that what Ricarda was doing for Uschi was right, that her mother had her hands full – and that the flatshare had altered things between them slightly.

Yet she had also noticed how fragile her daughter was at the moment. She had always regarded Stella as being strong and independent, which is why she'd always left her as much freedom as possible. Ricarda's own mother had been very possessive and demanding, and Ricarda

232

wanted to avoid reproducing that at all costs. Yet pregnancy seemed to be placing a burden on Stella – Ricarda had underestimated that. Her daughter needed her far more than she'd thought.

They hadn't been able to resolve or clear up all their problems during their conversation, of course they hadn't; but they had at least concluded that the pregnancy and the stroke had been part of an unfortunate chain of events, and that they were determined to be more attentive to each other's problems in the future. Yes, it was something they both wanted to work on.

She'd wanted to hug Stella goodbye. Stella wasn't prepared to do that, but they had established a kind of truce; that was at least a start.

How come everything she did at the moment was wrong? Philip had been keeping out of her way ever since she'd been incapable of uttering a single sensible word the morning before. He had either acted cool and composed, or else his door was shut. Had she wounded him so badly? Or did he blame her for Harry moving out? Whatever the reason, Philip hadn't shown his face since Harry left, spending long spells outside with Ralf and not even deigning to appear for dinner last night. She'd sat at the table with only Uschi and Eckart for company, the kitchen air heavy with reproachful silence. Or was it all in her imagination? She hadn't had the strength to enquire. Stella's words came to her mind: 'You never engage. What are you afraid of?' Well, what was she afraid of?

Overnight she'd grown uneasy, extremely uneasy. Might Philip's next words to her be to say that he was moving out too? The mere thought of it was unbearable. Suddenly she had to think back to after the wedding, when he'd revealed to Herbert and her that he was leaving for Mali.

It had come as a shock. She couldn't comprehend his decision. How could he go away? How could he leave them behind? But that was what he did. Two weeks later he really had boarded the plane and been gone. She had been in a kind of daze, her world turned upside down. She'd felt as if she'd been abandoned, betrayed. If she hadn't known better, she'd have thought it was lovesickness.

But then she'd pulled herself together. Pregnancy had played its part, and daily life took over; she had coped, and Philip had gradually faded from her heart. And now, thirty-five years later, in the middle of the night, she was struck by a sudden, overpowering resurgence of the old feeling she had so completely repressed.

It *was* lovesickness.

However defiantly she had kept Philip at arm's length over the preceding weeks, now he had a hold over her. She could spin it whichever way she wanted, but she was in love – and more than a little.

This morning she had ventured cautiously out of her room and knocked on his door, without any response. Philip was out with Ralf, Eckart called from the kitchen over the whistle of the kettle.

So she'd had breakfast and waited, but still he'd not returned. She'd gone back into her room and pulled out her old box from under the bed. She wanted to pick out a nice photo of the two of them and write him a letter to invite him to dinner. However, she had caught a touch of the blues when all the old photos lay spread out before her. So many emotions had welled up inside her – old feelings, longings, such young, joyous laughter everywhere – and she'd suddenly felt old. And worn out. She had had to weep.

Then, quite unexpectedly, a piece of paper had slid underneath the door. She had stared at it as if it had its own life, as if it were about to grow little legs and come scuttling towards her. She'd held her breath and listened for sounds outside. She heard Philip give a quick cough and take the key from the shelf, then the latch snapped in the lock.

She'd crawled over to the door and grabbed the piece of paper.

I'll be at the Park Café at 2 and would love to see you there. Philip.

She had read his handwritten note, traced the brisk calligraphy with her finger and read the words once more.

Would love to see you there ... see you there ... would love ...

She must have read the words five times to make sure that it really said what it said. And now here she was, lying on her back on the floor, her arms outstretched and her heart racing.

A funny feeling came over her.

At two. Park Café. Philip. Rendezvous. She tried to arrange her thoughts. What should she wear? Should she take a quick shower?

She glanced at the clock. Five to one. No time to waste. She jumped to her feet and rushed to the bathroom. She circled her hand over her pots of cream and tubes. Her beloved creams against the world; the receptacles of her soul. 'I-I-I-I have a cream,' she murmured, imagining how proud Martin Luther King would have been of her. She chose a foundation and set to work.

Eckart tapped on the door and announced, 'I'm taking Uschi to occupational therapy.'

'Okay,' she called out.

She clicked the top back on her lipstick and looked at herself in the mirror. 'So?' She rehearsed a smile; it looked good. She blew herself a kiss.

Flinging open the bathroom door, she tripped over Ralf, who had once again plumped himself down on the threshold.

'Come on,' she whispered to the dog in high spirits. Never in her life had she envisaged that she would one day confide in an overweight dachshund. But he had at least been lucky enough to go for two long walks with Philip yesterday, be Philip's confidant and hear what Philip was thinking. This dog knew things; Ralf must know things.

Ricarda grinned at these thoughts. Being in love made you silly – she'd almost forgotten that.

Ralf obediently trundled along into her room, and she shut her door behind them.

'I need your advice, Ralfie!' Oh, boy, now she was calling Ralf Ralfie too! He looked up at her ingenuously.

'I bet you were a really handsome dachshund in your prime, eh?' asked Ricarda. 'You have taste. You're a cosmopolitan dachshund, aren't you?'

Ralf looked down and sniffed the floorboards. It wasn't clear whether he found the compliment embarrassing or was simply bored.

Ricarda opened her wardrobe and ran her eyes over her clothes. She took out a green dress, put it on and examined herself in the mirror. She glanced down at Ralf, who was sitting patiently in front of her, his head cocked – was that critically? – to the right. She took off the dress again and reached for a blue one with white dots; it was tight around the hips, and even Ralf expressed fairly obvious reservations. He sat down and gawked out of the window. That was a statement too. She tried on a black one, her *petite robe noire*, but it felt a touch too elegant, even though Ralf – kindly – had now turned his attention back to her.

She felt a bit like Julia Roberts in *Pretty Woman*, only she was a little older, and Ralf wasn't Richard Gere. Details, details.

She took out the green dress again before opting for her light pink satin wraparound dress from the wardrobe. It had been her favourite, but she hadn't worn it in ages. She did up the small zip on the right hip and felt the precious fabric caress her figure. The dress still fitted her perfectly.

'Not bad, eh?' she said, admiring her reflection. Ralf amiably tilted his head to the right. She gave a half twirl to check out her bottom. It looked pretty delectable, actually.

She was almost finished and could be off, but there was one small snag to her looking so delectable in this light pink satin dress, which clung so gently to her hips and emphasised her cleavage, because underneath it – and here she bad-temperedly raised her dress – she was wearing a fairly large pair of control knickers.

'Do you think anything's going to happen?' she asked Ralf with a glance at the underwear. 'Today? Nah, unlikely.'

Despite being Philip's confidant, Ralf seemed to have no strong opinion; he cocked his head neither to the left nor to the right. He just sighed and looked out of the window again.

Ricarda swapped the oversized knickers for some red panties and twirled in the mirror once more. Not good. Not good at all. Drat. After a moment's contemplation, eye-to-eye with her reflection, she slipped out of the panties and squeezed herself back into the control knickers.

Richard 'Ralf' Gere shot Ricarda a quick glance and rolled over for a nap. Mission accomplished.

56

'The twenty-first of March 1973, around one p.m,' said Philip, leaning over the white railing.

Ricarda craned her neck and caught sight of him standing on the first-floor terrace. 'Is it really that long ago?' she called up to him.

He nodded.

She was actually there.

She scoured their surroundings. He pointed to a hole in the fence around the disused Park Café. The locked gate was draped with ivy. Ricarda slipped through the hole and slowly climbed the overgrown steps to the terrace of the former café.

'I had no idea it had closed down,' she said. 'It looks like someone cast a spell on it.' He was waiting for her at the top.

'We have one table for two left, madam.' Philip gave a small bow and led her to a weatherworn bench. She played along, as he conjured two miniature bottles of bubbly from his jacket pocket.

'Wow,' she said with a smile.

'The off-licence just outside the park,' he replied, producing two straws from his jacket too. 'I had no idea they'd closed here either.' They unscrewed the tops, dropped their straws into the bottles and clinked them together. The sparkling wine foamed on their tongues.

'I've a confession to make,' he said.

'Hm?'

'I'm nervous.'

'Me too.'

Ricarda drew on her straw again. His eyes were on her lips; she noticed his gaze and he laughed.

'Silly, isn't it?' he said.

'Certainly is,' she laughed back.

Philip was genuinely nervous, grasping for words and trying not to say anything stupid. The wind rustled the leaves of the old trees as a little white speedboat raced past on the Rhine below, unfurling waves in its wake.

'Why didn't you ever say anything?' she asked after a while.

'You were with Herbert . . . ' He broke off. It had been a huge struggle back then, for he had been deeply in love with Ricarda. The first time Herbert had brought Ricarda with him to the Park Café, right here, there had been a swift exchange of glances between them, and they had both flinched slightly. She too – he had observed it very clearly. Then the three of them had chatted, trying to make themselves heard above the music – a lot of small talk – and the force of that exchange of glances had dimmed and given way to curiosity, before being erased by the everyday setting. *Your best friend introduces you to his new girlfriend.* She was Herbert's new girlfriend, end of story. They made a nice couple, and Herbert was over the moon. *Give it no further thought. Nothing you can do about it.* So he became the friend of his best friend's girlfriend. It wasn't always easy, but it had its charms; it might even have been better that way. It was a well-known fact that friendship endured better – and unconsummated love endured longer.

Herbert, Ricarda and he quickly became inseparable. They studied together, protested, revised, laughed and partied together. He had occasionally weighed up whether he should tell Ricarda about his feelings for her. There had been moments when he'd got a sense that it was more than a friendship to her too. But only ever a vague sense. When he once tried something more concrete, she had evaded the issue and laughed it off.

Ricarda sucked on her straw.

'Do you remember that evening the Daddy Killers played at the student union?' he asked.

'At the medics' party?'

'We danced together,' he added, 'and suddenly I thought: I'm going to tell her, I'm going to tell her right now. Just then you leaned over to me and whispered, "I have to tell you something." I thought, this cannot be happening. Telepathic or what? I was sure you wanted to say the same thing to me as I wanted to say to you, but—' he gazed at her '—you didn't.'

Ricarda gasped.

'You whispered in my ear that you were pregnant.'

She lowered her gaze. 'You wanted to tell me that . . .'

'Yes.' He nodded.

She breathed in deeply and stared at the Rhine, where a huge barge was gliding slowly past, piled high with rusting multicoloured containers. For a long time they said nothing.

'It was an accident,' she finally blurted out. 'Herbert and I were going nowhere. Stella wasn't planned. I actually wanted to start working, but—' her expression darkened '—is anything ever planned?' She began to peel the label from the bottle, then looked up with confusion in her eyes. 'You live with decisions you never actually made, don't you?'

Philip shrugged his shoulders.

'Do you think I might even have always held it against Stella, unconsciously?'

'Rubbish,' he murmured, but it didn't seem implausible.

She was still picking at the label. 'You'll patch things up, Ric. She's a wonderful person. A truly wonderful person.'

Ricarda attempted a smile, but it lacked conviction. She raised the bottle. 'Got another one?'

'Unfortunately I haven't. But I could do with something a little stronger now. Let's go somewhere else.'

They stood up and went over to the café window. Ricarda rubbed a hole in the coating of grime with her finger. The counter where they had first met was still there, but the café was run-down and dusty, and the floor was covered with rubble.

'And did you go to Africa because . . . ' She blinked.

That's right, he nodded. *Tabula rasa*. He'd needed to get away. When she'd become pregnant, and it had therefore been clear that she had definitely opted for a life with Herbert, he'd had to get away. Far away.

Ricarda took an audible breath.

Yes, he thought. What a life they could have had together.

'Who knows what might have happened if I hadn't got pregnant,' she speculated.

'I wouldn't have saved lots of lives,' he said, grinning.

'That's true,' she mused. 'I can be very proud of myself, don't you think?'

'You bet!'

She smiled wistfully.

'I have an idea,' he said.

'Oh, yeah?'

He tapped on the glass. 'We simply turn back the clock. We take over this café, we get *behind* the counter – since it didn't work out for us in front of it – and we start again from scratch.'

He needed to dispel the nostalgia, and his silliness paid off.

'Sure,' she chuckled. 'We'll bake our own cakes and in the evening we'll serve—'

'Cheese and pineapple on cocktail sticks.'

'Cheese and pineapple? No! Oh, God, do you remember that?'

'And Hawaiian toast!'

'Ouch, I'd forgotten all that stuff. That's right, you always ordered Hawaiian toast!'

'No, *you* did!'

'No, Philip, I always ordered the soup of the day. I always had to keep an eye on my figure, so there's no way I'd ever have eaten lots of white bread with sugary-sweet tinned pineapple. Harry would always pig out on sausage and eggs, and Herbert . . . '

'Pâté on toast!'

'With onions!'

They chatted on and on, and Philip no longer really paid any attention to what they were saying. It was exactly as it used to be when they would stand at the counter and laugh, and one word would give rise to another. They had missed out on thirty-five years, but that didn't matter now. Right now, at this precise moment in time, that didn't matter in the slightest.

They were together. That was all that counted.

They carried their memories down the steps with them and crept through the hole in the wire fence, Philip first, then her. He offered her his hand and helped her through.

'And now to the off-licence!' she laughed.

'A bottle of bubbly and down to the Rhine? You're not serious, are you?'

'Oh, yes, I am!' she said with a sparkle in her voice. 'Today we're going to do exactly the same as we used to.'

'Exactly the same?' He feigned disappointment.

Hm. She grimaced and smiled. 'Okay, maybe not exactly. We might want to try ... something new.'

'I'm all for that!'

They ambled through the park to the off-licence that stood near the Zoo Bridge, and bought two miniature bottles of Jägermeister, a bottle of sparkling wine and a large bag of crisps. They sat down on a bench by the Rhine, laughed as they downed the Jägermeister in one, popped the cork of the wine, munched crisps and talked and talked. It was as if they were afraid, now that it was so close and no obstacles stood in their way. Afraid of their first kiss.

'Do you know what?' The wine was loosening her tongue. 'The last time you were back, at Christmas ten years ago ... You'd only just got back, and, when you left, I smoked.'

'Really?'

'I was sad, you know.'

'You seemed so detached.'

'Detached? No. I was extremely impressed. The way you talked about your work and about the people there. And then I went to get a drink and had a chat with Harry, and suddenly you were gone. To your mother's, so Herbert told me. You didn't even say goodbye.'

'You remember it that clearly?'

She nodded.

He felt a fresh surge of melancholy. He'd experienced sudden intermittent bouts of sadness ever since he'd been back and without his work routine to distract him. Sadness about the opportunities he might have missed, doubts as to whether his own course of action had been right. Did you always know what was right, whether your current actions were right? How many things you did were properly thought through? As Ricarda said: was anything ever planned?

He had often thought of Ricarda. When he'd received the news of Herbert's death five years earlier, he had thought long and hard about her, and wondered how she was coping. He would have liked to have come to the funeral, but he simply couldn't get away, so he wrote her a letter. Then he had been swallowed up by his everyday life again, with no time to think. His mother's health was still good; memories blurred; he'd thought there was so much time left. And what Ricarda had said was true: he found his work fulfilling. Even when he was doing his rounds of the other villages, his mind was constantly on the health post. In fact, it was *more* than fulfilling; he was completely absorbed by his work, to the point where he himself had virtually disappeared.

He reached into the crisp packet.

'I always thought that some day I would do this or that,' he said. 'When I "grow up" I'll do this and that. I didn't notice that, if I really wanted to do something, that "some day" had to be *now*. I just let time tick away. As if it would go on and on for ever, you know? And suddenly I'm past sixty. And now all that time has gone.' He laughed. 'Past sixty, Ric! Past sixty! I can't get used to the thought. How about you?'

'Nah.'

'I can't be sixty!'

She laughed out loud, but then she became pensive. 'Who cares how old you are, as long as you have no regrets?'

'You think so?'

Shrugging, she asked, 'Do you have any regrets?'

'Not about anything I've done,' he said after a moment, 'but about what I *didn't* do, yes. Not *once* did I take a break, or ask questions. I regret that, but otherwise ...' He shook his head. 'Everything turns out to make some kind of sense, though. We might not immediately recognise it, but . . . '

'Today's shit is tomorrow's . . . ' whispered Ricarda.

He nodded and took another swig from the bottle. 'I'm worried about Uschi.'

'Uschi feels guilty, but Harry would have moved out anyway. Harry needs his freedom.'

'Ric, she said again yesterday that she wants to go into a home.'

'She'll wither and die in a home.' She took the wine bottle from Philip's hand.

'She's not exactly in full bloom at the moment, though, is she?'

'We'll sort things out,' said Ricarda in her determined voice. 'Hm?' She waved the bottle at him invitingly. They stared into each other's eyes for a few seconds, and he had to smile.

'What?' she asked.

'I'd like to sort you out,' he whispered.

'Oh, yeah? Go on, then.'

Without taking her eyes off him, she set the wine bottle down on the bench beside her. He leaned forward, her face became a blur and he felt her breath. 'Why do we keep dodging our own luck?' he mumbled.

'We don't.' Ricarda's words landed softly on his lips. 'I'm feeling pretty lucky right now.'

Just as his lips were about to respond to the pressure of hers, a rollerblader raced past, missing them by a hair's breadth, and Ricarda knocked over the wine bottle in her fright. 'Oh, damn,' she said, leaping to her feet as the sparkling wine streamed down her dress.

'As I said,' laughed Philip, 'no luck.'

57

Harry parked Eckart's car under a plane tree, unlocked the front door of the house and went up, two steps at a time. Yes, there were advantages to not having to lug Uschi upstairs.

He was in good spirits. His return to the granny flat had worked out better than he'd expected. His daughter had made up his bed and had actually put three beers on ice for him. He'd played cards – a round of snap – with Timmy; and the man with the do-gooder's voice was away on a week's study trip – fantastic! Harry had slept in that morning, left the toilet seat up, left his coffee cup unwashed, smoked in the kitchen and turned the Stones up loud. Life could be good. No nagging, no duties, no . . .

He gave a start. He saw a wheelchair on the landing at the top of the dark staircase. On the very top step sat Uschi, looking down with a thousand-yard stare. Her left hand gripped the tyre, and one little push would send the thing careering down the stairs.

Harry gulped for air. One wrong move, one wrong word, the wrong tone of voice, and Uschi would make the wrong decision. Not a word out of place now. Not a word out of place. The sound of a vacuum cleaner issued from the flat.

'Too chicken?' he asked.

His voice actually sounded gruff. There was a brief glimmer in Uschi's eye, as he crept upwards, step by step. 'Do you love me that much? Damn, Uschi, no woman's ever done this for me before.' The rubbish you could come out with under pressure.

She stared at him, her eyes blank. 'Oh, Harry, there's no point to any of this.'

If Harry was honest, he felt exactly the same way, but still: that was no reason for her to attempt to take off from the top landing.

'You know what, Uschi? There's a trick I know.'

'What?' she asked softly.

Harry nodded. 'Breathing. Just keep breathing.'

Her nose wrinkled, and he knew that he was on the right path. He climbed another step, then another. 'Uschi, we'll be dead for long enough as it is. So please be a little patient, okay?' The last step and ... he grabbed the handle of the wheelchair, turned the damn thing away from the stairs and got his breath back. The vacuum cleaner rattled over the floorboards inside the flat. The door was ajar, so Harry pushed it open and shoved Uschi inside.

'Eckart!' called Harry.

Eckart spun around in fright.

'Wow, you startled me,' he said, switching off the vacuum cleaner with his foot.

'It happens,' mumbled Harry.

'Where have you two been?' Eckart asked in astonishment.

'Och, taking in a bit of the fresh stuff. Ain't that right, Uschi?' said Harry, while miming to Eckart what Uschi had been planning to do moments earlier. Eckart reacted with surprising presence of mind, although his talents as an actor left a lot to be desired.

'Oh, that's great!' he trilled woodenly, and pushed Uschi into her room, casting Harry a 'you-can't-be-serious' look over his shoulder.

Harry went into the kitchen, fetched himself a beer from the fridge and took a seat out on the balcony. It felt strange helping himself from the fridge – after all, this wasn't his home any more – but boy, had he earned this beer. Uschi's intended crash was a step too far, even for him. He crooked the cigarette lighter against the neck of the beer bottle, and flipped off the cap with a hiss.

The cool beer coursed down his throat. The sun hung low in the sky. All was peaceful. Two of Uschi's legendary transvestite cockerel egg cosies still lay on the little balcony table from breakfast. He took his tobacco from his pocket, rolled himself a cigarette and lit up.

'She's sleeping now.'

Eckart sat down beside him, and for some time neither of them said anything. The twittering of the birds was annoying.

'Why would she do that?' muttered Eckart.

'Have you fallen in love with our sausage lady?'

'Not my type.'

My, my! Harry was surprised at such sharp words from Eckart. Eckart picked up the cockerels from the table and absentmindedly converted them into finger puppets.

'I didn't find it easy here at the start,' he said, 'but Uschi had this ... Uschi was Uschi. She did me a power of good right from the start.'

'Until those rabbits on the table.'

'To be quite honest, if it hadn't been for Uschi I'd never have stayed. She reminds me a bit of Lotte.'

To Harry's amazement, Eckart's two finger puppets were virtually copulating by now. What message was Eckart's unconscious sending out?

'We've taken care of everything,' Eckart continued. 'So why's she giving up?' Eckart's voice was on the point of breaking now. 'Why, Harry?'

Oh, boy, no emotional bullshit now, thought Harry. 'Eckart, things'll straighten themselves out,' he said.

Eckart at last set the stupid cross-dressing cockerels to

one side and went inside to fetch himself a beer too. Harry grabbed the bottle and fizzed it open with his lighter. They clinked bottles and drank.

'We're a right bunch, aren't we?' said Eckart.

'You can say that again,' Harry agreed. 'Your teeth in the bathroom. Blimey, even I flinched.'

'Periodontitis.'

'I guessed you must have been in a few brawls when you were younger,' chuckled Harry.

Eckart sniggered. 'Oh, you know, you get into some odd habits living on your own.' He took another swig. 'Harry?'

'Yep?'

'I stayed.'

Oh, don't pull that one on me, thought Harry. He stubbed his cigarette out grouchily in Ricarda's flower box.

'But if you hadn't got here first when Uschi . . . '

'That's enough!' Harry didn't want to hear this. He didn't want to hear this, damn it. It was Eckart's way of saying, *Come back*. It was Eckart's damned soft, friendly, irrefutable way of saying, *We miss you*. 'Forget it!' he added.

Eckart stared at Harry's cigarette butt in the flower box. 'Can I ask you a favour?'

'Knock yourself out.' Harry glared at him.

'I wanted to buy a vault, but . . . '

'Have you got cancer?'

Eckart shook his head.

*

They stood in Eckart's room, heads bent, studying Lotte's tombstone, then Eckart moved the bonsai trees and candles out of the way. On the count of three, they gave each other a signal, lifted the stone, hauled it down the stairs and dumped it, with a groan, on Uschi's wheelchair. Harry stretched his limbs. Lotte weighed a ton. Almost as heavy as Uschi.

They pushed the headstone along the main shopping street to the cathedral and took a twenty-minute train ride with a class of noisy school kids through the city, past the last houses and out into the countryside, through a patchwork of fields and woodland. They got off, pushed the wheelchair with Lotte's headstone down a track until they reached a lone tree, heaved the stone out of the wheelchair and leaned it against the trunk.

No one had really paid any attention to them throughout the entire journey, as if pushing a headstone about in a wheelchair were the most natural thing in the world.

They gazed at the headstone for a while.

'She's in a good spot here,' said Eckart.

'Yep, she's in a good spot,' Harry repeated. 'A bit of fresh air.'

What else was there to say?

Returning to town, they went into Harry's favourite pub while the empty wheelchair stayed outside like a faithful dog. They sat down at the bar and raised their glasses. The fruit machine tootled away, and the cold beer slid down nicely as they both looked straight ahead, each lost in his own thoughts.

'You know, Harry,' said Eckart, 'you come into the world, spend eighty years collecting wrinkles, and then it's into the coffin and into the ground with you.'

'Too true,' nodded Harry.

'And one day someone puts a tool shed on top of you.'

'A tool shed?'

'Yes,' said Eckart.

Okay, thought Harry.

On the radio Freddie Mercury started to sing 'We Are the Champions' quietly, his words clear and precise, before filling his lungs and ... As the chorus kicked in – that wonderful, deliberately raucous chorus that made you want to growl along in an almost obscene celebration of the joys of being alive and being together – without a glance, the two of them started to sing. Quietly and calmly, each on his own, yet both together, about fighting on until the end.

58

The crockery tinkled as he pressed her up against the kitchen worktop. They were laughing tipsily between kisses. She felt his hand on her chest, first softly, then more firmly, while he slid his other hand down her hips, under her dress and up her leg. His tongue glided over her lips. They swayed a little, laughed again; the edge of the worktop was burrowing into her back, a vase fell over, her hand reached down for his trousers – he was aroused – seized his belt buckle and—

'Hi, Mum.'

The voice came from out on the balcony.

'No-o luck at all,' chuckled Philip.

Stella? What was she doing here? Ricarda straightened her dress, smoothed her hair into place and stepped out on to the balcony, leaving Philip in the kitchen.

Stella was sitting on the small wooden bench – or rather, on Fabian. There was a flicker of candlelight. Judging by their position, these two had been up to more or less the same thing as they had. At least her daughter had made her presence known *before* she potentially started rolling around on the kitchen floor with Philip. Still, how embarrassing.

'Well, I never,' she stammered. 'You too? I mean ... you're here too?'

They let out a guffaw of laughter. It was so absurd. Fabian fingered his chin uneasily.

'May I?' she asked him with a smile. She took Stella's head in her hands, planted a loving kiss on the top of her head and looked her in the eye – into the gorgeous hazel eyes of her wonderful daughter, whom she'd let down so badly. And had perhaps, in some small way, unconsciously blamed for holding her back in life? As a therapist, Ricarda was surprised this possibility had taken her so long to realise.

'I'd never seen that photo on your fridge before,' Stella ventured cautiously. Ricarda smiled. She'd stuck the beach photo of little Stella on the fridge with a heart magnet.

She stroked Stella's cheek. She loved this girl who had one day decided that she would never ever buy 'ready' shrimps again. Stella looked up at her and whispered, 'I love you too.'

It was only then that Ricarda realised how much the whole stand-off had been affecting her, and how relieved she was that Stella was speaking to her again.

'What are you two doing here anyway?' Philip called from the kitchen.

'Eckart and Harry had to take care of something,' said Fabian.

'And Uschi?' asked Ricarda.

'Has something happened?' Philip came out on to the balcony, brandishing a Post-it note in Harry's handwriting from the fridge.

Don't do anything stupid, Uschi.

59

Eckart was having some difficulty putting his key into the lock. He was 'toasted', as Harry had informed him. They had knocked back quite a few jars in Harry's old 'seminar room'.

Eckart had staggered somewhat on his way home. He was returning without Lotte, but it had been the right decision, and he would always be indebted to Harry for helping him to put his plan into action. And if he was honest he missed Harry more than Lotte, as he searched for the stupid keyhole. Not only because of his inability to get in the door by himself, no; his company too, especially as the gloom about Uschi still hung in the air. Her plan to throw herself down the stairs was not a good omen, and things looked pretty grim without Harry.

He'd hugged Harry when they said goodbye, and

thanked him. His words had been, 'You've taken a real weight off my mind.' Or something like that. 'At least there's more space in your room now,' Harry had said, snickering. Typical Harry: the best remedy for any form of world-weariness. As they parted, Harry pressed his little box of weed into Eckart's hand. 'For if things really get tough.' Another remedy.

At last the key slid into the door. Eckart unlocked it and went into the flat. He heard muted voices. He paused in the hallway for a second and peered through the darkness at the door of his room; he was scared of the empty space he would encounter there. Ralf came tottering bleary-eyed out of the kitchen and crumpled on to his back in the hope of getting a good stroke. Eckart patted the dog on the head. Uschi's door was ajar, allowing a sliver of light to spill into the hall.

'I didn't *want* children,' he heard Uschi say. 'That was uncommon back then. Terroristically we could have had one . . .'

'Theoretically?' Philip corrected her.

'You too?' asked Uschi.

Eckart chuckled at his flatmates' dialogue. He stuck his head around the door and was taken aback by what he saw. He'd been expecting a crisis meeting commensurate with the shock of Uschi's potentially fatal close encounter with the stairs, but the sight that met his eyes surpassed all his expectations.

Ricarda, Philip and Uschi were sitting under the sky-blue duvet on Uschi's bed, drinking tea. Ricarda was next to Uschi, and Philip was leaning against the foot end. Unbelievable! The three of them really were crammed into the narrow nursing bed, with the triangular trapeze hand-grip dangling between them.

'Eckart!' said Uschi, her eyes red from crying. He walked over to the bed and ran a hand over her hair.

'May I?' he asked.

'Sure.' Philip lifted the duvet. Eckart slid in beside him at the foot end of the bed and fetched the metal box out of his pocket.

'Harry sends his regards.'

'Dear me,' grinned Ricarda. 'He always has to have the final word, doesn't he? So, are you going to roll us one?'

'I can have a go,' said Eckart, setting to work with some assistance from Philip. 'Feeling better, Uschi?' he asked.

'I'm so sorry, Eckart,' she said remorsefully. 'I didn't mean to scare you, but . . . I'm just in your way here.'

'You'd have been in our way on the stairs too,' he quipped through his teeth. The others eyed him with some puzzlement, then they all burst out laughing, even Uschi. It was an expression worthy of Harry, and it worked. Eckart noticed his cheeks start to glow, and then he went bright red.

'Being squiffy suits you,' remarked Ricarda.

'Squiffy?' asked Philip. 'What kind of word is that?'

'A very pretty word,' she murmured, 'and now he's going to roll us a spliffy.'

There was something going on between the two of them, Eckart thought as he stuck the cigarette papers together.

'Hey, Uschi,' asked Philip, 'didn't your husband want children either?'

'Whether he liked it or not, Udo accepted it, but deep down he never forgave me. After he left, he shacked up with a woman who had a kid.'

'Did you ever regret it?' asked Philip. He helped Eckart with the weed. Uschi played restlessly with the duvet, smoothing non-existent creases.

'Um . . . I had my first doubts when I was fifty-two.'

Eckart looked up, and the three of them gave Uschi puzzled looks.

'A tad late, eh?' she grinned mischievously. The indomitable Uschi of old was back. She sighed. 'It isn't always easy to make the right decisions in life.'

'Can't argue with that.' Ricarda swept together a few strands of weed that Eckart had spilt. Was he imagining things, or had she just given Philip the eye?

'The result,' Uschi continued quietly, 'is that I've got no one, and I'm forced to be a burden on you.'

'Children are no guarantee either, mind you,' said Philip. 'I wasn't here when my mother died.'

Uschi reached across the duvet for his hand. 'Don't you worry your head about that: she passed away peacefully.'

They were all keeping one another's spirits up, thought Eckart, as though they were brothers and sisters. They were supporting each other in the face of parents, life and adversity.

'At least you saved people's lives, Philip,' he said, licking the glued strip and checking with his finger that the gossamer-thin paper was properly sealed. 'My son's growing kiwis. Now will you look at this!' He held up his handiwork. It was no masterpiece, but then it was a miracle that he'd made it at all. It felt good to have rolled it in Uschi's sky-blue bed with his 'brother and sisters', while making harmless cracks about his son. It felt really good.

The joint did the rounds, and it didn't take long to have an effect. By the second round the laughing fits had set in. 'It's actually a good thing Harry's not around,' said Uschi.

'Why's that?' asked Philip.

'Because there's no way we'd fit a fifth person in here!'

They all giggled like mad. Ricarda was bent double with laughter and almost knocked Eckart out of the narrow bed; he just about managed to grab hold of Uschi's handgrip in time.

'You never know what a thing like this might be good for,' he said, chortling.

'Stop laughing. Stop it! I need a wee!' Ricarda cackled with one hand near her crotch.

'Come on, jump!' cried Philip. Chubby Ralf was poised beside the nursing bed, gathering himself to leap. He didn't make it even an inch off the floor.

'Oh, help him up,' squeaked Uschi.

'Hey, Ralfie. Want some?' Philip leaned over the side of the bed and waved the joint in front of Ralf. Ralf merely coughed at it and jumped his habitual half-inch.

The four of them were creased up with laughter. They were behaving like schoolkids, but that was precisely what they all needed right now. They'd just experienced one of their toughest days as flatmates, and now the four of them were hanging out in a small nursing bed – without Harry, unfortunately – having a spliff and giggling at the tubby, trusting dachshund who was desperate to join them under Uschi's duvet. The gloom of an hour ago had lifted, and the shock of Uschi's plan was virtually forgotten, as was Eckart's sadness at having lost Lotte and Harry. This club of four suddenly felt as if they could take on the whole world, and – no, he hadn't been mistaken – Ricarda and Philip weren't just making eyes at each other; they were playing footsie under the covers.

'You'd have been in our way-hay on the stairs too,' cackled Ricarda, setting them all off again. 'Oooh, this feels good.'

Eckart languidly blew out another cloud of smoke. 'Boy, am I happy we got together.'

60

There were certainly more pleasant situations to be in. Philip had reckoned with many things when he founded the flatshare, but he hadn't counted on being naked one morning in the hallway while running into Eckart.

The reason for this encounter was the most wonderful one he could imagine: he had spent the night with Ricarda.

After their unorthodox bed-in she had crept furtively towards his room with him, and he had simply yanked her inside when Eckart was out of sight. There was a touch of the youth hostel about it, when the boys would sneak into the girls' dorm unseen. It was clear: no one ought ever to underestimate a flatshare's capacity to rejuvenate you.

They had laughed, dying to pick up where they'd left off in the kitchen. Ricarda pushed him up against the wing-back chair, kicked off her shoes and began to sway her hips.

'No ...?' He couldn't believe his eyes.

Oh, yes, said Ricarda's smile, as she leaned forward and urged him to clap the rhythm. Ricarda was doing Brigitte Bardot's wonderful mambo routine from *And God Created Woman*, a dance Ricarda had occasionally performed for friends when they were younger and had smoked a little weed. Now she was dancing for him – timidly at first, but then, with a laugh, she threw open her wraparound dress, like Bardot in the film. Legs bared, she sashayed to the rhythm of the mambo that beat in both their heads.

Was there anything more seductive than having a woman dance for you, completely absorbed in what she was doing, gliding her hands up the insides of her thighs, running them over her hips, up to her neck and through her hair?

Thank you, Harry. Thanks for that joint.

He stood up and laid his hands on her hips, and together they danced. He felt her body, so soft. She seemed to have shed all the tension of the preceding weeks.

'Am I in love with *you*?' she whispered, resting her head on his shoulder. 'Or with our younger days?'

'You're in love?'

'Better not be, eh?' Her mouth sought his lips. 'There's an article in Uschi's glossy magazine: "Making up with your ex: don't get trapped by nostalgia."'

'Ric, we were never together.'

'Oh, yeah?'

Oh, yeah. But at last he could change that. He launched

her softly on to the bed. He didn't feel entirely self-confident, and his movements seemed awkward even to him. He wanted to be at his best – always a handicap, for the brain needed disconnecting. But never mind: his tongue reached for hers, they kissed, he pushed his hand – at the second attempt! – under her dress, slid it up her legs and—

What the hell was that?

This thing his fingers had encountered could not really be described as underwear. It was a very tight, fairly large item. And this fairly large item was fairly firmly attached to Ricarda's body.

He tugged, trying to pull the thing down elegantly, but it wouldn't move.

'What kind of underwear is that?' he murmured.

'Oh, no,' Ricarda grunted, smoothing down her dress. 'I'd completely forgotten about that. I didn't think we'd get round to ... I bet you'll need some Viagra now?'

'Doesn't it pinch you?'

The struggle with her underwear had caused a slight slackening in his trousers. They looked at each other and couldn't help but laugh. They really weren't having much luck today.

'Oh, how embarrassing!' Ricarda slipped out of the bed.

'No, Ric, stay here.' He was quick enough to catch her hand, but she withdrew it and padded out of the room.

'Trust me, we'll get that thing off,' he mumbled, and let himself fall backwards on to the bed. He lay there for a second with her scent in the air, the feel of her skin on his. He flattened his hand against the wall with a grin. They'd fumbled it.

He got up, went over to her room and silently opened the door. She was standing in front of the mirror in the half-darkness, a finger to her lips.

'I don't need Viagra,' he whispered. He stood behind her; they looked at each other in the mirror; he gently unbuttoned the top of her dress and she moaned; he grew aroused, shut his eyes and pressed himself against her, sought her lips, looked in the mirror again; their eyes met; they paused, holding this moment of desire in the balance, then she took his hand and guided it slowly, very slowly down over her stomach, lower, under her dress and ... this time he was lucky: no knickers.

Upon waking, he felt a lancing pain in his head. He hadn't a clue whether it was the cheap sparkling wine or Harry's accursed weed; maybe he was simply too old for such revelries. But then his eyes came to rest on Ricarda. She was breathing regularly, oblivious of the hangover she was bound to wake up to any moment now.

What a night. After making love on the floor, they had lain on the bed and caressed each other – delicately, tentatively, almost reverently. Then they'd done it again. And again. In between, they dozed off, woke up and searched once more for the touch of each other's skin.

He turned on his side towards Ricarda, propped his head on his hand and observed her as she slept. Silently he watched her lips rise slightly as she breathed out; the wrinkles around her eyes; the slight quivering of her eyelids; the faintest hint of white at the hair roots; the tiny liver spots that irritated her so much.

Who knew what would become of them, or whether they really stood a chance, but, whatever might be coming their way, he knew one thing: he loved this woman. It was as simple as that. He had always loved her.

And he knew something else too: his bladder needed relieving.

He jumped up, and dashed over to the bathroom, the bathroom door opened and ... Eckart exited. In his chequered dressing gown.

Great. Fantastic timing. Philip was in the nude.

'Hi, Eckart. Good morning.' He didn't quite know where to look.

'Good morning, Philip.' Eckart didn't quite know where to look either.

'Anyway,' said Philip, 'see you at breakfast, okay?'

'Yeah, breakfast. That's right,' nodded Eckart, 'as usual.'

The situation was already ridiculous enough, but then they had trouble getting past each other. It was that famous left-right double-dodge, when each person tries to make room for the other, but both choose the same side at precisely the same moment. And one of them naked, to boot.

As previously mentioned, there were more pleasant situations than this.

Eventually they managed a right-hand combination, and Eckart slipped past him, though he looked around again when he reached his door.

'Philip?'

'Yes?'

'Congratulations.'

'Right. Thanks, Eckart,' he said, squeezing out a smile and covering himself with his hands.

'It was about time, eh?'

It was touching to hear that Eckart shared his excitement, but wasn't the man ever going to go back into his room?

'Yeah, it was about time,' Philip said with a nod. He wondered whether everything in life really had to be thrashed out in detail, or if you couldn't sometimes just . . . let things drop. He nodded politely again and finally disappeared, still completely exposed, into the bathroom.

61

Uschi raised and lowered her right and left arms. That's right: she was actually raising and lowering her right arm. Ralf's head tracked their movements. Up, down, up, down.

Uschi smiled at Eckart, who was sitting across the kitchen table from her, leading the mirror exercise. At right angles to her chest stood a mirror that reflected her left arm, the good one. She raised and lowered it, and in the mirror her right arm was raised and lowered too. Up, down, up, down.

For the first time Ralf was part of the action. He was perching on a bar stool that Uschi had drawn up to the table yesterday for him, as an equal member of the flat-share. It was as if they needed a fifth man around the table, though it might have been due to their guilty conscience after so shamelessly excluding him from their revelries the other night in Uschi's bed.

Up, down, up, down went his head, as it followed closely both of her arms. It did look good, but sadly it wasn't real. Her paralysed right arm was out of sight behind the mirror, where Eckart was lifting and lowering it in time with her left one. This stimulated the plasticity of the brain, according to the occupational therapist. Eckart was always highly conscientious and attentive; the rhythm had to be exactly right. Yet for the past three days, ever since Ricarda and Philip had finally got together, he had seemed absent and unfocused.

Yesterday he had driven Stella and Fabian and their bulky rucksacks to the station. They'd applied for some time off before Stella's pregnancy advanced. Four weeks Interrailing around France.

Eckart liked looking after the two of them – probably because he missed his son. Every day Eckart would peer into the letterbox and quickly sift through the mail. Gazing up at him from her wheelchair, Uschi knew that he wasn't on the lookout for bills.

He seemed particularly affected this morning, however. As Philip and Ricarda giggled and cooed as they cleared away breakfast, Eckart had grabbed a carrot and spiked it upright on to Philip's cutting board. As he rammed it down on to the nail, he'd suggested they make another trip out to the lake some time.

'Today?' said Philip, glancing up in disbelief as he stacked plates into the dishwasher.

'Um ... Philip and I had actually planned to go jogging today,' Ricarda had interjected, for which she was rewarded with an astonished look from Philip.

'Jogging?' said Eckart.

'Yep, jogging,' Ricarda nodded, screwing the lids on to the jam jars.

'We could of course put that off,' Philip added.

'No, no. You go ahead and ... *jog*.' Eckart stressed the word as if it were a disease. 'We'll go to the park for a bit. Hey, Uschi?' He shoved the carrot board towards her, and she nodded, but this was not a nice conversation. She picked up the peeler and scraped away at the carrot. Ricarda and Philip had gone out jogging and, partly for lack of a second pair of hands, Uschi and Eckart had ultimately stayed at home.

Uschi focused her attention on the false miracle again. She raised and lowered her left arm, and Ralf's and Eckart's heads moved up and down in time with its monotonous motion.

She could sense Eckart's disappointment. He had made a fresh attempt to breathe new life into the flatshare, but he had been put in his place by the innocent cruelty of a couple in love. It was normal for Philip and Ricarda to want to spend some time on their own at the beginning, but it was true that it had unbalanced the flatshare. Their relationship left everything else feeling ragged. Harry was gone, Stella and Fabian were away too, and in the heat of their passion Ricarda and Philip had not yet taken any steps to look for a new flatmate. There was a sense of things falling apart. Up, down, up, down. Uschi directed all her thoughts to her paralysed arm.

The front door opened. 'Jesus, Ric!' cried Philip. 'Couldn't you have suggested something *a little* less strenuous than jogg—' His voice trailed off; they had obviously noticed that Uschi and Eckart weren't at the park after all. They heard Ricarda whisper. Uschi squinted at Eckart. He pretended he hadn't heard and stoically lowered her arm.

'It'll do you good once in a while,' Ricarda called out with exaggerated cheerfulness. Philip and she came into the kitchen, panting. They both looked extremely sleek in their running gear, and they looked happier than ever. They looked in love. And sweaty. At least they really did go jogging, thought Uschi.

'Hi, you two!' said Ricarda. 'Everything okay?' She wiped the perspiration from her brow with a towel, then slung it casually around her neck.

'Everything's okay,' confirmed Uschi.

'A smoothie?' Philip asked Ricarda, picking up a banana.

'Banana and apple.' Ricarda put her arm around his waist and watched over his shoulder as he peeled the apple. Eckart's eyes swivelled towards them, then veered away again.

Philip heaped the bits of fruit into the mixer.

'You're pretty good at this,' grinned Ricarda. Philip twisted around and stole a kiss from her. She whispered something in his ear.

Up and down, up and down went Uschi's arm, and she noticed that Eckart's gaze kept wandering over to the couple. He was straining not to look, but he couldn't help himself.

Philip ran his hand over Ricarda's behind, but Ricarda swatted it away and glanced around. She obviously didn't want to flaunt their infatuation unnecessarily. Philip tried again. She giggled.

Ralf suddenly became tense, ears pricked, peering left and right, one moment at Uschi, the next at Eckart, then back at the arms on either side of the mirror. He sat up on his bar stool, padded on the spot and fixed them with his gaze. Uschi's arms were no longer synchronised, apparently; in fact, Eckart's attention was focused at that moment on Ricarda and Philip, who were whispering.

There was a sudden slapping noise. Ricarda and Philip spun around, and Ralf looked bemused.

'I'm sorry, Uschi,' said a startled Eckart.

'What for?'

'I'm so sorry.' He had obviously let go of her right arm. She couldn't feel anything, but she could see from his expression that he was squeezing her numb hand on the far side of the mirror. He gave her a quick nod and left the kitchen.

'Eckart,' Ricarda called after him. With a glance at Philip, she followed Eckart into his room. Philip leaned back against the worktop with a sigh. Uschi and he could hear the other two's voices.

'Eckart, what's wrong?' Ricarda asked.

'Nothing. Nothing's wrong.' replied Eckart.

'Do you miss Harry? Or ... if it's about Philip and me ... if it's about us, then ...'

'Forget it!'

Silence. Philip stared out the window.

'A game of whist, perhaps?' asked Ricarda, her words barely audible from the kitchen. Philip looked at Uschi and shrugged.

'Please, Ricarda,' said Eckart, 'I'd just like to be alone right now! Do you think that'd be possible?'

Philip hung his head. No, none of this was very nice. They were no longer in sync; the four of them had fallen completely out of sync.

'Philip?' said Uschi quietly. He looked up. 'Let me go. Please. It'd be better for everyone.'

62

The car sped along the street, its engine roaring. Harry accelerated even harder. Suddenly a bend appeared before them.

'Watch out, Grandpa!' screamed Timmy. Harry desperately tried to keep the car on track, but centrifugal force was pushing it off the road. The car smashed through the crash barrier, careered across a field and slammed into a tree. A column of smoke rose from the bonnet.

Silence.

'You were going too fast, Grandpa,' said Timmy, leaning forward on the couch and removing the PlayStation control pad from Harry's hand. 'You always go too fast.'

They were sitting side by side in Harry's granny flat. In front of them on the table stood a collection of empty beer and juice bottles. The Stones were singing 'Wild Horses' on the radio. Harry considered whether he should still nip over to the racecourse, but for some reason he didn't feel like it. He hadn't had the energy since moving back in here. Or maybe the incentive? Was it because no one here gave two hoots if he went to the races? *What are these strange thoughts popping into my head*, he thought.

He dug his hand into the crisp packet that lay on the couch between him and Timmy. These damn things: once you started, you just couldn't stop. Mick sang on through the radio about doing some living after we die ... and Timmy started a new race.

The doorbell rang. Harry checked his watch. A quarter of an hour early; the do-gooder was too early. Harry got grumpily to his feet, patted Timmy's head – the boy was already back on the track – and opened the door.

'Blimey! Eckart!' What a surprise. It really was Eckart standing outside. Harry was delighted. He was really delighted. 'Come in!'

He fetched two beers from the fridge, and Eckart greeted Timmy with a clumsy high five. The two men went out on to the small terrace, which Britta had furnished with two teak chairs and a blue metal table. Harry prised the first bottle open with his lighter and handed it to Eckart, who was admiring Britta's eco-garden. Harry popped open the second bottle, and they clinked them together.

'Good to see you,' he said.

Eckart nodded. He posed a few questions about the bushes, which Harry was incapable of answering. They sat down on the teak chairs and surveyed the garden with its rows of vegetables and beds of herbs.

'So?' said Eckart. 'How are things?'

'Oh,' said Harry. 'Good. Timmy's fun to be with. Yeah, it's okay. At least I can make sure his education doesn't suffer now.'

'His education?'

'My daughter's boyfriend is a bad influence.'

'Oh, yeah?' said Eckart, taking another sip from his bottle.

'He lectures Timmy. He only allows him one hour on the computer per day, or on the PlayStation. An hour in total. *More would be unhealthy.*'

'And the same applies to you?'

'He's hasn't gone that far yet,' Harry chuckled. 'No, he believes children shouldn't spend too much time in front of a computer.'

'He's not entirely wrong there,' Eckart remarked.

'Right, right you are,' Harry conceded. 'Sitting is the new smoking. Still. You have to give young men a bit of space. They have to find out for themselves that sitting in front of a screen eventually gets tedious. After an hour and a half Timmy goes out on to the playing fields with his friends anyway.'

He knew he was in the wrong, but he didn't care. For

him nothing was more fundamental than self-determination and personal freedom.

'And does this boyfriend have any children of his own?' asked Eckart. 'I mean, does he know what he's talking about?'

'No. He's a sociologist. When I see the kind of crap they research ... '

'But you studied sociology yourself?'

'Yep. And now I finally know why I dropped out.'

Eckart had to laugh. For a time the two of them stared out over the garden, and a crow landed next to the tomato plants.

'Psst,' went Harry. Bloody pests; he hated crows. 'What about you?' he asked. 'How are you all doing?'

'All right.' Eckart nodded. 'Fine.'

It wasn't particularly convincing. He studied Eckart's profile, but Eckart said nothing, instead raising the bottle to his lips again and taking three or four swigs. The beer gurgled in his throat. Harry had never seen Eckart put back so much beer in one go.

After staring out into the greenery for a little longer, Harry asked, 'Another beer?'

Eckart looked at his watch. 'Good gracious, no! I've got to go. Ricarda and Phil are ... ' He stood up. 'Sorry, Harry. Another time, with pleasure. I'm late. Uschi is ... My turn to cook.' He set the beer bottle down on the blue metal table with a clang, and went to shake Harry's hand.

As stiff as ever. Harry acted as if he hadn't spotted the hand, and clapped Eckart on the back by the door. A manly goodbye. Quick and painless. Eckart still had to learn that.

'See you soon,' he said.

'Maybe you can drop round once in a while?'

Harry nodded. Eckart walked down the short gravel path to the gate. He got into his car, started the engine, waved and drove off.

Quick and painless.

So what might Eckart be cooking for the others today?

Harry took another beer from the fridge. He detested being glum, but that was how he felt right now. Eckart had infected him with his sadness.

Timmy had fallen asleep on the couch, so he carefully carried the little boy into the bedroom and laid him on the bed. He pulled the covers over the kid, and sat there beside the sleeping child for a moment. His gaze fell on the bedside table, from where his former flatmates were smiling at him. He had put the picture of Uschi's 'thousand-star' hotel that they'd taken on self-timer in an old frame and placed it beside his bed. He picked it up and asked himself why he'd framed the stupid snapshot. Then he studied it more closely. Everyone was laughing; they were beaming.

Timmy opened his eyes. 'Grandpa?'

'Yes?'

'Why don't you live with them any more?'

Harry pondered what the best answer might be.

'Is it because Uschi peed in her trousers?' asked Timmy.

'Don't be silly.' He punched Timmy softly in the ribs and put the photo back on the bedside table. On the wall hung Timmy's drawing with the brightly coloured coffins.

63

'I'd like something sporty,' said Ricarda to the salesman. Ralf waddled through the shop, sniffing the tyres of the mobility scooters. They didn't smell of anything, apart from rubber.

The salesman invited Ricarda to sit on a wheelchair at first, then demonstrated the advantages of a wide red scooter. Ricarda climbed into the scooter and guided it up a small ramp and back down again. She buzzed around the shop – and almost ran over Ralf. She laughed.

'Right, Uschi! Right!' Ricarda shouted. Ralf looked up at the scene. The red scooter with Uschi on board bumped along the path through the park and curved off gently to the left.

Ricarda, Philip and Eckart stood on the edge of the path,

and leaned right – in the opposite direction to Uschi's circular course. Philip was swinging his arms in the opposite direction too.

'Right, Uschi. You've got to steer. R-i-i-ght!'

'I'm not as good at turning right,' called Uschi.

'I don't get it,' said Ricarda. 'The salesman expressly said that the paralysis had no effect on—'

'Aargh!' cried Uschi, suddenly speeding away across the lawn. The red scooter shot off into the distance like a rocket.

'Bra-ake! Brake, Uschi!' screamed Ricarda. The three of them raced after Uschi, with Ralf clinging to their heels, his ears flapping up and down. He had trouble keeping up, but at last something exciting was happening on one of his walks.

The scooter screeched to a halt, and Uschi was jolted forward; she had obviously located the brake pedal. Ralf came panting to a stop too. Uschi looked up at her flatmates, wide-eyed, and Eckart bent over her, gasping for air. 'You haven't got . . . your . . . driver's . . . licence . . . have you?'

Uschi shook her head.

Philip and Ricarda set about explaining the various switches and pedals to Uschi, while Eckart gave Ralf's tummy a good tickle.

'Not sure it's the answer, are you?'

Ralf basked in Eckart's affection, gazing up into the foliage overhead. He loved this park with its little grassy knolls, its magnificent old trees and thick rhododendron bushes lining the paths, sometimes adorned with dense pink clumps of flowers. In the mornings rabbits hopped across the misty lawns. He knew this park like the back of his paw. He was old and tired now, but when his former owner was still alive he had explored every corner of it, every rabbit hole, every anthill and every bench.

They continued their walk. 'Yes,' Philip congratulated Uschi. 'You can do it. Good. And that's the speedometer.' Uschi was driving alongside them, slowly and in a straight line.

Eckart lobbed a stick on to the grass. Ralf did him the favour of retrieving it. Eckart threw the stick again, and a second time Ralf retrieved it for him. Eckart was happy (*aha, now, all of a sudden!*), praised him, and threw the stick a third time. Ralf considered two stick throws quite sufficient; there was no need to overdo this kind of activity.

Eckart caught up with the others.

'Do you think you two might be able to get by without us for a weekend?' Ricarda asked him.

'Of course,' said Uschi, zigzagging along to test the steering.

'A friend of mine is celebrating her sixtieth in Rome,' Ricarda continued.

'Don't you worry,' said Uschi. 'Eckart and I will arrange a nice hormonious weekend for ourselves with Ralf.'

'Oh,' said Philip with a cheeky sideways glance at Eckart. 'Now there's a prospect.'

Eckart didn't seem to appreciate Philip's humour at this point, and he cast around grim-faced for another stick.

'Harmonious with an "a", Uschi,' said Ricarda, grinning. 'Harmonious.'

'Huh?' Uschi attempted to look over her shoulder at her friends, but she almost veered off the path in the process.

'Leave her be,' said Philip. 'Uschi's right: when the hormones are right, the harmony's right too.'

Ricarda pinched Philip in the side. 'Don't come over all Harry with us now!'

'Why not?' said Philip. 'Terroristically speaking, that's not a bad idea.'

'Are you lot taking the mickey out of me?' Uschi called back.

'Noooo! I wouldn't dare!' cried Philip, then bent down and gave her a hearty kiss on the cheek.

'Stop it,' squeaked Uschi.

'All your fault,' countered Philip. 'You're the one who stimulated my hormones!'

'Just you wait until we get home!' threatened Uschi.

Ricarda, Philip and Uschi burst out laughing, and Ralf joined in with a woof. He hadn't seen his owners looking so exuberant since the evening they'd all sat in Uschi's bed, smoking that funny cigarette. It was almost like it used to be when the whole club had moved into his flat.

He snooped around a bin. What a wonderful walk. The birds were chirping, the wind was streaming through the leaves, and in some places sweet scents would float past him. There was a hint of the old carefree days in the air.

'And how long are you going away for?'

Ralf flattened his ears and pulled in his tail. Eckart's voice sliced coldly through the air that Ralf was just enjoying and settled – he could see it in their eyes – like a pinch collar around Philip's and Ricarda's necks.

64

'It's working out pretty well. We've just got to take some of the weight off Eckart's shoulders.' Ricarda pecked Philip on the cheek and headed towards the fish stall.

'It isn't,' Philip said, 'and, to be totally honest, I don't feel like carrying on.' He grasped Ricarda's arm roughly. 'Come on, the queue at the vegetable stall's shorter.'

They forced their way through the crowd with their two baskets. The colourful market stalls were surrounded with people, and the vendors were shouting out their sales pitches.

Ricarda usually adored going shopping with Philip, but not so much today. He kept grumbling. About Eckart. She was trying to keep her composure.

For the past week she'd been on cloud nine. She was in love. Philip and she made love a lot, sometimes gently, sometimes passionately. They did it in the daytime too sometimes, when Eckart and Uschi were out. Once they even did it in the kitchen. What perhaps made it all the more special was that they couldn't always do it when they wanted to, so their passion had time to build up. Ricarda noticed how good she felt. Everything had become doable, feasible, manageable. Even her new daily run wasn't so much of a stretch. She seemed to be floating through life.

But now Eckart had started to mope. On the one hand she could understand him, but on the other she didn't want to. She was happy. Couldn't things just continue as they were now? Why couldn't feelings of bliss remain that way? Why did Eckart have to choose now to act up and make such an exhibition of his displeasure? To be honest, though, she was just as annoyed as Philip.

'Everything'll fall back into place, Phil,' she said.

They joined the queue. Ricarda examined the red tomatoes and colourful peppers. The celery looked good. A homeless man asked for a euro, so she took out her purse and pressed a coin into his hand.

'I can understand Eckart too,' Philip picked up. 'Better than you think. But that question: "And how long are you going away for?" Honestly! I'm sixty-one.'

'We'll look for someone to take Harry's room and—'

'Oh, great!' Philip exclaimed. 'Flatshare with stroke victim seeks affable new member. They'll be battering down our door!'

Ricarda put her purse away. She could feel the anger

building up inside her. Why was Philip being so grouchy? It didn't make things any better.

It was their turn, and the blonde saleswoman with funny plaits smiled and nodded to them. 'So? What can I get you today?'

'Four sticks of rhubarb, a bunch of carrots, a cauliflower, a bunch of mint and four lemons,' said Philip. It was more of a bark than an order.

'That was pretty rude,' said Ricarda, with an apologetic smile at the woman. 'Please.' The woman waved her remark away and began to collect the various bits of fruit and vegetables together.

'Ricarda,' said Philip. 'Uschi wants to go into a home.'

'Why bring Uschi up again?'

'She wants to go into a home. She says it at least once every day, but you never listen to her. Some people can accept help, others can't – and Uschi's one of the latter. Where's the problem?'

'Where's the problem? How selfish is that! She's just getting better!'

'Thanks to your stupid scooter, or what?'

That was below the belt. She reached for a mango and handed it to the vendor. 'She was there when your mother died.'

'For God's sake, Ric! Cut it out! Uschi. Wants. To. Go. Into. A. Home. Why can't you accept that? What's wrong with you?'

'That'll be nine euros.' The vendor passed them the bags, and Ricarda grabbed them. Now look – he'd got to her. She was fuming. 'What's wrong with *me*? Now *I'm* the one who's acting strangely, am I? That really takes the biscuit!'

Philip whipped out his wallet, apologised to the vendor for Ricarda's rude behaviour – *how dared he!* – and handed the woman a fifty-euro note.

'Ric,' he said softly, 'we missed out on each other for thirty-five years. Tomorrow we'll be dead.'

What kind of comment was *that*? Of course their intimacy was being tested right now. Of course they couldn't express their feelings to the full. Of course none of this was easy, but that was no reason to weasel out of their commitments at the drop of a hat.

'See! You want to get rid of her!' she snarled.

'I do not want to get rid of Uschi. I'm just trying to analyse the situation rationally from every angle, and . . . '

'Stop, Philip, stop!' She held up her hands. Not another word. She didn't want to listen to any more of his selfish prattle. She too had indulged in the same thought the previous evening. She had imagined how it might be if she and Philip lived on their own . . . yes, on their own. Like a real couple. Just the two of them. In a flat. With all the corresponding freedom. But she had immediately and fiercely rejected the thought. She was ashamed of herself.

And now here was Philip, acting as if it were a possibility, as if it really were possible for them to disband everything and move in together as a couple. Not only that, though! No, for him it was not just possible; he pretended that it would be the best thing for everyone. The best thing! For Eckart! For Uschi! For Uschi? How could he twist it in such a self-serving manner? She hadn't thought Philip capable of such selfishness.

The market seller was still rummaging in her till for change, and Philip was waiting. Ricarda looked at him, wanting to add something, but she really couldn't find the words. She strode off.

'Ric! Ric, come back! Wait!'

'You egotist!'

'What if I am?' he called after her. 'Yes, Ricarda, yes! I want to enjoy the rest of my life! Is that a crime?'

65

'Help! Fire! Fire! He-e-elp!'

Uschi's scream rang out around the flat. Ralf yelped. Philip sat up in bed with a jolt. He stumbled out of his room, and Eckart and Ricarda came running out of theirs towards the kitchen. They tore the door open and were met by a cloud of smoke. Ralf retreated, barking, into the hallway. Flames were raging on the stove.

Uschi was trying to reach the tap from her wheelchair, at the same time as she attempted to throw some dishcloths on the fire, but the blaze continued to spread.

'Fire! Fire!' she screamed.

Philip ran to the cupboard and pulled out the bucket, while Ricarda flung open the window, and Eckart pulled Uschi, who was trying to toss more dishcloths on the flames, away from the stove. Philip filled the bucket, and after a few pails of water the fire was out.

They slumped on the living room couch with exhaustion. Even with the windows wide open, smoke was still billowing above their heads.

'How did it happen?' Ricarda asked feebly.

'The dishcloth. The dishcloth caught fire,' mumbled Uschi.

'So why did you keep throwing the other dishcloths on top?' asked Eckart.

Uschi shook her head dejectedly. 'Those were the only things I could reach to dampen the flames.'

She'd dampened not just the flames, but the mood too.

66

Am I the hero a child wants to see . . . Eckart had removed the *Bach Fugues* CD from the player and had started humming Harry's favourite growling song, written by a dead friend of his. Harry was very attached to this song and had often played it when he lived there. Eckart knew the lyrics off by heart now too.

The others were already asleep. Well, they'd retired to their rooms in any case. It had been a tough day, and it seemed to have absolutely no intention of ending.

They had tried to get the kitchen looking halfway decent again. They'd done everything they could, airing and cleaning and scrubbing, all so they didn't have to consider what the small kitchen fire really spelled.

Now here he was, sitting in his room, in his armchair,

staring at the spot where Lotte's stone had stood until recently, drinking a glass of schnapps and listening to Harry's friend sing *Please don't miss me, there'll be drinks when we die.*

Why, he thought, in moments of great sadness, did our thoughts automatically turn to death, to the end of all things? Or was he the only one who thought like that? He poured himself another glass. Finally his eyelids were starting to droop.

The blackbird was complaining again. Eckart had been awake for a while. He felt no desire to get up. He was tired. He had no desire to go into the kitchen, no desire to see the others, no desire to start the day.

He raised himself to a sitting position, sat there for a while on the edge of the bed, went into the bathroom, showered, brushed his teeth, said good morning to Philip when he met him in the hall, got dressed, went into the kitchen, put on some coffee for the others and some water for boiled eggs, pricked the eggs, laid the table, said good morning to Ricarda when she came into the kitchen, dropped a teabag into his mug, and sat down at the kitchen table. Ricarda and Philip joined him, and they each seized a section of the newspaper and barricaded themselves away behind their morning read. Uschi was presumably still in her room.

Eckart cracked open his boiled egg. The doorbell rang.

Neither of the other two moved, so he got up, went over to the entrance door and pressed the intercom button.

'Yes?'

'This is the Salvation Army. We've come to pick up Mrs Müller.'

Before he could answer, Uschi came rolling out of her room into the hall, with her blue, flower-embroidered handbag on her lap. Ricarda and Philip appeared from the kitchen, and the three of them looked quizzically at Uschi. The doorbell rang again.

'Open it.' Uschi nodded to Eckart. He pushed the button to open the door.

'This may be a little sudden,' said Uschi, gazing guilelessly at the other three, 'but I had to take things in hand. You gave me no option.'

'No, Uschi,' Ricarda half-heartedly protested. 'No way – you're staying.'

'No, I'm going,' replied Uschi before attempting a joke. 'Well, rolling, actually.'

'Uschi . . . ' said Ricarda.

'I know you only want the best for me,' Uschi said softly, 'but only *I* know what's best for me. Hm? I'd like to thank you so much . . . I . . . for everything you've—' she sighed, lowered her eyes for a moment to gather herself and looked up again bravely '—you've do-done for me . . . nobody ever d-did that for me before. See?' She laughed. 'My speech impediment's back!'

Irony to counter sadness. *Oh, shit*, thought Eckart, *I'm pretty sure the fertiliser's not going to work this time.*

'Hello?' There was a knock on the door, and the man from the Salvation Army stuck his head through the gap.

The men carried Uschi downstairs in her wheelchair, with Eckart, Ricarda and Philip following on behind. Three flights that *they* had so often scaled and descended in recent months, in the widest possible range of positions and combinations. Eckart ran his hand along the wooden banister. The men set Uschi down outside, and one of them slid open the van's door. An elevator lifted the wheelchair into the vehicle with a whirr. All the difficulties that the flatmates had tackled so valiantly, day in day out, suddenly seemed like child's play. Two strong men, a small lift.

'I'll break a leg,' said Uschi, flashing them a smile from the back of the van. 'Give me three weeks before your first visit so I can introduce you to my new friends, okay? Three weeks. Promise?'

They nodded. The care worker slammed the door, jumped into the van, started it up and sped off past the plane trees. The vehicle grew smaller and then turned off.

'Satisfied?' Ricarda snapped bitterly at Philip, and went inside.

Philip looked up at the building opposite, where a young man was fitting a net curtain. Eckart knew that Philip had always kept an eye out for the old man. Now a young single man had moved in.

'I'll look for a place too. You two need a place to yourselves,' Eckart said. Philip wanted to object, but Eckart just shook his head gently, lightly squeezed Philip's arm and went into their building. *No buts*, he said to himself.

Eckart unlocked the letterbox. Between two bills lay a black postcard with 'New Zealand by night' printed on it in baroque gold lettering. He flipped the card over.

Hi, Dad,
   Warmest wishes from New Zealand. Thanks again for the money. Have fun in your vintage flatshare.
   Christoph
   PS. Love from Elena too.

The hall light went out. He stood holding the black postcard in the dark hallway, then went to the door, pressed down the brass handle and stepped back out into the bright street. He walked along the main shopping street to the cathedral and took a twenty-minute train ride with a group of noisy pensioners through the city, past the last houses and out into the countryside, through a patchwork of fields and woodland. Then he got off, walked down a track, still holding their son's postcard, to the tree against which Lotte's headstone rested, and informed her that Christoph had been in touch.

*

He spared himself the detour via the pub this time; he didn't feel like drinking without Harry. Later, he opened the door to the flat, and caught Ricarda's voice in the kitchen.

'It *could* have worked!'

'Could have!' Philip retorted. 'Of course it *could have*. But you just had this obsession. Were you really concerned about Uschi? Be honest. Was it really about Uschi? Or about yourself? Ricarda, you *wanted* it to work. But Uschi—'

'Don't be unfair now. For me Uschi's part of the family. She's ...'

Eckart went into his room. He slid the black postcard into the bookshelf between Peter Handke's *A Sorrow Beyond Dreams* and Erik Fosnes Hansen's *Psalm at Journey's End* – between farewell letters and certain doom.

He stood in the middle of the room, unsure what to do with himself. He sat down on his bed. Start again from scratch? The newspaper lay on his bedside table. He flicked through the small ads, running his finger over the house rentals section. *Soulmates wanted! We're all in our sixties, but feel younger than ever. If you enjoy cooking together, walking, going to concerts and ...*

Eckart let the newspaper sink on to his lap.

67

The air streamed through her hair, under her arms and under her dress, which she had to pull back down over her knees every few metres. Ricarda was cycling over the Hohenzollern Bridge. It was good to pedal and feel the wind and the sun on her skin.

She gazed over the Rhine. She loved this wide river and the way it simply went its own way, undeterred, oblivious to what was happening to the left and the right of it. The same as every river, of course, but she had grown up beside this one, and she felt a strong bond with it.

Whenever anything went wrong in her life, whenever she got the blues, she would always go to the Rhine, sit on the bank and wait until her thoughts had sorted themselves out or her anger had subsided, until her nerves had settled or the tears had dried up. This time too, as she crossed its waters, it granted her a break, some breathing space.

She felt uneasy. The day before, Philip had asked her in the kitchen whether, now that Uschi had left and Eckart was maybe on his way too, they shouldn't start afresh together, right from the beginning. He had looked at her with an almost distressing candour in his eye – a candour that, in truth, left no room for prevarication.

'Us two?' she'd asked, surprising even herself with the frailty of her voice. He had nodded, cautiously. She had sensed that he was scared of her answer, and she'd known why. She was scared of her answer, too.

'Phil, I love you,' she had said, groping for words to describe a feeling she had not yet defined for herself.

'But?' he'd said.

She'd given some thought to how best to express herself. Eckart hadn't moved out yet, and she was determined to do all she could to stop him from doing so. For she hadn't yet given up. Not by a long way. She liked sharing a flat. She liked sharing worries with others, and also joy. Laughing, comforting, being comforted. Arguing too. And making up. Playing cards, cooking together, watching the World Cup together, riding out to the lake.

Sure, they'd had a load of problems. But they had also successfully dealt with a load of problems, and had grown as a result. At least she thought they had. She had recently even caught herself imitating the thuds – BANG BANG BANG – of Harry's darts on the wall.

Even with the benefit of hindsight, there were very few

moments she regretted. But all the things she had gone through and experienced would not have happened to her in a conventional single life.

Since Philip's question the previous day, she had tried to imagine their living together in practical terms, but she simply couldn't see herself in a two-person flat: the two of them in a flat, where routine, or habit, would sooner or later move in with them. Of course, she had briefly dreamed of a two-person flatshare with Philip for a while, but the very term 'two-person flatshare' said it all really. Routine didn't stand a chance when several people shared a flat. The days were so wonderfully unpredictable. You got up in the morning without a clue what the day might bring. Maybe a tombstone would move in; skinned rabbits might cause outrage; the Jane Fonda VHS video would break into a drone; and Philip – oh-so-correct Philip of all people – might say, 'She's growing old too, at last.' You never knew whether Harry might toss his well-gnawed corn-on-the-cob towards the bin without Michael Jordan's accuracy; whether Eckart would suggest an outing to Bavaria and Uschi would squeal with delight that she'd finally get to visit Schloss Neuschweinsteiger; whether Harry would try out Uschi's motorised scooter, knocking over Eckart in the process; whether a Post-it note from Harry might be stuck to the fridge – their complaints box – with *'Uschi is dense'* written on it, because Uschi had elected Harry as her main helper up the stairs. And so on and so forth. No one had a clue. It was marvellous.

'Shouldn't we first wait and see if Eckart does move out?' she asked. Philip nodded and went over to stand by the window. The melodrama window.

'Have you noticed?' he said. 'The old man isn't there any more.' He made no comment on her answer. He'd turned her own weapon against her, countering her ambiguity with further ambiguity. This was precisely why she felt so anxious. She didn't know how he had taken her reply or how he might react. All she knew was that she had lied. Not really a real lie, but a white lie; not telling the truth was also lying. She had thus hurt him twice over: once by evading his question, and the second time because he had – of course – expected a romantic 'Yes, let's move in together'.

'Phil, I love you,' she had repeated.

'I love you too,' he had answered, without turning away from the window.

Now she must wait, wait and see whether he accepted her answer – or, to be more precise, her non-answer. Or not.

She arrived at the small open-air swimming pool. It wasn't very busy. It was late afternoon, and the children were still at school. She got off her bike and locked it up. She paid at the till in the little hut, changed, and walked across the grass to the small pool. She was met by a wave of shrill music. She recognised Fabian, standing on the side of the pool with a mint-green foam water woggle stick between his legs, and demonstrating to some oldies in the water how to use the flotation aids jutting out from between *their* legs.

She reached the pool to find four elderly ladies, a gentleman and Stella splashing about in the water. Ricarda nodded a quick greeting to Fabian, and lay down on her towel. Stella came out of the water in surprise with her pink flotation woggle.

'How come you're here?' Stella wrapped her towel around herself and sat down next to her mother.

'You didn't pick up, so I called Fabian.'

'Something up?'

'No, just felt like seeing you.'

One of the elderly women managed to slap herself around the ears with her sky-blue woggle, and her friends cackled. 'Concentrate, Erica!' called the old gentleman with a smile.

'Five of them, like your gang,' said Stella. 'You were a lovely bunch.'

The sky-blue woman was having trouble threading her woggle back between her legs. The lady next to her tried to lend a hand, but her own red woggle promptly popped out. There was more cackling. 'Erica!' the old man reprimanded her.

'Choose two new flatmates from that lot,' grinned Stella.

'You'll hardly believe it, but that's just the question at the moment. Start anew, or . . . give up.'

Had she really said 'give up'? Did moving in with Philip mean that she was giving up?

'Give up? You? You don't know how to give up!' said Stella. Ricarda noted the slightly sarcastic tone in her daughter's voice.

'Stella, I'm sorry. If I didn't give you enough attention, then I . . .'

'It would do you good for once, though.'

'What would?'

'To give up. Just give up for once, Mum! You're sixty-two. Let go.'

'Sixty-one,' Ricarda corrected her.

'Sixty-*one*? Right.' Stella grinned ironically. 'Of course. Well, in that case it's *much* too early.'

Ricarda gave a smile. It was nice to sit here on the lawn, with her daughter sniping at her, her tummy swelling already, and a charming young guy who was giving elderly ladies woggle lessons, and didn't mind if his girlfriend's baby was his or not. She reclined slightly.

She had come here to tell Stella something. She was just considering how she should broach the subject when she suddenly felt Stella's hand on hers. She twitched; it wasn't often that they touched.

'Stella, when I was pregnant with you, I . . . Those were different times. It was hard with a kid back then, and my life would have turned out completely differently if . . .'

'If I hadn't arrived,' said Stella. She stared out impassively at the coloured floats, and Ricarda swallowed hard.

'It did cross my mind, yes,' she said. There; it was out.

Stella nodded imperceptibly. Ricarda wanted to take her in her arms. 'I'm so happy I have you . . .' she muttered helplessly in a shaky voice. Another float popped out of the water.

Stella gave her hand a squeeze. 'It's good that you told me. It's good.'

Ricarda, on the verge of tears, glanced at her daughter. 'May I?' she asked. Stella nodded, and they embraced.

'I'm stronger than you think, Mum,' said Stella. 'I even go to Faye Dunaway's toilet now.'

'Faye Dunaway?'

'Forget it,' smiled Stella. The five oldies in the water were waving their foam floats above their heads.

'Stella, I wouldn't give you back for the world.'

'Bit late now.'

'Aaaand, wave your woggles in the air! Aaaand . . . thank you! See you next week!' Fabian called to his wogglers. They clapped, and Fabian cheerfully walked over to join Stella and Ricarda.

'Only to *him*,' smiled Ricarda.

'What are you two whispering about?' asked Fabian.

'Will he take you?' Ricarda asked Stella.

'No way!' said Fabian. '*She's* the one taking *me*.'

Oh, how gallant. They all laughed. And Stella, her little Stella, squeezed her hand.

68

The cheap large white tiles echoed under their feet. Older people turned their heads slowly in their direction, screwing up their eyes with curiosity and suspicion as they silently followed their footsteps. Philip had the impression that they were striding down the main street of a dusty one-horse town towards the saloon. *The Five Man Army*. Only they weren't wearing Stetsons and spurs or carrying Colts, and there weren't five of them but four. Ricarda, Eckart, himself – and Ralf. They had replaced their fourth man with a tubby dachshund, and were visiting the fifth man. Or rather, the fifth woman: Uschi.

Uschi Müller, who was not in captivity in some Mexican village in the Wild West, but in a bland retirement home somewhere out in the suburbs of Cologne. It was a very silly thought, but it helped Philip to rise above the bleak, unwelcoming surroundings and the futility of their roles.

It was their first visit; they had respected Uschi's wish to have three weeks to settle in.

Uschi was waiting for them in the coffee room, a large space with a low ceiling and strip lighting, faded Van Gogh prints on the light green walls, three large round tables and two artificial pot plants. A few residents, mostly women, were already sitting around the tables, drinking coffee and eating honey, cream and almond cake.

Uschi was in her wheelchair, glowing with happiness, and pointed proudly to the laid table, as though they were there to sample the retirement home's coffee. Each of them in turn bent down and gave her a hug. Uschi patted Ralf lovingly on the head.

'Come on, I'll show you my room.' With the Four Man Army in tow, she manoeuvred down the corridor and gestured towards an open door. It was a narrow room furnished with dark curtains, two white-painted nursing beds, a small table with two matching chairs, a light-veneered wardrobe and a wall-mounted television set. The detergent used on the grey PVC floor caused it to squeak under their shoes. A sausage trophy was poking out of a cardboard box on top of the wardrobe.

They said 'Nice' and 'Oh, it's fine', then hurried out again, longing for the much-heralded cake and coffee.

Uschi talked non-stop. She introduced the three women who were already seated at her table, and they gave them a friendly nod. She praised her carer, Veronica, a jovial fifty-year-old with dyed red hair who placed a coffee pot on their table. She explained how they were served this cake once a week, and she hoped they liked it. She mentioned the gymnastics she'd done earlier that morning; the large sheet they all held in a circle to roll and bounce a ball around; the clown who had come in the previous week because laughing was good for you; and the cream she had ordered especially for their visit. Uschi talked and talked – and said nothing.

Then they were finally seated at the table. They concentrated on the cake and praised Veronica's freshly whipped cream. There were ten seconds of silence, though they felt like five minutes to Philip. He was dying to ask Uschi how things were, besides bouncing balls on a taut sheet, and freshly whipped cream. He didn't know how to go about it. He took another sip of coffee.

'So? Who's moved into my room?' asked Uschi.

'No one,' said Ricarda. 'We're keeping it free for you.'

Philip conveyed a second sugar lump into his cup so that the coffee would at least taste of *something*.

'No chance! Don't you dare!' cried Uschi, shaking her head and laughing. 'They're looking after me a treat here.'

Philip pummelled the sugar lump to bits in his cup, Eckart scraped the remaining traces of cream from his plate, and Ricarda smiled at the other three ladies. 'What do you do during the day?' she asked them all, arching her eyebrows; she had put on her 'I'm-*so*-interested-in-you' face.

311

But Uschi had already told them everything. Philip was astonished to see Ricarda so helpless.

Uschi cast a searching glance at her 'new friends', but their sole utterance was the quiet sound of munching.

'Oh,' said Uschi, 'all kinds of things. Watching television, a little singing from time to time, exercises. How we laughed when the clown was here last week, didn't we? It's a very nice place really, eh?'

Uschi's 'friends' nodded. And chewed. One of them picked up her cup with stiff fingers, and brought it unsteadily towards her face. Philip caught himself imagining that she might miss her mouth.

'They're tired,' Uschi said with a wink. 'We had gymnastics earlier. I'm a bit fitter than the others.'

A rivulet of coffee ran out of the corner of Uschi's friend's mouth, but she was able to guide her cup relatively directly back to the saucer.

'There's only one thing I find a bit of a shame,' whispered Uschi.

'What's that?' asked Eckart.

'I've tried to teach them whist—' she grinned '—but they can't seem to get their heads around the trumps.'

When the plates had been scraped clean and the cups were empty, Eckart coughed and made for the toilets, and Ricarda helped the carer to clear up. Philip pushed Uschi's wheelchair over to the window, and crouched down in front of her.

'Now, tell me how you're doing.'

'Fine. I'm fine,' she said. 'Leave it. I'm doing really fine. This way at least, I only carry my own burden, not yours as well.'

She stared past him and grinned again. He looked around to spy an old couple walking along the corridor. It took him a second to realise what was going on: the lady actually had her hand in the gentleman's fly. With great calm, as if it were the most normal thing in the world. And so the two of them ambled across the hall, their faces a picture of serenity.

'See,' said Uschi, giving him a cheeky wink. 'There's always something going on here!'

'How about your therapy?'

'Fabian comes three times a week. Imagine that. Such a nice lad.'

Philip nodded. They paid Fabian a little for these visits. Uschi was unaware of this, but the cost of the retirement home had dented the amount of money available for her therapies.

After an hour they said goodbye, and one after the other they bent down to embrace her.

Ricarda gave Uschi a heartfelt kiss on the head, but her hands were trembling. 'I'll come again the day after tomorrow, okay? Take care, my love.' She fought back the tears. Philip had never seen her in such a state. Her idealism had come under heavy fire, and seeing Uschi here like this was the equivalent of a direct hit – and being sunk.

They waved and walked off along the corridor. The white-haired heads slowly followed their steps, as they echoed hollowly on the large white tiles. The Four Man Army was leaving town. An old man was tugging apathetically at a rubber plant.

Shortly before they reached the main entrance, they glanced back one last time.

'Bye. Goodbye, Ralf.' Uschi was waving cheerily after them.

The light was dazzling as they stepped outside. Even with rainclouds about, it was noticeably brighter than inside the home. There was a light drizzle, as if the weather had to rub salt into their wounds.

'Weren't you wearing a jacket?' asked Ricarda. She was right. Philip went back inside, and spotted his jacket hanging over a chair beside the dining table. Uschi was sitting staring out of the window. She was holding a handkerchief in her hand. He gulped. Uschi Müller, the finest sausage seller in the land, a woman who had put her great big heart and all her affection at the service of other people, was now hanging around with three 'friends' who didn't speak – and who also had problems telling the black queens apart.

Slowly he turned on his heel and, with his jacket draped over his arm, strode down the long grey corridor and out into the open air.

*

At least it had stopped drizzling. They walked home through the park. No one spoke, and Ralf kept his nose firmly to the ground, for the rain had infused it with the fresh aromas of flowers and wood.

They sat down behind the small rose garden on one of the red wrought-iron benches and studied the ancient trees. No one said anything.

A young woman with dark frizzy hair called to her dog, a small fox terrier that was gambolling on the lawn and showed not the slightest inclination to obey her commands. Ralf glanced up, then retreated behind their legs and lay down under the bench to doze.

'She hasn't even unpacked her sausage trophies,' Eckart remarked. 'The prospects aren't good.'

He too looked the worse for wear after their visit to Uschi. He had revealed to them that morning that he was on the lookout for a small flat; he didn't have the strength to try sharing a place again. Yet he seemed shocked by Uschi's solitude in the home.

'Picko! Picko! Come here now!' cried the woman with the frizzy hair. Picko ran as fast as he could – in the opposite direction.

'We had a dog once,' said Eckart after a while. 'He obeyed orders. Always. Every time. Without exception.' *Not like that one there*, said his expression.

'If you don't come here this minute, Picko! Heel!' The woman was giving it her all. In vain.

'Then one day,' Eckart continued, 'we were standing on the other side of the street and ... Lotte called him.'

Silence.

Eckart nodded. 'His name was Bill.'

Sure, sometimes it was better not to obey, thought Philip, but what should they do? They couldn't force Uschi. *Don't you dare*, she'd said.

'Picko! Here! Picko!'

Picko barked and cavorted to his heart's delight. He didn't give a fig about obeying; he was having fun. Ralf crept out from under the bench and trotted indecisively towards the lawn. Picko stopped, then slowly approached Ralf. They sniffed each other up and down.

'Let's find some new flatmates,' said Philip. He was surprised by how clear and firm his voice sounded.

Ricarda looked at him with amazement. *Really?* her eyes seemed to say. *Really!* he nodded. He had never been so certain of anything in all his life. Uschi's decision merited respect; it was painful, but it didn't stop them from moving ahead. Part of their plan had failed, but not the whole plan. Ricarda hugged him and buried her face in his neck.

'Love you,' she whispered in his ear.

'Sure?' asked Eckart.

'Sure,' Philip nodded over Ricarda's head. She peeled herself from his shoulder, and grasped Eckart's hand.

'Ralf,' she called. 'Ralf! Did you hear that?'

Ralf raised his head momentarily, then sniffed Picko a little more.

'We're going to carry on, Ralf,' Ricarda shouted over the lawn. Philip felt a sense of peace spread through his veins. He had last felt this way out in the bush after a successful operation on which everyone else had given up.

Finally, he had arrived.

69

Uschi's green frog with the bloated cheeks stared out from the windowsill over the kitchen table. Every day since Uschi's departure Eckart had dropped two euros into the froggy-bank so they could buy Uschi a nice present at some stage.

Today, however, the frog's expression was a little accusing, he thought. He was sitting at the kitchen table with Ricarda and Philip. They were studying the applications that had landed at their house in the wake of their advert for the flatshare. A good forty unopened envelopes still lay scattered over the table, and there was an even larger pile of rejections next to Philip's elbow.

'This one wants us to go jogging together every day. At eight in the morning,' read Philip.

Ricarda was studying another application and didn't even bother to look up. She shook her head.

'But you love jogging!' Eckart couldn't help butting in.

'Haha, very funny,' said Philip, and added the jogger's paperwork to the rejection pile.

'You prefer aerobics with Jane, do you?' Eckart quipped. Was he seeing things, or had Uschi's frog just flashed him a disapproving look? He picked up the next application. For once the covering letter and the CV weren't typed on a computer, but written in purple ink with a fountain pen. Not so common nowadays. This stirred his curiosity.

With a shake of her head Ricarda added an application to the pile of refusals. 'Smoker.'

Eckart skim-read the CV of the woman with the fountain pen. 'I've got a retired teacher here. A vegetarian who likes going to the theatre, organises a reading group, gets an organic box once a week which is too much for one person to eat ... blah-blah-blah ... favourite destination: Italy, Tuscany, where she knows an olive oil producer ... sixty-two years old.'

He held up her photo. The woman had short ginger hair, and was laughing at the camera, her expression friendly and candid. 'Seems perfect.'

Mm hm. Ricarda and Philip nodded equivocally.

'Seems,' said Philip.

'Who will probably want to force her oh-so-perfect lifestyle on us?' guessed Eckart.

'Probably,' Philip responded.

Ricarda shook her head. 'Forget it – one's enough.'

They all had to grin. They were almost telepathic by now. Eckart picked up the next envelope. Covering letter typed in Courier. Retired tax officer, a widower, an angling buff, three sons, all in good positions, two rabbits ... Rabbits! Eckart shuddered.

The kitchen door flew open. Harry. Harry?

It was indeed Harry standing there, with his lank, greasy hair and his faded blue and green lumberjack shirt.

'I heard this is a disaster zone. You obviously cannot cope without me!'

He snapped open his Zippo. His cigarette crackled as he raised the flame to it. Ricarda, Philip and Eckart stared at the door as if Harry were an extraterrestrial.

Harry hesitated. 'Where's Uschi?'

'Gone,' said Eckart.

'Dead?' asked Harry.

'In a home,' Eckart replied.

'In a home? Harry gave an audible gasp. 'In a home? That's no good at all. Uschi needs social care. Right, Ricarda?'

This was his way of apologising.

'Well?' Philip got to his feet. 'Does this mean you want to move back in?'

'If you'll still have me?' Harry's words sounded more like a threat than a polite request.

'Oh boy, Harry.' Eckart felt his tear ducts twitching. Ricarda stood up and went over to the window. Harry looked enquiringly at Philip.

'Um ... as far as I'm concerned, yes.' Philip nodded, glancing at Ricarda. She turned her back on them and gazed outside. 'Ric?'

No reaction. Eckart looked at Philip, and both of them looked at Harry. Harry furrowed his brow.

'What?' said Harry, while hiding his cigarette behind his back.

Do it, Eckart and Philip encouraged him.

Do I have to? suggested Harry's expression.

Yes, the two of them nodded.

Harry cleared his throat. 'Ric, I ... If I was sometimes a bit rude, then ... then ... well, then ...'

Carry on, signalled Eckart and Philip.

'Well, then ...' Harry was fighting the toughest battle of his life.

Then ... nodded Eckart and Philip.

'Then I'm sorry,' mumbled Harry. It was obvious that he couldn't bring himself to say any more. Philip grinned. Ricarda still gazed unwaveringly out of the window. She was quivering slightly. Was she weeping?

'Ric?' Philip put a hand on her shoulder. 'Is everything all right?'

'Everything's all right,' she said, turning around. She burst out laughing. For a second the others looked at her in amazement, then they all joined in with her laughter.

Harry patted Ralf. 'How about you? No opinion?' Ralf woofed. It sounded like approval.

'Good!' said Harry. 'All wrapped up, then. And now,' he said, eyes sparkling, 'we're going to fetch Uschi!'

Outrageous. The guy was simply outrageous, thought Eckart. Harry's taxi wound its way through the evening traffic, not always strictly by the book, but elegantly. Eckart was in the passenger seat with Ralf on his lap, while Ricarda and Philip were sitting side by side on the back seat. They had the windows down, and the air was whistling past their ears.

They were on their way to the retirement community. No long discussions, no beating around the bush, no getting rooms ready. No nothing. Uschi had to be brought home. For good. Not just for good, but *right now*. Typical Harry. Harry really was an extraterrestrial. Eckart had felt like leaping in the air when Harry came in earlier with his punky energy and said that he would stay. He had felt an indescribable urge to hug him, but he decided he ought not to. It wasn't really on to hug Mr Harry Markwand.

Harry did as he wished, and no more. But no less either. And, if he didn't want to do something, they knew that he wouldn't do it. Except for the little apology just now, that was. Eckart grinned.

Harry glanced at Ricarda and Philip in the rear-view mirror.

'So, have you finally . . . ?'

'Huh?' Philip leaned forward into the wind.

'Screwed!' Harry laughed his throaty laugh, and he steered them through the city streets in his spaceship.

70

The crumbs formed two parallel lines. Uschi pushed the bottom of each row into the middle until they formed a semi-circle: U.

She examined the U-shaped crumbs on the blue plastic tablecloth and wondered whether she had enough time to make an M for Müller before Veronica came over to tidy up. The carer was still feeding Mrs Gockel at the next table.

They had had crumble cake for dessert today – if you were charitable enough to call this dry mess a cake. She could have dished up something better with her one good arm, thought Uschi. And the less said about the limp sausage they were served for dinner, the better.

Her neighbours' heads had slumped forward; they tended to doze off at table. Almost as soon as they'd finished spooning up their dessert, their heads would sink gently forward. Every lunchtime.

Bad manners, actually, thought Uschi, and stole a few crumbs from her roommate, Mrs Fuchs, who was sitting to her right. She set about forming the third line of crumbs for the M.

'Mrs Müller?'

She was startled, because the deep voice was coming from right next to her ear. Slowly she looked around. No! It couldn't be!

It was. 'Harry?'

Yes, Harry was standing there.

'Cripes! Great atmosphere here.' He performed a perfect bow to her dozing neighbours. 'Ladies?' Mrs Fuchs woke with a start, and looked up in a daze at the long-haired man in the checked shirt.

'Uschi?' Harry turned her wheelchair to face him. 'I was disconcerted *not* to . . .' he paused for effect and narrowed his eyes menacingly ' . . . find you *at home*.'

'At home?'

What was Harry saying? In the last few weeks she had tried with all her might to drive that word out of her heart. She wanted nothing more to do with that word; she didn't even want to be reminded that the word existed.

Veronica and the others really did do their best; of that there was no doubt. They did what it was in their power to do, and the place was clean, but she had nonetheless immediately sensed that this retirement community would never be her home. Which meant that she would never again in her life have a real home.

She had attempted at least to bring a little warmth to her own room. She had begun to unpack her sausage trophies and had lined them up on the little sideboard. However, half of the sideboard belonged to Mrs Fuchs, who stored her medicine there, so Uschi had cleared her prizes away again. She couldn't place the trophies from her professional career, these reminders of the 'World's Best Cold Meats Counter', next to bladder medication, mountain pine tablets, disinfectant spray and haemorrhoid cream. Her wonderful cold meats counter deserved better.

She gradually grew accustomed to the greyness of the place. Her sadness at having lost her home waned with each passing day, and memories of the uproar of the shared flat faded from her mind.

'Home?' she muttered a second time, looking up at Harry.

'That's right,' he said tenderly.

'Uschi?'

'Ricarda?'

Only now did she notice Ricarda, Philip and Eckart. Ralf pattered excitedly towards her.

'You have to come home, Uschi!' Ricarda said.

'We miss you,' nodded Eckart.

'And we'll get your right side back in order,' Philip added with a smile.

Was she dreaming, or could this truly be happening?

'Enough of the emotional stuff. What now?' Harry scowled down at her. 'Home or not home?'

How dared he doubt her decision! 'Home, of course.'

'Told you so.' Harry nodded to the others. 'She wants to go home!' He spun her wheelchair around, and pushed it towards the exit.

'Hold on ... stop ... Harry,' she protested.' It's not that simple. You can't just ... '

'What are you doing?' Veronica blocked their path with a quizzical look on her face. 'Mrs Müller?'

'We'll come back to fetch Mrs Müller's things later. With your permission ... ' Eckart pushed the amiable carer a little to one side and placed Ralf on Uschi's lap. That cleared the path for Harry, and off they went.

'Veronica!' Uschi called over her shoulder. 'Thanks for everything. All the best! I'll come back and see you. All the very best!'

'But Mrs Müller ... ' she heard Veronica gasp in disbelief.

'Bye! Thanks for everything,' shouted Ricarda, and Philip managed at least to add a final friendly, 'Your cream was tops!'

'Yeah! Top of the pops!' laughed Harry. They raced out into the open air.

71

So they were all back on board. Ralf crouched on Uschi's knees, and together they were pushed to the car park. He felt like Little Lord Fauntleroy. Uschi, the woman with the world's most succulent sausage fingers, was back among them, tickling his ears, and everyone was in high spirits.

'One word: Thailand,' gushed Harry. 'They have immaculate retirement homes, with all the fittings – or rather, fit things! There'll be something for everyone!'

'No way,' Ricarda objected. 'I'm going to be a granny. We'll need to babysit.'

'That way we'll have the nappies ready for Uschi too,' laughed Harry.

'You—' Incensed, Uschi tried to punish Harry's insolence with a punch on the arm, but she couldn't reach. She exploded into gales of laughter. Just like the old days.

'Maybe we could swap flats with the students on the ground floor,' Eckart suggested. 'Or install a stair lift?'

'And meals on wheels,' Harry chimed in.

'In any case, Uschi, from now on you're only allowed in the bathtub with armbands on,' said Philip.

'How about hiring someone from Eastern Europe to help after all?' asked Ricarda. 'For a decent wage, of course! People don't have it easy over there.'

'Oh, yeah!' laughed Harry. 'A multi-purpose Polish woman!'

'Oh, Harry,' said Philip. 'Shut your dirty mouth for once!'

Uschi laughed. 'Do whatever you want. The main thing ...'

'... is not to urine ourselves!' shouted the others in unison.

This is more like it, thought Ralf. He wasn't an expert on the human species, but he liked this spirit. He liked it a lot.

Epilogue

Five weeks later.

'Do it again. Do it again,' said Harry. The four of them were bending over Uschi's right foot, their eyes glued to her big toe.

'Come on! Do it again,' cried Harry.

Uschi concentrated and . . .

'Ye-e-es!' Her big toe moved! Uschi really was wiggling her big toe. They stood upright again, proud as peacocks. Of Uschi – and of themselves.

One after another they hugged Uschi, then shook hands, one after another.

They'd done it. It was as if they'd just swum the Atlantic.